D0708928

Pineapple

Mystery Box

A Pineapple Port Mystery: Book Two

Amy Vansant

©2015 by Amy Vansant. All rights reserved.
No part of this book may be reproduced in any form, by any means, without the permission of the author. All characters appearing in this work are fictitious. Any resemblance to real persons, living or dead, is purely coincidental.

ISBN-10: 0983719187
ISBN-13: 978-0-9837191-8-2
Library of Congress: 2015916300

Vansant Creations, LLC / Amy Vansant
Annapolis, MD
http://www.AmyVansant.com
http://www.PineapplePort.com

Cover art by Farik Osman
Copy editing by Carolyn Steele.

Dedication

To Mom. The original Charlotte who's had the dubious distinction of having to read everything I've ever written since day one. Love you! (Not just for the reading, you fed me and whatnot, too.)

CONTENTS

Chapter One 1

Chapter Two 8

Chapter Three 16

Chapter Four 31

Chapter Five 35

Chapter Six 46

Chapter Seven 58

Chapter Eight..64

Chapter Nine 78

Chapter Ten..88

Chapter Eleven 97

Chapter Twelve 108

Chapter Thirteen 118

Chapter Fourteen 126

Chapter Fifteen 134

Chapter Sixteen...137

Chapter Seventeen 148

Chapter Eighteen 156

Chapter Nineteen 167

Chapter Twenty 176

Chapter Twenty-One 182

Chapter Twenty-Two 191

Chapter Twenty-Three 198

Chapter Twenty-Four 209

Chapter Twenty-Five 213

Chapter Twenty-Six 222

Chapter Twenty-Seven 230

Chapter Twenty-Eight 241

Chapter Twenty-Nine 248

Chapter Thirty 260

Chapter Thirty-One 266

Epilogue 273

ABOUT THE AUTHOR 276

Other Books by Amy Vansant 276

CHAPTER ONE

He didn't mean to kill her.

Well, he *did*, of course, but not that way. Not with a knife and not so soon. Now there was *ooze* all over his hand. The blood slipped down the back of the blade like a kid at a water park. His lip curled with disgust.

What a mess.

He'd spent a week researching sleeping medicines. *A week*. He hadn't spent that long studying for his GED exam. He'd spent *hours* driving to three different counties to buy the pills. *Real* sleeping pills, not capsules. Capsules would have been easier, crack them open and pour—but something in his gut told him she'd be able to taste whatever came out of a capsule. It must taste terrible or why stuff it in a gel cap?

He was half way home from the drug store before he realized he'd forgotten to wear the ball cap with the blond mullet flowing from the back to hide his mug from the cameras. *Idiot.* He pulled over and pictured his face on all those videos, like watching a tiny episode of *Dateline* in his head. After stressing for a good five minutes, he decided that returning *with* the mullet cap to buy new pills didn't make any sense.

He'd hit the gas. Nothing to do but hope he reached South America before the cops pieced together the mystery of Bobbi Marie's death. If his plan worked, the cops wouldn't even begin work on the outer edge of the puzzle. If his plan only *half* worked, he'd still be long gone before they completed the edges, started the center, and realized the picture was of him.

When *he* committed a crime it was like a puzzle of the *sky*. Sky puzzles were the hardest to solve. All blue, maybe some wispy clouds…

Yep.

I'm a sky puzzle.

Back at his apartment, he'd mashed his cache of sleeping pills with a mortar and pestle usually reserved for crushing mint leaves to make mojitos. Girls *loved* mojitos. His original plan had been to run to Mexico but he'd decided that was too predictable. *Everyone* ran to Mexico. And Brazilian girls probably liked mojitos, too. He'd started watching the Spanish television channels to learn the language. He'd be good either way.

After smashing half a sandwich bag of light blue powder, he rinsed his tools. Reaching to return the mortar to the cabinet, he paused, staring at the stone bowl. He'd crushed sleeping powder into every pore of the thing. Could he still take it to South America with him? He knew he'd knock the South American girls' socks off with his mojito recipe, but he didn't want to knock them—or himself—out. Did they have mortars and pestles in South America?

Dang. I should have done more research on South America.

He drove to a nearby strip mall, threw the bowl into a dumpster with a reverberating clang, and stopped at a store to buy a new set. This time he wore the mullet cap. It felt good to get some use out of it.

Back at home, he stirred the entire bag of sleeping powder into a pot of milk on the stove. He tasted it several times, adding a bit more milk here and a dash of sugar there until he found it drinkable. Bobbi would never notice a thing.

Sleepy-milk in a thermos, he drove to the old lady's apartment at *Casa Siesta*, letting himself in with the key he'd had cut while she napped one afternoon. She'd never noticed that he let himself in *or* that the woman assigned to her assisted living apartment had stopped visiting. He'd told the lazy nurse that he'd be taking over daily visits and she'd been more than happy to check Bobbi off her list.

"Hola! Ready for your warm milk, Bobbi?" He liked to practice his Spanish when he could.

Bobbi Marie glowered at him from her threadbare yellow sitting chair. She was a willful old broad, but her mind had been on vacation since he met her. She still puttered around the apartment and fed her ratty old cat, but the comfy chair absorbed most of her time. A small stroke had made it difficult for her to talk, so she barked everything in short staccato sentences that made him jump.

He was doing them both a favor by putting her out of her misery. Anyway, if anyone came around asking questions, the last thing he needed was her barking his name at the cops. If she even knew his name. He wasn't sure she knew her *own* name anymore. She only seemed to remember the dumbest things.

His eye fell on Friskie, napping in the window. The tabby's patchy fur looked worse than Bobbi's chair. The only thing *friskie* about that cat was its bladder.

I should send the cat with her. A nice bowl of sleepy milk for kitty...

"I'm practicing Spanish," he said, setting Bobbi's mail on her sofa table. "Thinking of moving to Brazil."

"Porch geese."

"What's that?"

"Porch geese. Not spansch."

He looked at the woman and noticed her misbuttoned dressing gown. It drove him crazy when she did that. "What are you moaning about now?"

She huffed and then barked again. "Brazil."

"What about Brazil?"

"Speak Port-chu-*geez*."

"Portuguese? Wait... You're saying they speak Portuguese in Brazil? Not Spanish?"

She nodded with one hard jerk of her head.

"Woman, you're crazy. You can't even button your dang housecoat. It's *South America*. Of course they speak Spanish. It's right next to Mexico, land of mojitos."

"Cuba."

"Right. Now they speak Cuban. Whatever."

Tucking the thermos under his arm, he patted her on the knee as he passed on his way to the kitchen. It had been a long four months, trying to get the information he needed out of the old cow. He'd threatened, cajoled, and finally discovered that adding a bit of booze to her milk loosened her tongue. Unfortunately, the only thing he was sure of was that his father had given Bobbi a *box*. The old man mentioned it in the last conversation they'd had before he died. He didn't know how big or what it looked like, but it had to be worth a fortune. He *knew* it. Why else would Pop give it to her to hide?

His father had bragged about the box, then went and got himself shivved by another inmate before he'd had a chance to share any details about his treasure chest.

Pop never did have any luck.

By the time he found his grandmother Bobbi, she'd lost her mind and didn't seem to know what was in the box or what she did with it.

Some days she remembered leaving it at the old house.

9

Other days she thought she sold it or gave it to someone.

That theory just about made him sick to his stomach. The idea that someone else might have the goods his father had worked so hard to steal...

Once Bobbi claimed Indiana Jones stole the box. That's when he gave up trying to get a straight answer out of her.

"Tea."

He was unscrewing the thermos when she said it.

"What?"

"Tea."

"What about tea?"

"*Tea.*"

He poked his head out of the kitchen.

"You want tea?"

She grunted.

"But you *always* have warm milk."

"Tea after church."

"After—"

She turned her head away from him and crossed her arms against her chest.

He rubbed his temple with one hand. The crazy old bird thought it was Sunday. Probably thought it was nineteen seventy-six, too, because she hadn't been to church in all the time he'd known her.

He looked at the thermos, sitting there with all his hard work inside. He yawned.

What a day for her to switch to tea.

"Do you want milk in your tea?"

"Yes."

Fine. At least he could put his sleepy milk in the tea. Maybe it would be enough. If not, he'd just have to keep slipping it into everything he could until it did the job.

Yawning again, he reached into the kitchen cabinet

and found a box of tea still sealed in plastic wrap. He picked at the edge of the box with his short fingernail. Frustrated, he pulled a long knife from the butcher's block and stabbed at it until it tore open.

He opened another cabinet in search of a teacup but found none. He opened another and another, finding nothing but yellowed Tupperware containers warped by the microwave and enough cat food to keep a pride of lions alive for a year. He whirled and stormed back into the front room.

"Dang it, Bobbi, where do you keep—"

Oh…

His face was inches from Bobbi's.

She'd gotten out of her chair and they'd almost run smack into each other. Only the knife in his hand—the knife he hadn't realized he was holding—kept her from hitting him.

He looked down and watched as a rivulet of blood rode the blade from where the tip pierced her midsection.

Her height had done her in. A shorter gal would have taken it in the ribs. The knife might have bounced off the bone. But Bobbi was nearly six feet tall.

He considered pulling out the weapon, but it was too late now.

Instead, he *pushed.*

Bobbi Marie barely made a sound. Just sucked in a little wind. Her face fell slack as the knife in his hand reached the wooden hilt. He froze and they stood that way, eyes locked on each other. He could feel her lean against the blade and his wrist trembled with the strain of holding her weight. Her legs buckled and he withdrew. She fell to the ground in a curled clump.

Standing over her, he watched the blood drip from the knife to the floor. He sidled past her and sat in the chair where she'd been only a moment before.

He didn't mean to kill her.

Well, he *had*, of course, but not that way. Not with a knife.

His eyelids felt like they weighed a thousand pounds. In a situation like this, having just stabbed a woman to death, he felt as if he should be more *awake*. Wired, even. Instead, he wanted to sleep. Let his mind rest for a bit.

He closed his lids.

Maybe he'd taste-tested a little too much of the sleepy milk.

A moment later he was snoring.

CHAPTER TWO

Charlotte's pulse quickened as she walked the final block to her destination. She was running the gauntlet. Succeeding against all odds. Soaring like a hawk full of helium with tiny rockets strapped to her talons.

Or...

...she was failing like a rainy Fourth of July.

It was hard to tell.

The sun reflected off the back of a molded plastic squirrel sitting at the edge of Mrs. Mann's garden. The rodent eyed her, preparing to gnaw his plastic acorn, a treat destined never to reach his squirrelly lips.

Hm. That's one.

Charlotte's gaze moved to Mann's mailbox. One of the yellow Rudbeckia flowers beneath it had lost its head. Not a single golden petal of the missing bloom remained; the executioner had carried it off whole.

Strange... Let's say two.

A peculiar alligator-shaped patch of dead grass marred the Sykes' otherwise perfect square of turf.

Three.

Two pugs guarded the steps of Mrs. Maggliozi's porch like chubby little pagodas, their bulging eyes following her as she strode the last few feet.

Four?

Charlotte stopped at the end of the block where Seamus stood waiting for her, his muscular arms crossed against his chest. He peered down his nose at her, one bushy black eyebrow hiked higher than its twin.

"Are you ready?" he asked.

She met his steely gaze with a metaphorical metal squint of her own.

A titanium stare.

"I am."

He nodded. "*Go.*"

She took a deep breath.

"At Mann's you faced the squirrel in the opposite direction and yanked the head from one of her mailbox flowers—she's going to kill you for that, by the way. You stole the Sykes' alligator, Snappy, and one of Mrs. Maggliozi's three pugs went missing. I don't know if you had anything to do with that or if he just wandered inside, but there you go."

Seamus' serious demeanor cracked into a million-watt smile. "Beautiful!"

She grinned, preparing to accept his praise with great humility.

"Too bad you're dead," he added, slapping her on the shoulder.

The smile melted from her face.

"What?"

He looked past her and barked a single word.

"Jackie!"

Charlotte followed his gaze to a pile of brush tucked behind a plastic storage box on the side of Maggliozi's lime green modular home. The pile of grass grunted and stood to assume a humanoid shape. It looked like Big Foot covered in Spanish moss.

"Gotcha."

The monster pushed brown netting from its head to reveal a human face hidden beneath the nest of weeds. Jackie, Seamus' girlfriend and a fellow resident of

Pineapple Port, looked as if she'd rolled in a swamp and the whole thing had stuck to her. In her grassy paw, she held a two-inch wide, foot-long wooden dowel, painted black.

Charlotte grimaced. "Jackie, I don't know how to tell you this, but you need a wax."

"It's a ghillie suit. Isn't it cool?" Jackie bowed her legs and bobbed from her left foot to her right, weedy fringe dangling from her outstretched arms.

"It looks pretty hot, actually."

"You're right. I'm dying in here."

"What's with the black stick in your hand?"

"I gave her that to simulate a rifle," said Seamus. "You noticed all the changes I made but you didn't see the woman on the ground in the ghillie suit with the rifle, the *one* thing that could have killed you."

"She was there when we started so I didn't notice any change. That shouldn't count."

"She wasn't aiming at you when we started."

"Well I wasn't expecting an *armed* pile of brush."

"But that's just the thing. Nobody ever *expects* an armed pile of brush. That's why you have to notice *everything*."

He pulled a small pad of paper from his pocket.

"Observational skill tests number one: I'm going to give you a C-plus for noticing the missing flower—"

"Right before I was shot to death by a pile of hay."

"Bingo."

Charlotte sighed. When she asked her boyfriend's uncle to train her to be a top-notch investigator, she hadn't expected the man to be so diabolical.

Her *boyfriend*. The phrase sounded funny; part grade-school label, part serious romance. She assumed Declan was her boyfriend. It wasn't like he'd given her a ring or a varsity letter or anything, but they'd gone out a few times in the weeks since solving the mystery of his mother's disappearance and their courtship seemed to be blossoming. Still, Declan was difficult to read and romance was hard anyway. So many things could make a relationship awkward: jealous exes, disapproving friends, the fact that she'd found his mother's bones in her backyard...

Offering Declan a cocktail and then casually strolling to her lanai where they could overlook his mother's former grave definitely qualified as *awkward*. But maybe finding his mother had nothing to do with the fact that their romance was moving at the pace of a snail cattle drive. Maybe it had more to do with the facts that Uncle Seamus was living with Declan and her own house was under constant surveillance by her mother-hen neighbors Mariska and Darla. At twenty-six, she was the youngest person in Pineapple Port and the subject of some local fascination.

When people asked how she lived in a retirement community, she told them she'd been grandmothered-in.

Ha!

Nobody ever got the joke, but in all fairness, it didn't make sense until she explained. Her parents had died, forcing her to move in with her grandmother in the retirement community. Then her grandmother had died. Rather than ship her off to an orphanage, Pineapple Port unofficially adopted her, pulled some strings, and enabled her to grow up amongst them, like Jane Goodall with the apes.

The residents didn't like that joke either.

Charlotte had lived there long enough to grow accustomed to the scrutiny, but it was a whole new world for Declan. Dating in Pineapple Port was like trying to make out in a basement while your parents, grandparents, brothers, sisters, and a hundred or so aunts or uncles mingled upstairs.

Not sexy.

Then again, maybe the less-than-whirlwind nature of their romance was her fault. She'd been busy. She'd never felt so alive as she had while trying to unlock the mystery surrounding Declan's mother's death and now that it was over, she wanted to solve more puzzles. That's where Seamus and his fiendish training came in handy.

"I hear your flyers didn't turn out so well," said Seamus.

She threw her head back and huffed. Declan must have told him she'd slipped flyers into her neighbors' mailboxes to advertise her investigative services. She'd thought she was being enterprising. Aware of her potential clients' proclivities, she'd even included a *clip-and-save twenty-percent off.* coupon. She wasn't an idiot. Some of the Pineapple Portians would buy a wet suit in the Sahara if they had a coupon for it.

After a week of waiting for clients to come rolling in, only one crime had been committed: Someone put unstamped detective agency flyers in people's mailboxes.

"Come on. Who knew it's a federal offense to put mail in people's mailboxes?"

"Mr. Caslin, apparently. The better question is: who knew you had a retired postman in the neighborhood?"

"Tell me about it. He felt duty-bound to lecture me on the dos and don'ts of mailbox laws for an *hour*."

"Is he going to turn you in?"

"No. I begged Mariska to help me make a pie for him. She said he'd only threatened to report me in the *hopes* of getting a pie in the first place, but she helped me anyway."

"He's a notorious food grubber," said Jackie, trying to

unzip the ghillie suit. "I've seen that man eat an entire pie by himself. He ate it one slice at a time so people wouldn't notice, but I noticed."

"Maybe I should be training you," said Seamus with a wink.

Charlotte tried not to take his comment as personally as it was probably meant and continued to whine about her failed marketing campaign.

"In hindsight, I did think it was a little weird that Mr. Caslin mentioned lemon meringue pie *four times* in a speech about mailboxes." Charlotte lowered her voice to mimic the retired postman. *"Say someone sends you two lemon meringue pies...you find one in your mailbox in a temperature controlled box* with *postage, and the other—this one with those little dollops of whipped cream around the edge—you find* without *postage..."*

She'd only been operating a freelance detective agency for a few days and she'd already lost money on flyers, lemons and Crisco *and* committed two crimes herself. Turns out, she needed a *license* to be a private investigator, too. Crime number two. At this rate she'd be in prison by the end of the month.

"Maybe being a detective is a stupid idea. What's the point? I can't be a private investigator without a license, and to get a license I need at least forty hours of experience as an intern for a *real* private investigator and there aren't any around here."

"Yes there are," said Seamus, grunting as he helped Jackie out of the ghillie suit. The zipper had stuck in her fringe.

"Where?"

"About two feet away from you."

"Huh?"

Jackie let out a little scream. "I swear, if you don't get

me out of this suit I am going to *freak out.*"

"Shush, Jackie, you just shot me dead. You don't get to complain. Seamus, what are you talking about?"

The zipper gave away and Seamus took a step back as Jackie thrashed. He ducked to avoid her flailing grassy arms. She dropped to her knees and collapsed sideways, squirming from the suit like a snake shedding its skin.

The sight was so pathetic Charlotte couldn't help but pity her pretend-murderer. "Aren't you going to help her?"

Seamus held a hand in Jackie's direction as she squirmed across the lawn. "And miss this?"

Jackie rolled to her back, kicking her feet in the air as best she could with her ankles bound together by the suit.

Charlotte shrugged. "Okay, so what are you talking about? Who's a private investigator?"

Seamus tapped his chest. "I am."

"You are? *Licensed?*"

"Licensed."

"Really? Or are you a private investigator in the same way you said you were a cop in Miami when you were really a glorified informant?"

"Oh, you cut me to the quick, lass. I thought we were friends…you know I only fibbed to appear an upstanding citizen to my nephew."

"So you're *really* an investigator?"

"Sure. I did the paperwork while I was still in Miami right before I came up here. I even took a few side jobs. The cops didn't pay *all* my bills."

"Why didn't you say so?"

"You didn't ask."

"Can I be your intern?"

He shrugged. "Sure. Unpaid, of course."

"Naturally. All right." She saluted him. "What's my

first assignment, sir?"

He jerked a thumb behind him.

"Locate a glass of water for her."

Jackie's face was flush and her shirt soaked with perspiration. She stood and began stomping on the ghillie suit with her right leg as she strained to yank away her left ankle.

"Jackie? Would you like some water?"

Jackie glared at her. "You two can play cops and robbers all you like, just leave me *out of it* from now on. This thing is some kind of alien…" She stomped on the suit one last time and then pounded toward her house, one leg dragging the deflated ghillie suit behind her.

Seamus chuckled.

"I couldn't believe it when she agreed to wear that thing. This is going to give me material for *weeks*."

He clapped Charlotte on the back and jogged after his girlfriend.

"Your shadow's looking a little furry there," he called.

"Shut *up*!" screamed Jackie.

CHAPTER THREE

Charlotte heard the wailing from her bedroom, even with one ear pressed against her pillow and her soft-coated Wheaton terrier's chin resting on the other.

"She's gone! Someone stole her!"

She tried to rise but Abby fought her, pressing her furry face against Charlotte's in an attempt to pin her human pillow to the mattress. She slipped out from under the Wheaton, who grunted and rolled onto her back, legs falling open to expose her pink belly. Charlotte offered a conciliatory tummy rub before throwing on shorts and a tee and heading for the door.

Outside, she looked down her street and saw a small crowd gathering in front of her friend Darla's house. Charlotte felt her stomach lurch. In a retirement community, curious people outside someone's home rarely turned out to be a good thing. At least she didn't see an ambulance. Not yet.

Mariska burst out of her own home the moment Charlotte's foot hit the asphalt. Mariska lived directly across the street from her. She wore a thin housedress and slippers.

"Uh…bra?" suggested Charlotte.

"Oh, phooey," said Mariska, slapping an arm across her breasts to still the impression of puppies in a laundry bag. "We have to hurry."

"What's the ruckus? Do you know?"

"No, I don't know. That's why I'm rushing."

"Is it Darla?"

"I don't *know*."

"Well come on. You're supposed to know everything."

"I know, I know."

The two of them wove through the crowd until they spotted Darla standing in her front yard. She wore a black tee shirt with *Sea Hag* scrawled in white letters across the chest. Her husband, Sheriff Frank, had bought it for her after she insisted he take her on a fishing trip. She didn't catch anything except a sunburn and never asked to go again, but she loved the tee.

"Darla, what is it?" asked Charlotte.

Darla shook her fist, the grimace on her face making her lips thin and white.

"Someone stole Witchy-Poo."

She thrust an accusatory finger at the roof as if it was the culprit.

The giant inflatable witch that always perched on Darla's roof during the Halloween season had disappeared. Charlotte kicked herself for not noticing. She'd done well spotting tiny changes during Seamus' test and then failed to notice the absence of a seven-foot-tall witch with striped socks and a wart the size of a blueberry muffin on her nose. Clearly, she still had work to do.

"They switched my flag," said someone else deep in the crowd. "I'm not a Raven's fan. They're in my division for crying out loud. I'm from Pittsburgh."

"My gazing ball is gone," said another. "Now I've got gnomes."

Mariska tittered. "That sounds serious."

"Does the gnome have a hoe?" asked someone nearby.

"I'm not touching that," mumbled Charlotte.

"I have a frog where my ducks used to be," said

another voice.

"A frog?" roared Darla's husband, Frank. "Lil' Frankie. I was so mad about the witch I didn't even notice Lil' Frankie was missing."

In the spot where Frank's fishing frog, Lil' Frankie once sat, the fishing pole string no longer floated in the tiny manmade pond. Now, Mrs. Mann's plastic squirrel struggled to nibble his acorn while standing tail-deep in water.

"Someone switched all the lawn decorations?" asked Charlotte.

Mariska gasped and grabbed her arm. "It's a mystery. You've got your first case."

Charlotte shook her head. "All we have to do is switch them back."

"Yes, but who did it? And what about Witchy-Poo? I don't see anything in her place. And what's to stop these vandals from doing it again?"

"I suppose Frank should do something—" began Darla, who had moved to take her usual place beside Mariska.

Mariska elbowed her.

"Ow. Oh… Right. Frank's busy. He doesn't have time for this. We need a detective. Like Sherlock Holmes. Only maybe cuter."

She winked at Charlotte.

Charlotte suspected the ladies were patronizing her, but Mariska had a point. No one would hire her to find out who switched the lawn decoration, but if she solved the case, it would prove to the whole neighborhood that she had *skills*. It would be like handing out freebees in the hopes of selling more in the future.

"You're right. I'll take the case."

"Go get 'em," said Darla. "Find Witchy-Poo and arrest

the heartless jerk who stole her."

"I don't think I can arrest anyone."

"Then just beat 'em up."

"I don't think she should *beat up* anyone…" said Mariska.

"Well, maybe just *rough* them up."

"What's the difference?"

As the two women bickered over what constituted a beating, Charlotte gazed at Darla's empty roof. "Hey… does anyone else have a *big* decoration like Witchy—er, the *witch?*" She hated the name Witchy-Poo and refused to say it.

Darla stopped arguing long enough to look at her. "Only *I* have Witchy-Poo. She's one of a kind."

"And only *I* have to climb my old butt up there once a year and blow her up," said Frank. "I'm going to go get Lil' Frank from Sally's house."

Darla rolled her eyes. "You do that, hon. That frog is probably homesick and panicky."

Frank glared at her, hitched his belt and wandered off.

"Charlotte's going to figure out who did this," said Mariska.

"Yes. Go get 'em Char," said Darla. "Just make sure you concentrate on Witchy-Poo."

Charlotte patted Darla on the shoulder and jogged back to her house to grab a pen and paper. She wanted to let Abby out for her morning bathroom break and then note the switched items so she could search for any patterns.

She let the dog out the back and grabbed a notepad and a pen. She considered hopping into her golf cart to begin her investigation, but worried she might miss a clue by speeding by it. No, she would *walk* the neighborhood and knock on every door.

Wait—time to start using official investigator language.

She wouldn't walk. She would *canvass* the neighborhood. Canvass for clues.

She felt very official, until she realized the pen she'd grabbed looked like a palm tree, with green, plastic fronds flopping from the top.

Sherlock Holmes would never use a palm tree pen.

She grabbed another, much more *official*-looking pen, and the game was afoot.

Well…she was afoot, anyway.

Someone had to have seen *something*. People couldn't wander the streets of Pineapple Port with gnomes and giant inflatable witches tucked under their arms without someone noticing. The Port had more busy-bodies per capita than any other place in the United States. At least according to her own unofficial statistics.

An hour later, as Charlotte climbed the steps to old Dottie's house, she knew solving the caper wouldn't be as easy as she'd hoped. Her notes said she'd discovered precious little.

1. Two Republicans turned into Democrats and vice versa. *Politically motivated?*
2. Three flowerpots switched with birdbaths. *Theme? Or just too many flowerpots and birdbaths?*
3. George Sambrooke's golf cart half off the curb and pressed against his wife's sedan. *Had a few too many last night?*

The last item probably had nothing to do with her case. Things hadn't been great at the Sambrooke's lately, but that was gossip, not a crime.

She knocked on Dottie Parson's door. She waited a minute and then knocked again. She was about to leave when the door jerked open and slammed against the interior wall of the home. Dottie caught it with the side of her walker and elbowed it back into the wall repeatedly until she'd wedged the walker tight enough to keep the bouncing to a minimum. Charlotte sneaked a peek behind the hinge and saw a pre-formed hole in the drywall holding the doorknob. That explained the strange metallic ding of the door's bounce; it had been striking a metal joist inside the wall.

"Hi Dottie, sorry to bother you."

The old woman grunted. "I was *busy.*"

Charlotte took a deep breath and decided it would be unwise to start an argument. Dottie was probably "busy" lifting small trucks off the ground. Her arms were freakishly strong, as if the strength in her legs hadn't so much left her as packed up and moved to her biceps. She wished the old woman would invite her in so she could peek in the back rooms, see what sort of workout equipment she had, and sell the secret to an NFL football team.

"Sorry. I just wanted to know if you've noticed any of your lawn items missing or replaced?"

Dottie glowered at her. Charlotte calculated how long the woman's arms were and took half a step back to be safe.

"Why should I tell you?"

"You don't have to tell me. I could arm wrestle you for it."

"What?"

"Never mind. Just kidding. You don't have to tell me, but I wish you would. I'm trying to find out if anyone saw anything suspicious last night. A bunch of people had their lawn decorations stolen."

"I don't have any lawn decorations. Lawns are for *grass. Grass* is the decoration."

"And you didn't see anything?"

"No. Someone stole the tennis balls off my walker a while back. I didn't see you here then."

"Really?" She looked down and saw Dottie was sporting brand new Wilsons, sliced down the center so they could cuddle the feet of her walker.

Who would steal an old lady's walker balls?

"I'm sorry to hear that. I didn't know."

"Uh huh. That it?"

"Um…yep. Thank you."

Dottie took a wobbly step backwards and then slammed the door so hard the house shook.

Charlotte stared at the door until it finished vibrating.

I pity the person who stole those balls.

Charlotte wiped her brow and realized how hot it was. As the first flush of investigative excitement began to melt from her bones beneath the Florida sun, she understood why people said police work was mostly drudgery. She'd hoped being a private investigator was all grand discoveries and foot chases. Foot chases after very slow, small, *weak* criminals ready to turn themselves in at the slightest provocation.

Maybe I should have become a grade school truant officer.

She knocked on the edge of Gloria Abernathy's screened porch door. On a flag hanging from a wooden pole beside her, a bright red parrot held aloft a coconut with a festive drink umbrella hanging from its shaved rim. Neon pink script along the bottom of the flag announced *It's Five o'Clock Somewhere.* She wasn't sure, but she thought Gloria had a different flag. Gloria was new to the neighborhood, and didn't seem like the drunken-parrot-flag sort. Of course, in Florida, parrots drinking rum concoctions from coconuts were as common as sunglass-wearing lizards tanning on the beach. Maybe everyone who moved to Florida received a parrot flag at the border.

Both Gloria's car and golf cart were in her driveway, but no one answered. Charlotte tugged on the screened porch door and found it open. She moved to the inner door and knocked again. Nothing.

Leaning to the right, she peeked through the window. A flash of movement caught her eye, something moving low to the ground.

Did Gloria have a dog?

"Gloria?" she called, rapping on the window.

A head popped up from behind a floral-patterned sofa and then disappeared. It was like peering in on a life-sized game of whack-a-mole.

Was sixty-six-year-old Gloria Abernathy crouching behind her sofa?

Charlotte pressed her face against the window. "Gloria—It's Charlotte. Are you okay?"

Gloria's face popped into view like a meerkat on high alert.

"Charlotte?"

"Yes. I came to talk to you for a second. Are you hurt? Can you get up?"

Gloria stood and opened her door.

"Are you alone?" she asked, peering past Charlotte.

"Yes. Are you okay?"

Gloria took a tentative step onto the porch.

"Look around outside there. Do you see anyone?"

Charlotte walked back to the outer edge of the porch and looked left and right, beginning to feel paranoid that somehow she *wasn't* alone.

"I don't see anyone...am I looking for anyone in particular?"

Gloria moved to the screen door and latched the

hook.

"Okay. Come in, quick."

She grabbed Charlotte's arm, tugging her into the house, through the kitchen, down the hall and into a spare bedroom. Charlotte flipped on the light. Gloria lunged to shut it off.

"Don't."

Charlotte snatched away her hand and studied Gloria's face. The woman's bottom lip had swallowed her top and nearly touched her nose. Her eyes were wide. She looked worried.

No, she looked terrified.

She'd known residents in the community who had fallen to dementia. Gloria seemed too young but…something had to be wrong.

"Gloria…can I ask what's wrong?"

"They're trying to kill me," she whispered.

"Who?" *Maybe she saw someone swapping her flag and thought they were trying to get in her home?* "Did you see someone? Was it someone swapping out your flag?"

Gloria's expression flashed from fear to annoyance. "Swapped my flag? My granddaughter gave me that for my birthday."

Gloria's top lip remerged somewhat less neon pink after its manhandling by the bottom. It made Charlotte wonder how much lipstick the average woman swallowed in a lifetime.

I'll Google that later.

Right now, she had to divine what had upset Gloria. The woman seemed much less confused. Now she seemed peeved, and about something that made *sense.* That was a good sign.

She pointed toward the front of the house. "The parrot drinking cocktails. Is that your flag?"

"What? No. Why would my daughter let my sweet seven-year-old granddaughter buy me a flag with a boozehound parrot on it?"

"Fair enough."

"*My* flag is a pair of flip flops and underneath it says *Life's a Beach.*"

Charlotte smiled. *Ah. A flag with a cutesy swap-out for a curse word. Much better seven-year-old material.* She touched Gloria's shoulder. "Don't worry about your flag. I'm pretty sure I can find it. Did you see them take it?"

"No. What are you talking about?"

"Vandals switched a bunch of decorations last night and you ended up with a parrot. Someone else in the neighborhood has your flag. That's why I'm here; trying to find the culprits and Darla's witch."

"Witchy-Poo is missing?"

Charlotte sighed. "I refuse to call her that, but yes."

"Oh that's terrible."

Gloria put her hand on her chest and took a deep breath. In her Hawaiian flowered shirt she had more in common with the drinking parrot than she knew. She was an adorable woman; the human equivalent of a Pomeranian puppy with soft, tawny hair and large brown eyes. It made Charlotte want to cuddle her and tell her everything would be fine.

"So everyone got death threats?"

Charlotte straightened. "What?"

"Follow me." Gloria tiptoed back to her kitchen, retrieved a piece of paper from her island and handed it to Charlotte.

Colorful letters clipped from magazines covered the lined yellow sheet, arranged to spell *Give me whats mine or your dead.* The good news was Gloria wasn't losing her mind. Someone really had threatened her.

"You're dead," mumbled Charlotte.

Gloria gasped. "What?"

"It says *your* dead, y-o-u-r. Should be you're dead, apostrophe r-e. They forgot the apostrophe in *what's*, too."

"Will any of that make me *less* dead?"

"I suppose not. I guess it just means they couldn't find apostrophes to clip out."

"What do they want?"

"I have no idea. Do you?"

Gloria shook her head. "I can't imagine."

Charlotte read the note several times and then picked at the edge of one of the pasted letters. "I thought only movie people cut letters out of magazines...and even then, only for ransom notes."

"Nobody told me this neighborhood was so dangerous."

"I wouldn't worry. It must be kids playing a prank. Hey, did they put it in the mailbox? If they did it's a federal offense."

"No, it was slipped under my porch door."

"Hm." Charlotte noticed a partial fingerprint pressed into the glue. "Looks like there's a—*shoot*." She dropped the paper to the counter as if it had burned her fingers. "I shouldn't be touching it; it's evidence. We have to give this to Frank so they can dust it for fingerprints."

She rapped herself on the side of the head with her knuckles. *Rookie mistake.*

Gloria scowled. "Why do you need fingerprints? I thought you said it was kids playing a prank?"

"It probably is. This and the flags being switched and whatnot..."

"So they aren't targeting me?"

"No...but...so far you're the only one who received a

death threat."

The blood drained from Gloria's face and her eyes grew even larger. Clinging to a tree she'd pass for a bush baby.

"So it *is* just me."

"As far as I know. I haven't talked to half the residents yet."

Gloria nodded, pushed past her and slipped into the spare bedroom. The door shut with the soft click of a lock turning. Charlotte followed and called through the door.

"Gloria, you can't stay in your spare room for the rest of your life."

"There are fewer windows in here."

"So?"

"*Snipers.*"

"I don't think there are snipers after you. They said they're coming for you, not that they're *aiming* for you."

"It would take a lot of patience to cut all those letters out and arrange them on a paper. Don't you think?"

Charlotte shrugged. "I suppose…"

"You know who else has a lot of patience?"

"Who?"

"*Snipers.*"

"Gloria, can you think of any reason why someone would…*sniper* you?"

"Call the sheriff," she said after a moment. "We need to do the fingerprints right away."

"You didn't answer. Do you have enemies who—"

"Call Frank. I want police protection."

"Okay. You sit tight." Charlotte fished in her pocket for her phone and dialed the sheriff's office. While waiting for the operator to locate Frank, she spotted a head bobbing past by the side window of Gloria's home.

She gasped and slapped her hand over her mouth. The last thing she needed to do was further terrify the tiny woman cowering in her guest room.

"Gloria, I'll be right back."

Charlotte ran through the kitchen and fumbled with the latch on the porch door before bursting onto the front walk. She rounded the house in time to spot two figures making their way through the underbrush separating the back of Gloria's home from the farmland adjacent to Pineapple Port. They appeared to be young men, both wearing jeans and hoodies, hoods up. It was eighty-two degrees outside and while it wasn't as humid as it could be, their clothing seemed unnecessarily heavy.

"Stop," she called, nearly toppling into the runoff pond on the side of the house.

One of the boys looked at her. She saw a flash of white skin and brown hair, but little else that could be useful for identification. He took flight, crashing through the brush with his friend tight on his heels. Charlotte ran after them, pulling up short when she reached the natural barrier. It was full of thorny bushes and she was wearing shorts and flip-flops. She gritted her teeth. On one hand, she wanted to be a good detective; on the other, she didn't want to flay all the skin from her legs. Who knew what Floridian horrors might be lurking in the swampy hell beneath the brush? She peered through the scraggly foliage and caught a glimpse of the two boys sprinting across the open field beyond.

She was out of breath. She hadn't run that fast since forgetting to set her golf cart's parking brake on the only hill in the neighborhood. The boys were distant specks now. She'd never catch them. Even if she did, what could she do? Tackle them and demand they wear more weather-appropriate clothing?

Grunting with frustration, she heard a tinny voice calling her name. It took her a moment to realize it emanated from her phone. She put it to her ear.

"Hello?"

"Charlotte? Is that you?"

"Oh, Frank, yes. Sorry. I was running after some kids."

"What are you talking about?"

"I'm at Gloria Abernathy's. She received a death threat. It's made out of clipped letters from magazines, like a ransom note."

"Clipped out letters? I thought that was only in the movies."

"That's what I said. Anyway, she's terrified and wants to talk to you. I saw some kids outside her house and chased them, but they got away through the brush that separates her house from the cow pasture."

"You stay out of there. We've been having a bit of a wild boar problem in that area."

"Seriously? I thought if I made it past the snakes, spiders and gators I was home free."

Charlotte glanced back at the underbrush as if it were trying to sneak up on her and moved toward the front door.

"Let her know I'll be there in a bit," barked Frank. "I'm sure it's just a prank."

"Will do." She reentered Gloria's and tapped on the door of the spare bedroom. "Gloria? Frank's on his way."

"Thank you. Where'd you go?"

"I ran after some kids I saw outside."

"Did you catch them?"

"No."

"But that's good, right? It probably *is* just kids?"

"Probably. Don't you think this conversation would

be easier with you on *this* side of the door?"

"Not really."

"Okay... Hey, have you ever seen any wild boars around here?"

"Wild what?"

"Never mind. Do you want me to wait here with you?"

"Yes."

Charlotte wandered back out to the kitchen and noticed a plate of brownies covered in plastic wrap.

"Can I have a brownie?" she called over her shoulder.

"Yes. I left out the walnuts so if you have an allergy, don't worry."

"Nobody likes walnuts. Why do recipes always tell you to put them in brownies?"

"I don't know."

"Walnuts in perfectly good brownies. Now *that* would be a reason to threaten someone," she mumbled as she sat at the counter and unwrapped the treats.

Delicious.

Being a detective *did* have its perks.

CHAPTER FOUR

His eyes fluttered open and for a moment, he didn't know where he was.

The dead body on the floor reminded him.

Oh, Bobbi. It could have gone so much easier.

He whispered a profanity and stared at the old woman nestled in a halo of blood. He'd done what he came to do, but now he had a mess. Now he had to get rid of a body.

How?

Drive her down to Alligator Alley. Throw her in the swamp. If the gators don't get her, the pythons will.

He tapped on his lips, trying to think through all the complications. He'd have to carry the body to the car without anyone seeing. No matter how careful he tried to be, there would be blood in his trunk, and he'd planned to drive his car to South America by way of Mexico. And what if he was pulled over for something stupid while he had the body? So many things could go wrong.

Deep in thought, he noticed something unexpected.

Bobbi Marie's arm moved.

He gasped and froze, his gaze locked on the body. Curled in the fetal position, her expression remained hidden from his perspective. Was she alive? He saw no other evidence of life. Her chest didn't rise and fall. Yet…

Her arm moved again and he slapped his hand over his mouth.

Please don't make me stab her again.

With his thumb pressed against his nose, he found it

hard to breathe, which gave him an idea.

Suffocate her.

Another flash of movement near the body caught his eye, but this time it wasn't her arm moving. This thing was...*fuzzy?*

Dropping his hand from his face, he stood and peered over the body.

Bobbi's cat stared back at him, his face and front paws covered in blood.

Friskie.

Gross.

He moved to gain a better view as the cat ignored him and returned to business. Friskie had torn through Bobbi's housedress and nibbled the edges of the knife wound until what was once a smooth slit had transformed into a ragged hole.

The cat was eating her.

He looked at the cat's bowl in the kitchen and thought about the bags of food he'd seen in the cupboards. Unopened bags.

Bobbi Marie, in her dementia, must have forgotten to feed the cat. Friskie must have been starving. In the few weeks he'd been visiting, he'd just assumed the old lady was taking care of her usual business. She'd seemed confused, but able to move, eat and use the toilet. Maybe the caretaker he'd dismissed had been feeding the cat? Maybe part of Bobbi's illness made the cat invisible to her? Maybe she thought Indian Jones was feeding him? Now that he thought about it, he didn't recall seeing food in the cat's bowl.

He put his hands on his hips and watched with morbid fascination as the cat continued to snack.

An idea began to form.

This is my out.

What if Bobbi Marie died from natural causes and the cat ate her? Why did it have to be a murder at all? The tabby had already eaten most of the knife wound evidence... By the time anyone found the body he'd be long gone, having retrieved his box. He'd be in South America and any evidence of murder would be in the fat cat's belly.

He stepped over the cat, careful to avoid the blood, and cleaned the kitchen of his presence. The thermos of sleepy-milk went back into the plastic bag he'd used to transport it and he wiped down anything he thought he'd touched, just in case.

In mid-polish, he paused as a disturbing new thought crossed his mind.

The caretaker assigned to check in on Bobbi Marie had seen his face.

Did he need to kill her too?

He shook his head.

Nah. Too risky. They'd never consider Bobbi's death a homicide anyway. They'd assume she died of old age and the cat got hungry. Case closed. Anyway, hopefully, in a day he'd have his prize and be gone. They probably wouldn't even find her body for a few days. Maybe a few weeks.

I'll be drinking mojitos.

Thinking he had everything, he headed for the front door.

Then he remembered.

The knife.

The most important piece of evidence and he'd almost forgotten it.

Idiot.

He found it beside the chair where he'd fallen asleep, wrapped it in a paper towel and put it in the plastic bag.

The smudge of blood on the carpet wouldn't be a problem. In a day or two, bloody paw prints would *paint* the apartment.

Too bad he hadn't taken more time to pet the cat during his visits. Kitty was solving *all* his problems. He owed it.

Pulling the sleeve of his thin hoodie over his hand to open the door, he paused a moment to survey the apartment a final time. Friskie peered over Bobbi's arm.

"Bone appetite, cat."

He wiped the knob and closed the door.

Rushing to his car, he placed the plastic bag on the floor of the passenger side. He was about to close his door when he saw an orange cat sitting on the cement outside another resident's room.

Stepping back out of the car, he scooped up the cat and returned to Bobbi's door. He opened it, threw in the cat, and locked it once more.

If one cat was good, surely two cats were better. There wouldn't be an *ounce* of evidence that made sense by the time the two little monsters were done.

Chuckling to himself, he again wiped down the knob and hopped into his car. Nothing left to do but follow the box to its last known location.

Pineapple Port.

CHAPTER FIVE

Declan locked the door of his home, his mind running through his to-do list. It was going to be a busy day. First, he had to work, open his pawnshop, the Hock o' Bell, and sit; waiting to see what treasures the local community would bring his way.

He needed to dust the shop. Due to the abundance of local retirement villages, he had more furniture than the average pawnshop and the trails left by the fingertips of idle shoppers crisscrossed the tops of his bureaus and tables like snake trails.

After work, he hoped to grab dinner with Charlotte. They were due some quality time. When they went to her house, she seemed jumpy. He understood why; knowing the prying eyes of an entire neighborhood were monitoring your social life would be unsettling for anyone. Even a public restaurant might be more soothing.

They couldn't find any privacy at his house, thanks to Seamus. He needed to get on the real estate web sites and find his uncle some place to live. Maybe he could print out some spots and leave them scattered around the house in conspicuous places, like Seamus' pillow, or the bathroom. His uncle certainly spent enough time in *there*. He was going to have to repaint the room when he left.

Declan's phone rang and he paused beside his car to answer it.

"Hey," said Charlotte.

"Hey, what's up?"

"Guess what I'm doing?"

"I wouldn't hazard a guess."

"Interviewing everyone in the neighborhood to try and find out who stole a witch."

"A what? I—"

Declan cut his thought short as he watched a car pull into his driveway. A blonde sat behind the wheel.

No...

He pushed down his sunglasses to get a better look.

It couldn't be.

He swallowed, only to find he had no moisture left in his mouth.

Stephanie.

The ex.

He hadn't seen her in over a year. He'd read about natural disasters all over the globe though, and assumed she'd been *there*.

"Charlotte, can I call you back?"

"Sure. I just—"

"Okay, thanks."

It didn't occur to him that she'd been about to say something until he'd hung up. He winced and looked at his phone. He hadn't meant to be rude. He'd tell her later that a demon had rolled into his driveway and he'd had to call an exorcist. She'd understand. You didn't want to leave evil unattended until heads started spinning and your good furniture was covered in pea soup.

The door of Stephanie's red Dodge Viper opened and a long, tan leg capped by a black four-inch-heeled sandal slithered out. She stood and smiled at him, bleach-white teeth flashing beneath her Ray-Ban Aviators.

"Hey baby, you miss me?" she purred.

Declan felt a growl rumbling in his chest.

"I wake up to find you gone a *year* ago, along with all the money in my cash drawer and my favorite three wood, and you come back with *hey baby*?"

She shrugged. "I didn't have a three wood."

"You didn't *need* a three wood. *You don't play golf.* I don't have a cricket bat because *I don't play cricket.* That's how *not* playing a sport works."

"Well...I was thinking about taking lessons."

"So buy your own."

The corner of her mouth curled into a smile. Thanks to the plunging neckline of her tight-fitting red blouse, he had full view of the inside curve of her breasts. The right one bobbed up and down as she winked.

The movement was what Stephanie called a "bink"—short for "boob wink."

He shook his head and crossed his arms against his chest. "Don't bink at me. That isn't going to even come close to working."

"You used to love a good binking..." She walked toward him with her arms outstretched. "Come on...don't be like that..."

He took a step back, clipping the back of the low stone wall surrounding his front garden against his calf. He flailed and fell backwards, landing tush-first in the dirt. He lifted his right hand to find a flattened geranium beneath his palm, its hot pink petals strewn like confetti.

Stephanie giggled and held out a hand to help him up. He pushed away her fingers and climbed out of the garden, furiously wiping the back of his shorts.

"Now I'm going to have to change. Why are you here anyway? It's almost Halloween. Maybe there's a witch convention in town?"

"My mother died. I'm here to take care of her affairs."

"Oh...I'm sorry to hear that."

"I'm not. She was long overdue."

"Well...still. But now I need you to go *away*."

He turned and strode towards his front door.

"I came to tell you important news," she called after him.

He could hear the click of her heels on his stone walkway and increased his speed.

"I'm your boss."

He stopped, his hand on his door, and turned. "You know, you shouldn't be drinking and driving. Especially this early in the morn—"

"I found the will."

She ceased her pursuit and smoothed her skirt as if anything that form fitting could raise a crease.

Declan put his left hand against his abdomen. It felt as though a giant spatula had stabbed into his guts and flipped his stomach.

His uncle Seamus and Seamus' business partner, Bonehead O'Malley, had once owned his pawnshop. When Seamus moved to Miami, he made a deal with Bonehead that Declan would inherit the shop. The deal was scrawled on a bar napkin now framed on the wall of the Hock o' Bell's office.

Stephanie's mother, Bonehead's ex-girlfriend, had once claimed, during a drunken, post-funeral tirade, that she possessed a will stating Bonehead had left the shop to her. The next day she admitted she'd been lying. With Declan already running the store as if it were his own, life went on as usual.

Now Stephanie had returned, much like a nasty case of shingles, invoking the threat of the will.

Had she found it? Did it really exist?

Declan wondered if it was too late to fall on the ground and play dead until she left. It worked with bears.

"What are you talking about?" he asked.

"I came back to take care of Mom's funeral and found

Bonehead's will in her papers. So... looks like you work for me now."

"That's not true. Even if you do have an old will, Bonehead and Seamus made a deal and he changed his wishes."

"Did he? What do you have to prove that? A framed note scrawled on a napkin?"

Declan's stomach spatula went back to work and flipped his guts back to their original side. Stephanie was a lawyer, capable of mounting her case at no expense. Even if he won the battle, it would cost him a fortune.

"Why would you want the pawnshop? It doesn't mean anything to you."

"Neither did the three wood."

She smiled and he felt like throwing up in the surviving geraniums. He held very still, hoping she wouldn't notice him and wander off.

When was the last time I breathed? Do I have to breathe? Is that an everyday thing? It doesn't seem right but I'm feeling kind of dizzy...maybe I should breathe...

She waved a hand at him. "Don't worry. I don't want to take the shop from you."

He took a gasp of air.

Yep. Need to breathe.

"You don't? Let me guess... You want me to buy you out?"

"Nope. I don't want you to buy me out either."

He grimaced. This was going to end badly. He could feel it.

"You know I can't afford to fight you in court."

"I know."

"So what do you want?"

"I want to own the pawnshop *together*. I don't want anything to do with it...but I want everything to do with *you.*" She pointed an index finger at him, her long red nails flashing in the morning sun like the blood-tipped claws of a velociraptor. "And of course twenty percent off the top."

He swallowed. "You've got to be kidding. I ended our relationship the night I discovered you'd been sleeping with my best friend and that was the *last* of me having anything to do with you or him."

Her eyes flashed. "I remember. That was the first time anyone ever broke up with me, and since then *two* people have dumped me. You ruined my perfect record. You cursed me somehow."

"I'd blame that on karma, not me. If you dated people for love instead of money, you might find they stick around. And I don't care. We're *done*."

"I don't think so…" she said in a sing-song tone as she pulled a plastic tube from her purse and waved it in the air. "The paper in here says we'll be partners or you lose the pawnshop."

"We're not going to be partners."

"Then I hope you have a good lawyer and a lot of spare cash."

She winked and the mound of her enhanced breast bobbed beneath her blouse.

"Stop that."

She turned on her heel to leave.

"Stephanie, wait."

He jogged after her.

"What can I do to make this go away? You don't need the pawnshop. You have your own career."

She paused and slowly turned to face him. "I want a date."

"A what?"

"A date. You. Me. Out on a date."

He barked one loud *ha!* in her direction, so visceral even she lost her cool and paled.

"I'm not going out with you. I'd rather take a *wolverine* to a drive-in movie. In a very small car. Wearing a meat suit. It would be safer."

Stephanie set her jaw and glared at him.

"We're going out. And while we're out, we'll discuss things. Maybe it will all go away for the price of a few cocktails."

"Why do I suspect that isn't how things will go?"

She put her palms on his chest and stared at him with her big blue eyes.

He realized she smelled like candy. Much like the house in *Hansel and Gretel* must have.

"Maybe I just want an opportunity to apologize," she said, her voice dropping to a whisper.

He couldn't move.

This must be what it's like being hypnotized by a cobra.

Stephanie pushed the hair back from her face, revealing a heart-shaped scar above her left cheekbone. They'd been kids when that happened. He'd been on his way to find her when she'd run out of a store, stolen candy in her hand, the shop owner screaming at her in the background. She took the corner onto the sidewalk too fast, slipped, and clipped the side of her face on the low fence. She didn't cry. She picked herself off the ground, cradling her cheek with one hand, and stared at him. When the shop owner came barreling out of his store, Stephanie pushed Declan behind her, leaving a bloody hand print on his favorite shirt. She ran away, and the man accused him of being her accomplice, when all he'd been was an impromptu speed bump to slow her pursuer.

Strangely, it made him feel as if he had *saved* her

somehow, and he'd liked the feeling.

When they first started dating, their entanglement seemed like an inevitable fate. They'd known each other for so long. On and off through high school and into early adulthood they'd danced. Between his grandmother moving him to Tampa and Stephanie attending college and law school, it took him too long to realize that he was nothing more to her than a safe port between conquests.

Using him to seduce his wealthy friend had been the last straw. Finally, he realized he'd always be the one sacrificed while she ran away with the candy.

He'd realized her happiness wasn't his responsibility.

It made her *furious*.

"Apologize for what? Being who you are?" he asked.

She stared into his eyes a moment longer, turned and opened her car door.

The Viper roared to life and the window slid down.

"We need to talk," she said. "You pick the day, but be sure it's *this* week."

There were many things he wanted to say and none of them were nice, but she had him over a barrel. He *had* to be accommodating. Had to play along until he could coerce her into signing off on any claim she might have on his store. He wasn't sure if his napkin contract would stand under scrutiny.

"Bring the will. I don't even know if it's real. I want to see it," he said.

"Oh it's real." She again waved the tube at him. Stuffing it back in her bag, she blew him a kiss and he threw his head to the side to avoid it.

"See you soon, lover."

She pulled out of the driveway and sped away.

Declan dropped his head and stared at a dandelion

growing through a crack in his walkway.

Weeds. You never know where they will sprout. Your house…your business…your love life…

Someone cleared a throat and he turned to spot Seamus grinning at him, leaning against the tired VW Jetta he'd bought for a thousand dollars after arriving in Charity. Declan sighed and rubbed his eye with his left palm.

"Okay, let's get this over with. How much did you see?"

His uncle strolled toward him.

"That was quite a lady."

"She's not a lady. Charles Manson in drag is more of a lady than her."

"I dunno…she's certainly a fine thing."

"Don't do that."

"What?"

"Don't give her credit for what she was born with. Everything she has any *control* over is a nightmare. She's certifiably insane."

"So, ex-girlfriend I assume?"

"Yes, and you know her. She's Bonehead's ex-girlfriend's daughter, Stephanie."

"That's Stephanie?" Seamus looked down the street after a car that was long gone. He held a face-down palm out at hip level. "Little Stephanie? The one that used to run around the shop with you when you were kids?"

"Yup. Now she's a full-grown psychopath."

"Just like her mother. Bonehead broke up with her because she tried to run him down with his John Deere. Thank the heavens lawn tractors are loud; he was a little deaf. If she'd gone after him with one of those electric cars he'd be dead."

"Stephanie's usually more diabolical than lawnmower

hit-and-runs. When we were kids, she locked me in that treasure chest you had in the shop. She left me there for *three hours*. That should have been my first hint."

"I remember that. When we heard you yelling she said she'd lost the key and had been too scared to tell us."

"And you believed her. Trusting morons like you helped convince her she could cause havoc without consequences."

Seamus chuckled. "Most things are my fault in the end. So, what does she want this time?"

Declan felt ridiculous, but there was no way he could hide his embarrassment from his uncle forever. The man was clever, street smart and constantly nearby, living in his house and drinking his beer. Whenever he suggested Seamus buy his own beer, the wily Irishman pulled him into a shady bar game or card trick and he ended up paying for it anyway. He wouldn't be able to hide anything from him for long.

"She said she found a will stating Bonehead left the pawnshop to her mother."

"What? Bah…she's off her nut."

"I told you that."

"You still have the napkin?"

"Yes. Of course. It's on the wall, framed in the…"

Declan's voice faded. He could feel the blood draining from his face and his cheeks began to tingle.

"What is it?"

"She said *framed*."

"What?"

"While she was here. She said, *What proof do you have? A framed napkin?*"

"So?"

"*So*, she just got back to town. I moved the shop into the old Taco Bell *after* we broke up and it was *then* that I framed the napkin. How could she know it was framed?"

"She must have visited. Maybe you were waiting on someone and didn't see her?"

Declan shook his head. "I would have felt the icy breeze." He covered his mouth with his hand. "Oh no."

"What?"

"The napkin is hanging in the office, in the back. She couldn't have seen it from the floor. That means she went into the office. That means she was *looking for it*."

"Oh. That's not good."

"I have a bad feeling about this. I have to get to the shop."

He gave the seat of his shorts one last brushing and ran to his car.

CHAPTER SIX

Charlotte patted Abby on the head and walked outside to where Mariska and Darla sat in Mariska's golf cart waiting to chauffeur her to water aerobics. She took her usual place on the rumble seat and Mariska stomped on the gas.

"Did you get your investigating finished?" asked Mariska.

"More importantly, did you find Witchy-Poo?" asked Darla.

"I didn't find your witch. I'm only about half way through the neighborhood though. I needed a break. So far I've identified about ten switched items, but I did have something interesting pop up with Gloria."

"Short Gloria or chubby Gloria?" asked Darla.

"Short. Someone sent her a death threat."

"A death threat? What does that mean?" asked Mariska.

"It means someone wants to kill you," said Darla.

Mariska shot her a look and nearly hit the curb sidelong as her arms followed her gaze. With a jerk of the wheel, she adjusted the trajectory and Charlotte scrambled to catch her towel as it attempted a suicide leap from the back seat.

"Frank thinks it's kids being stupid," said Charlotte.

"Frank knows about it? Then I'll get to the bottom of it," said Darla. "That man pretends he's a vault but he *loves* telling me about his police stuff. Especially if I promise him some sugar."

Charlotte stuck out her tongue. "Oh, *gross*. Too much information."

"No, I mean *actual* sugar. He isn't supposed to have it but if I want to know something I throw him some cookies. When you're young it's all sex, sex, sex, but when you're old just letting them use real salt does the trick."

"I'll make a note of that."

"So do you think it's just kids?" asked Mariska. "Gloria's so sweet."

"I saw some teens outside her house while I was there. I chased them but they went through the trees to the cow pasture."

"You chased them? What were you thinking?"

"It's sort of my job now. Fighting crime and whatnot."

"Well, I don't like that one bit. And I don't like someone threatening Gloria either. This place is turning into New York City."

"The real victim of this nonsense is Witchy-Poo," grumbled Darla. "Let's not forget that."

Mariska parked at the pool and they piled off the cart with bags, towels and floaty noodles in tow. Jackie was poolside, her boom box at the ready. She hated being in charge of water aerobics, but she'd volunteered years ago and now no one would agree to take her place.

"Ready for some water aerobics?" Charlotte asked, teasing.

Jackie rolled her eyes. "I'm going to push play but I'm out of commission. I think I tore something in my shoulder trying to get out of that stupid ghouly suit."

"*Ghillie* suit."

"Whatever."

"I'd say I'm sorry but you *did* shoot me dead."

Jackie chuckled. "Did you figure out who's up to the mischief?"

"Kids we think. I saw them running away from Gloria's house but I couldn't catch them. She's having some…uh…issues, and it may all be related."

"Big-eyes Gloria or big-nose Gloria?"

"Big-eyes." Charlotte considered telling Jackie about the death threat letter, but decided there was no reason to cause alarm. Pineapple Port was too small. If she told one person, soon the whole neighborhood would be in a sweat, frightened to check their mailboxes. Telling Darla and Mariska wasn't the smartest idea, but she figured Frank would tell Darla anyway. "Well, I hope you feel better."

Jackie nodded and prepared her well-worn aerobics cassette.

Charlotte was about to step into the pool when a scream made everyone jump.

"Fire!"

Heads in the pool swiveled. Having just launched the water aerobics routine, Jackie pressed the button on her boom box to stop the musical instruction.

"Smoke!" said Darla, all gazes following her pointing finger toward the sky. A billowing cloud of gray smoke filled the air beyond the roofline of the clubhouse.

The fire was *close*.

"Mariska, I'm going to borrow your golf cart," said Charlotte.

"Oooh… *Be careful!*"

Wrestling to slip into her cover-up, Charlotte bolted to the parking lot and jumped into the cart, nearly toppling it over as she hooked sharp right onto the street at top speed. She kept her eyes on the column of smoke. The fire was definitely nearby. Definitely in Pineapple Port.

Sirens blared in the distance as she sped toward a crowd gathering in the street in front of a house. She recognized the drinking parrot on the flag, still working to finish his piña colada.

Gloria's house.

She stopped the cart with a screech of tires.

"Where's Gloria?" she yelled.

Everyone looked around at each other. Gloria was nowhere to be seen.

"Is she still inside?"

"Is anyone inside?" said 'Mac' MacBrady pulling up on his own golf cart.

In another life, Mac had been a Boston firefighter. His red golf cart had a siren on top and *Pineapple Port Fire Brigade* stenciled on the side in gold leaf, compliments of his wife. Charlotte noted that he'd forgotten to turn on the flashing light, but figured they probably didn't want an honorary fireman who took the time to turn on his toy siren during a real emergency.

"I just got here but no one seems to know where Gloria is," she said.

Mac yanked on the screened porch door and, finding it hook-locked, gave it another mighty tug to pull it free. Striding through the inner portal, he left the flimsy porch door hanging skewed from its hinges. He put his hand on the front door and then tested the knob. It was also locked.

"Stand back!"

Mac was a burly man and, well into his sixties, still appeared as though he could carry two people from a burning building, one under each arm. He took a step back and kicked the door near the lock. The door shuddered, but stood strong. On his next kick, the lock splintered from the frame, and he rammed his shoulder into it to finish his attack. As the door gave way, he stumbled inside. Charlotte shadowed him.

She didn't see any flames, but a haze of smoke filled the living room. "Check the first bedroom on the right; she's been hiding there," she called over the sirens blaring outside as she tried to move past him down the hall.

Mac thrust out an arm to block her progress and she had to throw on the brakes to avoid being beheaded. He shot her a look that made her rethink her plan.

"What are you doing in here? Get out."

"I had to tell you where she was."

Mac grimaced. "Stay behind me. Stay near the front door."

Charlotte took a step back and watched as Mac tested the spare bedroom door and tried the knob. Outside, the real fire trucks arrived and cut their sirens.

"Stand back," Mac screamed at the door. The bedroom door proved flimsier than the front, giving way with a single kick of Mac's size twelve tennis shoe. Sneakers weren't official fireman footwear, but secured to the bottom of his sturdy legs, they got the job done.

Charlotte heard a scream as Mac disappeared into the bedroom. A moment later, he reappeared with Gloria cradled in his arms like a baby. Gloria's eyes had gone from bush baby-size to Betty Boop.

"Is there anyone else?" asked Mac.

"No, no…what is going on?" said Gloria, clinging to his neck.

Mac paused in the kitchen, looking like a carved marble firefighting memorial as he surveyed the home for other victims. Gloria slid a hand down his chest, rested her head against his pectoral muscle and smiled.

"My…you're *so* strong…" She winked at Charlotte, who turned away to keep from laughing. Gloria segued from terrified to flirty as easily as shifting a gear. The woman was a puzzle.

"Charlotte, *out*," said Mac as he passed her, unaware that he was being felt up.

Charlotte spotted the plate of brownies she'd enjoyed the day before and considered saving them. *But*…something didn't feel right about Mac risking his life to save Gloria and her popping out behind him with a plate full of brownies. *Might be bad for business.* She left them.

Paramedics rushed to take Gloria from Mac. The fire brigade had a hose wrapped to the back of the building. Confident that Gloria was safe, Charlotte followed the hose. She was so intent on her path that she didn't see a fireman round the corner from the back of the house and they slammed into each other. She stumbled back and then caught her balance. He didn't seem to budge.

He removed his helmet.

He was *gorgeous.*

Sexy fireman? How cliché…but…

He grinned, his gaze sweeping from Charlotte's eyes to her toes and back again. She did the same to him. He put his helmet on the ground and slipped out of his jacket, revealing a white tank undershirt tight against his muscular chest. She forced her gaze away from him, but it soon swiveled back.

How predictable. Right? How—

He lifted both arms to ruffle his sweaty hair, blue veins crisscrossing beneath his tanned skin like a roadmap.

How…

Hm.

How does he make his biceps look like wire cables like that?

"Hey," he said, staring at her as if he wanted to sweep her into his arms, carry her away, and ravish her beneath the soft glow of a burning building.

At least that's how she read it.

He reached out, slid his hand from her hip to the small of her back, and led her away from the fire.

"Miss, you should probably stay clear of the area."

She allowed him to guide her to the sidewalk.

"Um, is it bad?" she asked.

"What?"

"The fire."

"Oh, right." He shook his head. "It's out. It was a cardboard box full of leaves in the middle of her backyard. Someone lit it on fire. Lot of smoke."

"Can you tell what started it?"

"Depends...do you want to get a drink some time? I'm Jason." He thrust out his hand and Charlotte shook it.

Why did things like this never happen *before* she had a boyfriend?

"I'm Charlotte."

"That's a pretty name."

"Thank you."

"So how about that drink?"

"Oh... That's really sweet of you but I can't. I have a boyfriend...I think..."

Damn.

She hadn't meant to say the last bit out loud. A little thief named *doubt* had stolen her confidence in her new relationship with Declan. She cringed to realize how easily she'd betrayed her insecurity and shot the fireman a look, hoping he hadn't heard.

He was already laughing, his hazel eyes twinkling with flecks of gray. "You *think*? Sounds like a lousy boyfriend."

She raised her palms and shook her head as a mea culpa. "No, I *do* have a boyfriend... I don't know why I said that. But, seriously, do you know how the fire started?"

Change the subject back to the fire…there you go…

"Seriously, I'll tell you if you'll get a drink with me. One tiny cocktail."

She smiled and hoped she wasn't blushing. She didn't often come in contact with men her own age, but she couldn't let one handsome fireman throw her into a tizzy. "Come on. Just tell me. What started the fire?"

He crossed his arms across his chest, the grin never leaving his face. "I don't think so…"

She shrugged. "Fine. I guess you probably couldn't *tell* what started it…"

His smile dissolved like a sand castle swallowed by the rising tide. Apparently he didn't like having his prowess questioned.

A person didn't have to be a private eye to unravel the mystery of the male ego.

"I know how it started," he said, a little too loudly. "Someone filled a box with a bunch of brush and set it on fire. *Bam!*" He threw an imaginary object to the ground and lifted his splayed fingers into the air to create the effect of an explosion. "And no accelerant was used. How about them apples? *Shazam!* See? I know all this stuff."

"So it was intentional? Like…fire vandalism?"

Or a like sending a message…

"Yep. The lady in this house might want to watch out."

Charlotte looked away, her mind whirring. She knew Gloria hadn't been burning leaves. Someone *was* trying to send her a message. First a note, then a fire. Things were ramping up…*what next?*

"So pick you up around five?"

She returned her attention to Jason. "What?"

"Drinks? Around five?"

She shook her head. "No, I can't. I'm sorry. But I really do appreciate your help."

He rubbed his hand on his chest as if trying to draw her attention to all she would be missing. "Stickin' with the *maybe boyfriend*, eh? Well, if you ever figure out if you're dating anyone or not, stop by the Stone Yard and ask for Jason. That's where I work."

"The Stone Yard? Is it a bar?"

"No, it's a real stone yard. We sell stones. Like, for landscaping."

He pointed to a truck parked on the curb with *The Stone Yard* emblazoned on the side.

"I thought you were a fireman?"

"Volunteer."

"Oh."

Charlotte spotted Mariska and Darla headed in her direction. Jason followed her gaze and then turned back to her.

"Well, maybe I'll see you," he said opening his truck's door. A landslide of soda cans, wadded fast food wrappers and spare clothing poured from the seat to the ground at Charlotte's feet. She stared at the pile, noticing two nudie magazines splayed with the rest of the rubble. The page edges on both were curled and worn.

Jason dropped to a squat to snatch the trash into his arms before throwing it back into the truck. He slammed the door to keep the rising tide of junk at bay.

"I share this truck with all the guys at the yard. They're kind of a mess," he said, appearing flustered.

Charlotte nodded.

"Sorry. I'll…I'll see you around." He jogged to the other side of the truck to hop in. The truck roared to life and he drove off.

"Who was that?" asked Mariska arriving beside her.

"Fireman Jason."

She strolled to where she'd left Mariska's golf cart parked and Darla joined them there. "How did you two get here?"

"We hopped a ride on Julia's cart," said Darla. "I saw that guy you were talking to. That fireman was smokin'."

"Ba dum dum. I guess; if you like that beefcake kind of thing."

"So what happened?" asked Mariska. "Is Gloria okay?"

"She's fine. Jason said someone set a fire in her backyard."

"Oh *Jason* did, did he?" asked Darla, a teasing lilt in her voice.

"Yes, *Jason* did. He's a fireman. That's what they do. Anyway, Gloria was asleep in the spare room. Mac broke in there and pulled her out."

"Mac? Speaking of hunks…" mumbled Darla.

"You smell like smoke," said Mariska.

"I went in too."

"Oh Charlotte…are you crazy? In that gauzy cover-up? You could have gone up like a Roman candle."

"The fire was outside. Just the smoke was inside."

"I'm sure you didn't know that when you went in."

Charlotte shrugged and changed the subject.

"Someone is trying to scare Gloria. First she gets a threatening letter and now someone's tried to burn down her house. Or at least imply that they could burn down her house."

They turned to look at Gloria, who sat on the back of the ambulance with an oxygen mask over her face. She waved to them and they waved back.

"I need to talk to her," said Charlotte.

"She looks a little busy right now."

"I guess it can wait..." As if on cue, paramedics removed her mask.

Nope. Can't wait.

"Just a second..."

She jogged over to the ambulance.

"Gloria, you weren't burning leaves in your backyard, were you?"

"No. The firemen asked me that, too. Why would I burn leaves? I have a lawn service. And where would I get leaves? I don't have trees that drop leaves. Isn't that supposed to be one of the perks of retiring in Florida?"

Charlotte thought about Jason's description of the fire. He'd said someone had set ablaze a *box* of leaves. The person who set the fire must have carted his own fuel.

"I'm afraid this fire might be related to your threat."

"Frank said he can't give me police protection. He says he thinks it's kids."

"I know. He might change his mind now. Either way, I'd like to help you."

"Because you're a detective now?"

"Trying to be. It isn't official yet. But I really want to help you, okay?"

"I'd like that. This would be exciting if I wasn't so scared."

"Do you have family you could go to visit for a while?"

"No. My only boy is in Germany. He works for one of those techy firms."

"Okay. Well...maybe later today we could talk if you feel up to it?"

She nodded. "I don't think they're taking me to the hospital. I told them I'm fine, thanks to Mac." Her eyes darted left and right and she leaned towards Charlotte, dropping her voice to a conspiratorial whisper. "Did you ever notice how big and strong Mac is?"

Charlotte laughed. "Easy there... He's married."

"I heard she was having heart trouble."

"Gloria. What a thing to say."

"I'm not wishing her dead. It was just the last bit of gossip I heard about her. My goodness..." She patted her chest and looked flustered. "I didn't mean it *that* way."

"Of course not." Charlotte eyed her, and she looked away. "Well, we'll talk in a bit."

Charlotte patted her on the knee and walked back to Darla and Mariska. The three of them piled onto Mariska's golf cart and headed for home. They'd had enough excitement for one morning.

They could skip water aerobics.

CHAPTER SEVEN

The loud rapping of knuckles on glass made Declan jump. Seamus was standing outside his car, banging to get his attention.

He lowered the window.

"What?"

"You think Stephanie took the napkin?"

"Yes. Now let me *go*. I have to get to the shop and check."

"I'm coming with."

Seamus jogged behind the car to keep Declan from pulling out of the driveway and then let himself in the passenger door.

"Why are you coming? I'm not bringing you back. You'll be stranded at the shop all day."

"That's okay. I've got nothing better to do."

"Really? What about house hunting?"

Seamus stared at his nails as if they needed a buff. "What's that now?"

Declan sighed and slammed his car into reverse. He reached the Hock o' Bell in record time and jumped out of the car. Fiddling with his keys in the lock for what felt like an eternity, the door finally gave way and he punched in his alarm code before bolting to his office.

He was staring at the frame on the wall when he felt Seamus enter the room.

"It's still there," said Seamus pointing at the framed napkin. "Tragedy averted."

"No. It's not the right napkin. She switched it. That's a

napkin from our favorite restaurant."

"*Our* favorite restaurant? I didn't know we had one."

"Stephanie and me. We used to get takeout from a little Italian place, Romanesque's, every Friday. It's a napkin from there."

"How's the pizza? We should get it some time."

"It's been closed for years."

"Then how did she—"

"I told you she's nuts. She *plans*. She's probably had that napkin in a jar next to her eye of newt just waiting for the moment it would come in handy."

"Eye of newt?"

"It's a witch thing."

"Oh."

Seamus grunted and scratched his head. "Well, for what it's worth, it's a lovely frame."

"I'm going to kill her. How did she break in here? I have an alarm system."

"She probably didn't break in. She probably had someone distract you while she slipped back here and switched the napkins."

"But I have a—"

Declan recalled entering the store.

No bell. He hadn't heard the familiar jingle of his door bell.

And here was Seamus, who'd also entered the shop without a sound.

No bell.

"Looking for something?" said a voice behind them.

Both men turned to find Stephanie standing at the threshold of the office. She'd entered like a ghost. No warning.

No bell.

Declan felt his face pinch, eyes narrowing. "I guess it would be too much to ask you to *wear* the bell you stole from my door?"

"Like a naughty kitty?" she asked in a low, sexy voice.

"Oh my," said Seamus.

"I didn't steal your bell," she added, turning and pointing to the front of the store. Declan followed her gesture and spotted the tiny gold bell hanging in its usual place above the door.

"I *did* get a new necklace though," she added, shaking the thin chain around her neck.

Hanging from it was the bell's clapper.

"Well look at you," said Seamus, grinning. "You would have been just my type when I was a younger man. Nutty as a squirrel's winter nest."

Stephanie rolled her eyes. "I've done May-December romances, old man, but I'm afraid you don't fit the bill. Or should I say, you can't *pay* the bills."

Seamus licked the fingers on his left hand and smoothed the hair above his ear. He stepped toward Stephanie and leaned in close. She stood her ground, as if to prove he didn't scare her.

"Ah…but I'm *filthy* with personality…" he purred in her ear.

Declan was mortified. "I thought you preferred older women?" It took every shred of willpower not to grab his uncle's arm and yank him away from his ex. He couldn't stand the idea of anyone playing into her hands. He couldn't turn back his own history but he could spend the rest of his life saving others.

Seamus stepped back and winked at Declan. "It's a man's prerogative to change his mind, isn't it?"

Declan opened his mouth and then shut it with plans to deal with Seamus later. He trained his gaze back on Stephanie. "Where is it?"

She rolled the bell clapper between her fingers.

"Where's what?"

"The napkin."

She looked at the frame. "Why it's right there, silly."

"That isn't it and you know it."

"Did you look behind the desk? Maybe it slid…"

"Stephanie, I'm not playing these games with you. Give me back the napkin."

"I will. I might. I don't really need it. What *I* have is ironclad. A real will trumps the scrawlings of two drunken Irishmen."

"I resent the implication. Who said we were drinking?" asked Seamus.

"It's a *bar* napkin."

"You've never heard of tonic water?" He waited a beat before continuing. "Just kidding. We were snockered." He turned to Declan. "Sorry, I couldn't keep a straight face any longer."

"Don't give her more ammunition. Knowing her, she's probably recording us."

"That would be inadmissible in court, so no point, really," she said.

"Why are you here?"

"I missed you. And I need a lamp for my new house. Mom's stuff was all junk. Thought I'd pick one up here…"

"There'll be no shopping today, missy," said Seamus taking a step forward. "I think you've made your point. You can go now."

"But—"

Seamus shooed her along and she began a slow, slinky walk toward the front door.

"Fine," she said. "I'll see you soon, baby. Pick me out a lamp."

Declan watched from his office. She turned and waved

to him as Seamus ushered her out the front door and locked it behind her.

"We can't keep the door locked. We're open," said Declan.

"Let's give it a second. Until she's gone."

"What, are you afraid of her now? A minute ago you were flirting with her."

Seamus laughed. "I wasn't flirting." He reached into his pocket and pulled out a square napkin covered in blue ink.

Declan gasped. "Is that—"

"It is. I'm a bit of a dip."

Declan raised his eyebrows. "Well I can't argue with that."

Seamus grinned and then sobered.

"I meant a *dipper*. A fingersmith."

Declan continued to stare.

"Which is to say I'm a bit of a *pickpocket*. I wasn't flirting. I was *distracting*."

"Ah. Why am I not surprised? Give it to me. That's going right in the safe. How did you know it was *my* napkin?"

"I saw the paper in her handbag and thought it might be it. Worst case scenario it turned out to be a dirty tissue."

"Gross."

"Indeed."

"She has the will in her purse too. In a plastic tube. I don't suppose you grabbed that while you were at it?"

Seamus grimaced. "No. I wish you'd told me she's keeping it close before I showed my hand. Once she realizes we have the napkin she'll be more careful."

"Hm. Still… I'm relieved. I was a little horrified by your behavior."

"No worries…she's not my type. I do like them older, but no less crazy, I'll give her that. Makin' a necklace outta your bell clapper…she's a right nutter. Clever though. Gotta give her that."

Declan opened the safe and set the napkin inside. "It must give her a thrill to keep what we want so close and then not give it to us."

"Or she knows how easy it would be to ransack her house in her absence."

A car pulled into the shop's lot and Declan stared at it, rubbing the back of his neck. He could already feel the tension in his shoulders growing. "I've got customers. I have to open the shop. Do you want to help me dust today?"

Seamus grimaced.

"I was thinking I'd borrow your computer and look for a house. It's about time I gave you your space."

Declan headed towards the door to unlock it. "I mention dusting and *now* you want to look for a house. You're a wily old coot."

He turned in time to see Seamus grin.

CHAPTER EIGHT

Charlotte tried Declan's cell phone again but he didn't answer. He'd said he'd call back, but that had been hours ago. Now she had to tell him about the case of the stolen witch *and* death threats *and* the fire. Things were piling up. She considered calling his shop but decided against it. It felt a little stalky. She didn't want to be that annoying girlfriend, hunting him down. He'd probably gotten some customers and forgotten or was just too busy.

Be patient.

She changed out of her bathing suit and redressed to continue canvassing the neighborhood for clues. As she left the house, she stared at her phone, willing it to ring. They needed some alone time. A romantic outing. Who was supposed to run point on something like that? Traditionally, men were in charge of planning romantic outings...but... *why?* After all, they were in this together.

She sighed. The phrase *in this together* made their burgeoning romance sound as if they were plane crash survivors in search of rescue before they were forced to eat each other.

Maybe she should let him handle the romantic bits. He had to be better at them than she was. On the other hand...maybe some gentle poking...

She texted him *Crazy things happening today!* as she walked to the next house on her list.

Maybe it was okay to be *slightly* stalky.

By the time she'd knocked on every door, Charlotte

had twenty-two switched items in her official notebook. No one had seen anything odd or bumped into a giant inflatable witch. Her only leads were two hooded youths and the fact that someone wanted to kill Gloria, which, when she thought about it, seemed a little more important than a missing witch did.

Not that she'd ever share that thought with Darla.

Detecting was hard work in the Florida sun and thanks to Gloria's fire, she smelled like a hot dog.

Why does smoke make people smell like hot dogs? If I dated a fireman, would it make me like hot dogs more, or less? If a fireman broke up with me, would I feel sad every time I went to a barbeque?

She took a quick shower to remove the hot dog perfume and the sheen of salt covering her body.

Feeling refreshed, she decorated her home for Halloween. She owned a box full of ghosts, skeletons and other scary doo-dads. Thanks to the ladies in the neighborhood, she had enough ghouls to decorate fifteen houses. The locals *loved* giving holiday-themed gifts, so she had a dozen crocheted pumpkins in both 3D round and flat coaster-style, scarecrows in various sizes, a never-ending array of ceramic witches and ghosts (some that served as salt and pepper shakers), and a plastic flamingo zombie she'd bought herself. She didn't always decorate but thought Declan might get a kick out of her collection. Thanks to his pawnshop, and generosity, she had new furniture which meant a plethora of new, flat surfaces to cover with terrifying kitsch.

She grabbed a few of the smaller pieces and placed them around the room. Abby stuck her head in the box, nipped a crocheted ghost between her front teeth and wandered down the hall. The next time Charlotte peeked at the dog she was laying with her chin on the flattened remains of the ghost, stuffing strewn around her head.

"I saw you take it, you're not that sneaky," she mumbled to the dog.

Abby grunted and rolled to her side, stretching.

Charlotte passed her chalkboard wall and paused. A few coats of chalkboard paint had provided her with a place to keep organized and the list was impossible to avoid, serving as a giant constant reminder of things to be done. Misplacing a notepad could kill a day's productivity. She couldn't misplace a wall.

She wrote "Current Casework" at eye level. That sounded official. Beneath that, she made her list:

1. Find Darla's witch
2. Find who switched all the decorations
3. Find who is threatening Gloria

No. That wasn't the right order.
Possible homicides should go first.

She erased them and reversed the order. Then she added an addendum to two items.

1. Find who is trying to kill Gloria (and why)
2. Find Darla's witch
3. Find who switched all the decorations (and why)

She didn't need to write *why* next to Witchy-Poo's line item. That thing was obnoxious. *Why not* was more like it.

There was a knock on the door and Abby bolted from the hallway to bark her unalarmed-but-compulsory staccato woofs. Charlotte peeked through her window before answering. Normally she wouldn't think twice about her safety in Pineapple Port, but things seemed different. Maybe that was the downside of crime investigation; suddenly, everything appeared more sinister.

She spotted little Gloria standing on her porch. The woman's ruffled, flowered tank top and neon, *differently* flowered skirt did little to distract from the red canvas suitcase in her hand, her large, green-rimmed sunglasses and the waist-length dark wig covering her tawny helmet of hair. She looked as if someone had shrunk Cher, dragged her through a flower patch and then kicked her to the curb.

She pushed Abby back with her leg and opened the door.

"I was just thinking about you…" Charlotte's gaze fell to the suitcase as she undertook the Herculean task of not ogling the wig. The sheer ugliness of the hairpiece was nothing compared to the strange and barely-controllable urge she felt to *braid* it. "Uh…how are you?"

Gloria flipped up her glasses.

"It's me, Gloria."

"I know."

"Even in the disguise?"

"Yep."

Gloria's shoulders sagged. "Shoot."

"What's up?"

"You said you wanted to talk to me."

"I do I—I'm sorry…is that a suitcase? Are you going somewhere?"

"Well, I wanted to talk to you about that. Can I come in?"

Charlotte searched for potential murderers and Sonny Bono impersonators in search of a partner. The coast was clear.

"Of course."

Gloria stepped inside and took a seat on the sofa. No sooner had her tush hit the cushions than Abby hopped beside her and plopped her head on her lap. Gloria stroked the dog's ears as if they performed the routine daily.

Abby was shameless that way.

Gloria tried to slide her sunglasses to her head and, realizing the task couldn't be completed without pushing the wig off her skull, instead placed them on the living room table. Her fingers lingered on the wood as she stared at the furniture.

"Is this Holly's table?" she asked.

"What's that?"

"Holly Thompson. Remember her? She lived down the street from me. Died six months ago? Emphysema."

People in Pineapple Port never mentioned a deceased person without including the cause of death. Many searched the Internet daily for the various ways they might meet their end. Noting how other people died also gave friends new things to talk about with their doctors. A typical exchange went something like:

Pineapple Port Resident #1: *Remember Bob? Cerebral Autosomal Dominant Arteriopathy with Subcortical Infarcts Leukoencephalopathy?*

Pineapple Port Resident #2: *Ooh, I'll have to look that one up. I wonder if my doctor knows about it. I better ask. How do you spell Leukoencephalopathy?*

Charlotte looked at her table with new eyes. "I didn't know Holly well. Why?"

"This looks just like her coffee table..."

Charlotte grimaced. "I don't know. I guess it could be. I got it from Declan's pawnshop..."

Oh boy. All my furniture is from dead people. Why did I waste time putting out Halloween decorations when my actual furniture is probably haunted?

Gloria shrugged and sat back. A silence fell, awkward to everyone but Abby who leaned into her ear scratching. She stretched out a paw to untangle it from Gloria's Cher wig and pulled the whole mop askew, leaving the center part shifted to the right.

"Can I get you anything?"

"Do you have any sweet tea?"

"I have unsweetened..."

Gloria grimaced as if she'd been offered cyanide.

"I could put a Sweet-n-Low in it?"

"Oh, yes. That will work."

Charlotte stood. "I got you, babe."

"What?"

"Nothing. I'll be right back."

As Charlotte poured the iced tea she noticed the light in the house changing. She didn't think much of it, clouds were as common as sun in Florida, but when she turned to reenter the living room, all her blinds had been closed.

She put the tea on the sofa table using a book as a coaster. Glancing at the chalkboard wall, she wondered if it would be rude to take a moment to jot down *coasters* on her shopping list. Declan probably had some at the shop but she didn't want any more dead people items in the house. There had to be a scientific ratio of dead-people-items to ghosts-attached-to-them and if she wasn't haunted yet, she didn't want to push her luck.

Charlotte sat in the deep reading chair Declan had given her. She loved the chair, but now she wondered who'd been sitting in it before her and what had taken the sitter's life.

"Is this Holly's chair?" she asked.

Gloria studied it. "I don't think so."

Good. Maybe the former owner just didn't appreciate it.

"Is the tea sweet enough?"

Gloria nodded, mid-sip. "Oh yes, perfect, thank you."

The room again fell silent. After a few minutes, Charlotte couldn't take it any longer.

"Gloria...we need to talk about the elephants in the room."

"What?"

"You have a suitcase and you've scalped Cher."

"Oh..." Gloria's hand fluttered to her head. "Yes..." She slid the wig off the back of her head and leaned forward to set her tea on the book-coaster. "I guess I don't need to wear this here, but you can't blame me for being careful; someone's trying to kill me."

"That's what I wanted to talk to you about. Who do you think?" She grabbed a notepad from the table beside her and held a pen poised to jot down the particulars of Gloria's case.

"Who what?"

"Who's trying to kill you?"

"Oh, I don't know..." Gloria looked down and fiddled with Abby's ear.

"You have no idea? There must be *something*. People don't usually threaten people unless they have some reason. And they definitely don't then try to burn down their house."

"It was just a box of leaves."

"Still..."

Gloria sighed. "Well...I guess there might be a couple possibilities..."

"A *couple*? Like what?"

"Well...I used to be in real estate..."

Charlotte waited for more but nothing came. She needed to coax more information from the little woman before Gloria stole her dog's love from her forever.

"Last I checked, selling houses isn't a capital offense."

"No, but selling someone a snake house doesn't put you on their Christmas card list, either."

Charlotte sat up in her chair. "Did you say a *snake* house?"

Gloria nodded. "The house had a bit of a snake problem. Basement was full of them. Every time the owners reached for the TV remote *whoops!* it's a snake. Need an umbrella? Too bad, it's a snake. That's what they said, anyway. Sounded like a bit of a stretch to me. Though…I believe them about hearing them in the walls. There were an awful lot of them in the walls…black ones, brown ones, little ones, big ones…"

"Cripes. You *knew* about them?"

"Yes… At first I refused to take the listing but then…"

Gloria leaned forward to reclaim her tea. Charlotte shifted to the edge of her seat.

"But then *what?*"

"But then I got this awful client. A capital B-rhymes-with-witch if you know what I mean."

"Got it. I'm a detective, remember."

"I figured she *deserved* the snake house. When I showed her the house I went to the appointment early and scared the stragglers back into the walls before she came to view it."

Charlotte slapped her hand to her cheek, speechless and tried to shake the image of snakes crawling through her walls before continuing.

"Okay…so…I can see how the lady who bought your snake house *might* be a little angry. How long ago was this?"

"Oh, twenty-odd years ago."

"Hm. That seems like a long time to collect magazines for a threatening collage, though I'm not going to take her off the suspect list. Anyone else?"

"My ex-husbands…"

"Husbands with an 's?' What did you do to *them*?"

"Well, one went bankrupt…"

"That's not your f—"

"…after selling a house full of snakes."

Instead of finishing the word *fault*, Charlotte made an airy *fuhhh* noise like a deflating balloon. "Wait. You said *you* sold the house full of snakes."

"I did, but my husband owned the real estate office where I worked."

"And he knew about the snakes, too?"

"No, he had no idea."

"But…*he* went bankrupt?"

Gloria nodded. "And did a little jail time."

"He went to jail?"

"I might have *implied* to the judge that my husband changed the contract and removed the bit where the seller revealed the house was full of snakes."

"I'm going to go out on a limb here and guess he *didn't* change the contract?"

"No. I changed the contract. And once they looked into him they found all sort of other things wrong with the way he ran his business. Oh, and he was cheating on me. Did I mention that?"

"No… But back to the snakes. Did it ever occur to you to pay someone to remove the snakes?"

"Do you know how expensive it is to remove two hundred snakes from a house?"

Charlotte's jaw fell. "*Two hundred?*"

"Give or take. Apparently, when snakes find a nice spot they send little messages to all the other snakes to stop by. They're like scaly little hippies that way. Did you know that?"

"I did not. But thank you for killing any chance I had of ever sleeping again."

"And in all fairness, the woman's family were *pet* people. You know?"

"She had a family?"

"Oh yes. Couple of kids, a dog, a cat and two hamsters and…um…well…they *had* two hamsters…"

Gloria looked away and began chewing on her nail.

"Oh no…don't tell me—"

Gloria dropped her hand on the sofa cushion and both Charlotte and the dog jumped. "Who takes hamsters into a house full of snakes?"

"I don't know…maybe a person who is *unaware* their house is full of snakes?"

Gloria sighed and the agitation in her voice fell away to her usual squeaky tone.

"I didn't know snakes ate hamsters. I thought they were too furry. They were teddy bear hamsters. Live and learn. I heard the cat had quite a scare too…"

Charlotte realized Abby, the furry love of her life, was lying on the lap of a woman who once fed a happy family and their pets to a serpent commune.

"Hey Abby, come here. Why don't you give Miss Gloria some space?"

Charlotte snapped her fingers until the Wheaton jumped off the sofa and came to lie at her feet. She glanced at her notepad. She hadn't written anything, but somehow she didn't think she'd have any trouble remembering the story.

"I can't tell you how frightened I am to ask about your *other* husband."

Gloria waved a hand at her. "Oh it couldn't be him.

He's dead."

"Please tell me it didn't have anything to do with snakes."

"Ha. No. Don't be silly. He died of a heart attack."

"Oh thank goodness. No one can blame you for that."

Gloria bit her lip and the smile melted from Charlotte's face.

"Oh no. Please tell me it wasn't your fault."

"Well...he had the heart attack while he was fixing the television antenna on the roof."

"That's not your fault."

"I insisted he fix it..."

"That still doesn't make it your fault. It was an accid—"

"...during a lightning storm."

"You sent him to the roof to adjust a metal antenna *during a lightning storm?*"

"Well, there was a lightning storm *coming.*"

"Did you know that?"

"Yes."

"Did he?"

"No. He never cared about the weather. He was always saying things like, *Who cares about the forecast? It will be what it is when it gets here.* Oh, did I mention he was cheating on me?"

"Naturally."

"And *Murder She Wrote* was on. I loved that show."

Charlotte heard her pen fall but she didn't pick it up. She couldn't take her eyes off Gloria. For her own safety, she wasn't sure she should.

"You know what's funny?" said Gloria with a dreamy look on her face. She sat back and crossed her legs. "You'd think it'd be the fall from the roof that killed him, or that he'd be blown up by the lightning, but nope, in the end, it was a heart attack. And that was days later."

As she said *blown up* she threw both hands in the air and splayed all her fingers, not unlike a magician after a particularly flashy trick.

Charlotte nodded slowly.

"Well…that *is* funny. Not in a ha-ha way, but in an *isn't-it-funny-the-many-ways-my-husband-could-have-died* way. But on the upside, as you said, I guess he can't be the one after you."

"No…but his sister is still pretty angry with me. She thinks the stress of the fall caused the heart attack."

"I suppose falling off a roof could be stressful."

"It was a rancher. He fell fifteen feet and slightly twisted one ankle. I think fifty odd years of bacon and cigarettes are more likely culprits than me."

She picked up her pen and jotted down *snake lady, first husband* and *second husband's sister*.

"So… Is that all? You didn't accidentally kill anyone or anything else?"

"No…well…do lizards count?"

Charlotte swallowed. "Go on…"

"Well, remember when I was working at the food store?"

"Yes?"

"I told everyone I quit, but really I was fired."

"For killing lizards?"

"No silly. For telling a woman her kids were too fat for donuts."

"Yikes."

"It isn't like I didn't suggest some alternatives. I must have rattled off half a dozen healthy treats but darn if that woman didn't complain to my manager anyway."

"The nerve."

"Exactly."

"And you think *that* woman wants you dead?"

"No. But after they fired me I accidentally ran my car over a lizard and then I took its little squished body and put it in their pre-made fruit salad."

Charlotte gasped. "The fresh fruit salad?"

"Right, but not at the buffet. The cut-fruit they put on the shelf in nice, clear plastic bins so you can spot a dead lizard in one from a hundred yards away."

"Ohhh, you mean like the canister I have in my refrigerator that I'm going to throw away the first chance I get. Gotcha."

Gloria tilted her head and ran her nails through her hair.

"Thing is, I should have waited a few days. It was serendipity that I ran over the lizard the same day I was fired... Cosmic justice."

"Like the lightning."

"Exactly. But I should have waited on the lizard so it wasn't so obvious who did it. It's not like I had to feed him. I could have kept his little squished body in a baggie or something."

"Hindsight is twenty-twenty."

"Exactly."

Charlotte dropped her face into her palm and took a deep breath. "Is that it?"

"I think so."

"Okay...well...if you think of anything else give me a call and I'll come over tomorrow..."

Gloria jumped.

"No. That's what I came over to tell you. I'm going to stay here for a few days."

"*What?*" The word came out a little screechier than Charlotte intended and she cleared her throat. "I mean, come again?"

Gloria put her hands over her heart.

"It's too dangerous to stay in my house. And I figured since you're my detective…"

"I'm not *your* detective. I mean, even if I—"

"And that's the other thing… I brought you this…"

Gloria stood and fished in her pocket. Charlotte winced; afraid she'd pull out a gun or a deadly asp.

"Here." Gloria held out a crisp hundred-dollar bill.

"What's this?"

"Your retainer while you work on my case."

"My retainer?"

Charlotte took it. It was her first paying case. She stared at the bill in her hand.

My first official case.

"I… I guess you can stay in the spare room."

"Great. Where is it? Down the hall?"

Gloria grabbed the handle of her suitcase and started walking to the back of the house. Abby stood, picked up the wig in her teeth and trotted after her, nub of a tail wagging.

"First door on the right."

"Got it," called Gloria.

"Just try not to kill anything…" Charlotte added, mumbling.

CHAPTER NINE

"Hello?"

"Hey," said Declan, sounding as sexy as a man saying *hey* could. Charlotte felt a bolt of excitement shoot through her.

Finally.

"There you are. I thought you'd never call me back."

She slapped her hand to her mouth. That was exactly what she *didn't* want to say.

"I mean, not that I was hanging here waiting or anything…you're just usually faster so I was a little worried, like, for your safety…"

Much better. Smooth.

"I'm sorry…"

She smiled. His unrequired apology made her feel both better and stupid for worrying. "Oh jeeze. Don't apologize."

He sighed. "No, believe me; I wanted nothing more than to find a quiet moment to call you. It's been crazy around here today. You have no idea."

"You sound tired."

"I'm exhausted."

"Are you still at the shop?"

"I was just locking up. I was thinking about coming to your house if you don't mind? Maybe I could pick up some dinner?"

"Oh, sure, that would be—"

"Charlotte?" echoed a voice from down the hall, cutting her comment short.

Oh right. Gloria.

She stared forlornly at the hundred-dollar bill sitting on her table. She had client responsibilities now.

"Do you have a washcloth I could borrow?" called Gloria.

"Charlotte?" said Declan in her other ear.

"Oh never mind, I found one in your closet."

She heard a click as Gloria closed the bathroom door.

Charlotte tried to remember if Sherlock Holmes' clients ever moved in with him. She thought not. Of course, he had Watson and Mrs. Hudson milling around all the time. No wonder he never had a love life.

She walked towards her lanai to keep Gloria from overhearing her conversation. No one knew better than she that old ladies could be diabolical when it came to eavesdropping. Mariska had pulled the *I'm in the shower how could I possibly overhear anything?* trick on her before, unaware of how red her ears glowed after pressing them against the bathroom door.

Declan's voice called from the phone again. "Charlotte?"

"Sorry, just a second, I'm moving."

"Moving?"

"Into another room."

She felt confident Gloria wouldn't have an electronic listening device like the one Darla bought at an estate sale. She'd claimed the purchase was for Frank and had *nothing* to do with the fact that Charlotte, high school-aged at the time, had started dating a boy.

Riiight.

Darla also swore she didn't use her new toy to overhear what people said about her cooking during cooking club. Yet when she excused herself to go to the ladies' room in the middle of the first course, everyone heard noises in the next room. The rustlings sounded suspiciously like a woman trying to slide on earphones without messing up her hairdo.

All's fair in love and the pursuit of gossip.

She sat in her lounger and put the phone back to her ear. "There's nothing I'd like better than to have you come over."

"But…?"

"There is one tiny complication. I have a guest."

"Who?"

"Gloria from the neighborhood. Little Gloria, not big Gloria."

"I don't know either."

"No, I didn't think you knew her. At least I *hope* you're not on her radar. It would be safer for you if you never meet her."

"What's that supposed to mean?"

"It's a long story. Maybe I could swing by your house instead?"

Declan sniffed. "Speaking of guests…"

"Oh right. *Seamus.* Has he started looking for houses yet?"

"He said he was today, though I'm ninety-nine percent sure it was just an excuse to get out of dusting. What if we met at sushi? It isn't the most romantic place but it will feel like *our* time."

"That could work…"

"Unless you have to play host?"

"No. Gloria already ate all my tuna on crackers for dinner and now she's getting a shower and going to bed. I'll have Abby here to protect her."

"Protect her? What does that mean?"

"I'll tell you when I see you."

"Okay. I'll pick you up in ten minutes?"

"See you then."

Charlotte listened at the bathroom door and heard that the shower wasn't running. She called to Gloria that she was going out for a bit.

The door cracked open and Gloria popped out her head, water dripping from her hair.

"You're leaving me?"

"No one knows you're here and you've got Abby to let you know if anyone gets near the house. I left my cell number on the counter if you need anything."

Gloria's big eyes swiveled as she gazed down the hallway.

"There are no ninjas sneaking around the house," said Charlotte.

The eyes swiveled back and locked on her own.

"You don't think it's ninjas, do you?"

Charlotte laughed. "No. I was only kid— Wait. You never exacted your particular brand of revenge on a *ninja*, did you?"

"I don't know any ninjas."

"Good. Well…I'll be back before you know it."

"Okay. I'm going to bed anyway. Being hunted is exhausting."

"I imagine. See you soon."

Charlotte grabbed her handbag and headed outside to wait. As she strolled to the bottom of her driveway, she noticed a red car parked across the street and fifty feet from her home. It seemed unusually sporty for the neighborhood. She suspected someone was in the car; the brake lights were glowing, but the person wasn't visible.

Just as she began to wonder if she *should* stay and watch over Gloria, the car pulled away from her and disappeared around the corner.

Probably someone checking directions. People often pulled

into the neighborhood to get their bearings straight. They definitely weren't looking for Pineapple Port with a racy car like that. Though, every once in a while a resident would go through a second or third midlife crisis and things got a little weird.

A few minutes later Declan arrived and she hopped into the passenger seat.

"Hey," she said.

He leaned towards her, his eyes closing and lips puckering. They kissed and he lingered a moment before sitting back.

"Well *hello* sailor," she said.

He smiled. "I needed that. I need a hug too but seatbelts make that difficult."

"I know. What good is safety when it keeps hugs at bay?"

"Seriously."

"So, tell me about your crazy day."

"You go first."

As they drove to dinner she told him about the missing witch, switched lawn decorations, Gloria's threatening note and the fire.

"Jeeze," he muttered as they got out of the car to walk into Katana Kuts. "Your day is putting mine to shame. Now I feel stupid. You're hiding a woman that someone wants to kill in your *home*?"

"When you say it like that it sounds like a bad idea."

"Um, *yes*. How did *you* see it?"

"Like having a sweet old lady puttering around my home asking for bath towels. I'm sure it will turn out to be nothing. Frank thinks it's kids playing pranks. Oh. And it's my first paying detective job, so that part is kind of exciting."

"Ah…" he took his seat at the counter. "Sounds more

like your first paying bed and breakfast job."

"But potentially deadly."

"Right. Bonus."

Charlotte arched an eyebrow at him.

"I'm detecting a note of sarcasm."

Declan exhaled and rubbed his eye with the heel of his palm.

"I'm sorry. I'm not belittling what you're trying to do. I'm just…worried for you."

Charlotte felt a breeze rustling the hair on her forearm and looked down to find Kim, Katana Kuts' tiny, close-talking waitress, standing beside her.

She looked at Declan and motioned to Kim with her eyes.

"Hey Kim," he said.

"Hello Mr. Declan," said Kim, a nervous giggle in her voice.

"It's good to see you," said Charlotte.

"Good to see you Miss Charlotte."

Charlotte ordered some saki for them to share. Declan and she had been to the restaurant a few times since their first visit and now had a pattern; a bottle of unfiltered saki, three rolls (which rotated between five favorite choices) and a smattering of sashimi depending on their mood. If they didn't order anything too odd, it kept Kim from crawling in their laps to read the menu out loud as she tried to memorize their order.

Charlotte turned back to Declan. "There's nothing to worry about."

"You're probably right. Why would anyone want to kill a little old lady?"

Charlotte chose not to enumerate the multitude of ways Gloria might have attracted the ire of others. First, it would only worry him. Second, it would take the rest of the evening to list them all.

Her hand was resting on her thigh and his came to rest on it. He curled his fingers beneath hers.

"I've missed you," he said.

She felt a wave of emotion. "I feel like it's been weird between us. Has it?"

"No, I mean…yes, I know what you mean but not bad weird. We've just had a lot going on and a lot of visitors. There hasn't been much time for us."

She nodded. "That's it. Good. I mean, good we're on the same page. Romantically speaking."

He nodded. "Same page. And I don't mean to be unsupportive, *ever*, but do know going forward that I'm a little worried. I know you're new to the job, but don't forget private investigator *is* a dangerous occupation. You need to be careful."

"Are you saying you'd miss me if something happened?"

He smirked. "Maybe."

He pulled her toward him and kissed her on the forehead. His lips felt soft and her shoulders relaxed. If he could bottle whatever he had done, chiropractors would be out of business. She wanted to fall into him and take a nap. It had been a busy day and curling up with him would feel *amazing*.

"Maybe we could move Gloria in with Seamus and you could come and stay with me instead," she mumbled.

He rubbed his cheek against hers and she rested her head on his shoulder. She spotted Kim just outside the kitchen staring and as their eyes met, Kim covered her mouth, tittering at their public display of affection.

PDA. The acronym from grade school rang through her mind. Turned out PDA wasn't as awful as the kids in grade school made it seem.

The bartender placed a boat of sushi in front of them and they sat back to enjoy it. Charlotte picked up her saki cup and tried to take a sip, the grin on her face making it difficult to wrap her lips on the edge of the cup.

Ochoko.

She said the Japanese name word for the saki cup in her head to distract herself from how much she wanted to grab Declan and kiss him. She'd Googled the name of it the last time they'd stopped by the restaurant.

Ochoko. Ochoko. OchokoOchokoochokoochokoochoko…

She sneaked a glimpse of him as he stirred wasabi in his soy sauce and watched the sinews in his neck move beneath his tan skin.

I might have to say it a few hundred more times…

Distracting herself with Japanese language trivia wasn't going to cut it. She still wanted to grab him. That's when she remembered he'd had a big day as well.

"Oh. You have to tell me about your day," she said.

He nodded and put down his own *ochoko* with his well-manicured yet manly fingers…

OchokoOchokoochokoochokoochoko…

"My day? Well, my ex-girlfriend stopped by to tell me she technically owns my pawn shop."

Ocho— wait, what was that now?

Her perma-grin tilted on her face like a hung painting in an earthquake.

Ex-girlfriend?

She took a deep breath and then exhaled slowly.

"Wow. I didn't think there was any way you could top my day."

"You don't know how sorry I am to disappoint you."

"This wouldn't be the crazy ex-girlfriend you told me about, would it?"

"It would."

"Oh. Yikes."

"*Yikes* would be one way of saying it...emergency sirens wailing would be another..."

"How is this possible?"

"To prove I own the shop *I* have drunken scrawlings on a napkin—her words—and *she* claims to have a *real* will stating Bonehead left the shop to her mother, who, if I never mentioned it, was *his* ex-girlfriend."

"Lot of ex-girlfriends in this story."

"Yup."

"It doesn't sound good."

"Nope."

"What are you going to do?"

He put his elbows on the bar and dropped his head into his hands.

"I don't know. I probably need to talk to a lawyer, but lawyers are expensive. This whole thing is going to end up costing me a fortune. I know it."

Charlotte stared at the bar top for a few minutes and then jumped, an idea shooting through her as if she was strapped to an electric chair and someone had just flipped the switch.

"You could talk to Tilly."

"Who?"

"Tilly. She's the neighborhood busybody but she was also a lawyer. Possibly for the mob."

"For the mob? Seriously?"

Charlotte shrugged. "I mean, she doesn't introduce herself as *Hi, I'm Tilly who worked for the mob*, but yes. There's talk she might be in witness protection, but who knows...when rumors get flying around here it's best not to assume anything. Once we weed through the exaggeration we could find out she was a plumber in Kansas."

"But you're pretty sure she's a lawyer?"

"Yes...retired of course. When people talk about lawyer-stuff my eyes glass over but I think she did something with property...or business...I dunno. Either way, she might be able to help."

"Do you think it's too late to see her now?"

She looked at her watch. "It's seven...that's pushing it around here...we could give it a shot though. She wasn't home when I tried to talk to her earlier so I need to interview her anyway. Maybe she's back now."

They scarfed down the rest of their sushi, paid their tab, checked their pockets to be sure Kim hadn't accidentally slipped inside of them, and headed back to Pineapple Port.

CHAPTER TEN

Tilly's ancient Ford Taurus, rusty and missing all four hubcaps, sat in her driveway. Charlotte stared at it and then looked at Declan.

"Maybe she wasn't that *great* a lawyer."

"Any help would be welcome."

They parked and knocked on the door.

Tilly answered wearing black yoga pants that accentuated her knobby knees. Her oversized tee featured a glitter-covered sand dollar. The word *Sanibel* blazed beneath the shell in orange script. Her dark hair was short and spiky and the Florida sun had turned her skin the color of nutmeg.

"Hi Tilly," said Charlotte. "I stopped by earlier but you weren't around."

Tilly cocked her hip and rested her knuckles on it.

"I know. I wasn't here so I remember being somewhere else."

Her voice was low and smoky. She looked at Declan. "You got your hair cut," she said, jutting her chin in his direction.

Declan's hand rose to touch his hair.

"Couple of days ago... Have we met?"

She snorted a laugh and then turned back to Charlotte. "Whaddya need?"

"Well, two things. I came earlier to ask you if you'd seen anyone suspicious in the neighborhood."

"You'll have to be more specific."

Charlotte's gaze shot to the closed-circuit television

camera above her head. Tilly had cameras everywhere, some at her home and some hidden around the neighborhood. Little escaped her attention. Rumor had it she owned a mythical tome known as The Book, in which she noted everything of interest that happened in Pineapple Port. No matter how sneaky people thought they were, their shenanigans were probably logged in The Book. In a way, Tilly served as a minor deity; people didn't misbehave for fear she was watching.

Some residents knew about her surveillance, but few minded. Not many of them had things they needed to hide, and she'd become the head of the unofficial neighborhood watch. Her vigilant observation served as a free security program and it helped that she wasn't a gossip. She'd answer questions about the comings and goings of the neighborhood if asked, but never *offered* information.

"Someone switched the lawn decorations. People with gazing balls woke up to find fishing frogs, people with sports flags had flamingo flags, that sort of thing."

"Last night?"

Charlotte nodded.

"I was out of town. I haven't had a chance to review the tapes. I'll have to check the feeds but if someone was messing with things, I'll find them."

"That would be great." Charlotte fished in her purse and found her notebook. "Here's the list of people who reported changes." She handed it to Tilly, who looked it over and then returned it.

"Got it."

"Don't you want to keep it?"

Tilly rolled her eyes.

Charlotte slipped the notebook back in her purse. "Okay…I have one other question for you."

"I'm going to have to start charging you."

"You can, if you like," said Declan. "It's a law question."

She waved a hand at him. "I'm kidding. What else do I have to do? Hit me."

Declan looked at Charlotte and then continued.

"I inherited my shop from my uncle's business partner, Bonehead—"

"Who would go into business with a man named Bonehead?" asked Tilly.

"It's a nickname my uncle Seamus gave him; something to do with head-butting people back in Ireland. Anyway, his real name was Tommy O'Malley. He and Seamus owned the shop together, and made a deal that my uncle wouldn't take his full share when he left town under the condition that the shop would go to *me* if Tommy died. Tommy didn't have any kids, so when he died of cancer, I took over the shop. I have the napkin they signed when they agreed upon it. So I was wondering—"

"It's a holographic will," said Tilly, cutting him short.

"What?"

"Holographic. It means a handwritten will. Florida doesn't recognize them."

"*What?*"

"The shop was never yours. What'd you do? Just start paying the bills?"

"I...basically, yes. I even closed up the original shop and moved it across town, all at my expense."

"And someone is contesting?"

"Yes. Maybe. I'm not sure yet. Bonehead's ex-girlfriend might have had an official will stating *she* inherited the shop."

"Might have *had?*"

"She died."

"Gotcha. Go on."

"She mentioned the will after Bonehead's funeral, but she's a bit of a nut, so no one believed her and then she admitted to lying about it anyway. But now her daughter contacted me, claiming she found the will and plans to use it."

"Is she Bonehead's kid?"

"Stephanie? No. She was little when her mom started dating Bonehead. Her real father is the devil, more than likely."

"Well, I hate to say it, kid, but if she's got a real will signed by two witnesses, she's probably going to win this fight. She could even try to sue you for selling the original shop and moving it. Damages. Whatever. Hopefully she likes you."

"It's his ex-girlfriend," said Charlotte.

"Ha. Oh, you're in trouble, buddy."

The blood drained from Declan's face. "I feel sick."

"Now…I've got some old friends who could take care of this problem of yours…if you're not particular on how it gets done. They could make her an offer she can't refuse…"

Declan, holding his stomach, peered down at Tilly.

"Uh… That's sweet, and it *is* tempting, but—"

Tilly cackled and slapped his arm. "I'm *kidding*. Everyone thinks I used to work for the mob."

"So you didn't?" asked Charlotte.

"No. Not *me*, personally. Why don't you two come in for a second? I'll run through my footage and see what I find."

She turned and rolled toward the back of her home on her skinny, bowed legs, beckoning them to enter by shaking her hand over her shoulder as she went.

Charlotte and Declan stepped inside the foyer as Tilly disappeared into the back of her home. It smelled like lavender and stale cigarette smoke.

"What does *not me, personally* mean?" whispered Declan.

"I don't know. It wasn't exactly a definitive *I'm not connected to the mob*, was it?"

Declan sighed. "This holographic will stuff isn't good news. What am I going to do?"

She rubbed his back with the flat of her hand. "We'll figure something out."

He groaned and she hugged him. He wrapped his arms around her and they rocked back and forth for a moment.

"Hey Char," called Tilly. "Quit lovin' on your man. I think I have something. C'mere."

Charlotte and Declan jumped back from each other.

"Does she have cameras in *here?*" whispered Declan.

"Yes, I have cameras everywhere," said the husky voice from down the hall.

Charlotte offered Declan a froggy *yikes!* face and walked down the hall to Tilly's office, first door on the right, like most of the homes in Pineapple Port. The room held only a large desk, a rack of humming electronic equipment and the framed black and white photo of a young man propped beside an older model desktop computer. Above his head, a large sign said *Fralin* in script font. Even framed, she could see the photograph had one ragged edge, as if someone had ripped the person standing to the left of the man from the scene.

"Is that your son?"

Tilly looked at the picture and then glared at Charlotte.

"Look at how old that photo is. How old do you think I am for crying out loud? Plus you know I don't have any kids."

"Oh, no, I didn't. Thought maybe you'd ripped out a girlfriend of his you didn't like or something."

"No. I tore off myself. I was standing next to him."

"Bad hair day?"

Tilly arched an eyebrow. "You want to see this video or not?

"Sorry. Yes. Whatcha got?"

She pointed at a paused video. "Recognize anyone?" She hit play.

Charlotte watched as a familiar figure waddled toward a collection of gnomes and gathered them in her arms. Behind her, another person entered the screen holding a round sphere in front of her like a mystic priestess, except, she wasn't wearing a priestess gown. She was wearing a black tee shirt with white lettering that said *Sea Hag*.

"Mariska and Darla," she mumbled. "I'm going to kill them."

Tilly attempted a chuckle that morphed into a rattly cough.

"Is there any way you could send me a clip of this to my phone?"

"Sure."

"Do you have any footage of Gloria's house?"

"Sweet Gloria or crazy Gloria?"

"Sweet."

"No, you know, I don't have any cameras over there. She's over in the older section, right?"

"Yes. You wouldn't happen to know a reason why anyone would want to kill her, do you?"

She expected Tilly to laugh, but instead she pulled at her chin, seemingly deep in thought. After a moment, she clicked through files on her screen until she found the one she wanted.

"Well, there's this…"

She double-clicked a video file and expanded black and white footage of the parking lot outside the recreational building. Gloria appeared, scurrying toward a white car. She stood beside it and looked around before squatting and making a stabbing motion. After four thrusts, she stood and wandered out of frame.

"What was *that?*"

"She flattened Trey Oakford's whitewall."

"What? Why?"

Tilly used the mouse to close the video and then circled the name of the file with the glowing pointer.

Charlotte leaned forward to read it.

Gloria A - Bingo dispute.

"She stabbed his tire for something that happened at bingo?"

Tilly nodded.

Charlotte thought about her dog, home alone with her houseguest. Hopefully, Abby hadn't cheated during a game of fetch.

"So you're a detective now?" asked Tilly.

"Not officially. I'm interning though, so I can get my license."

"With who?"

"Declan's uncle has a license."

"The same guy who likes to work with boneheads?"

"Very funny."

Tilly chuckled at her own joke. "Well, if you ever need anything, just call. I've got the Port wired, as you know."

"Thank you. I definitely will," Charlotte looked around the room, admiring the high-tech equipment. "Whatever made you do all this?"

"Habit from my youth."

"When you worked for the mob?"

Tilly made a noise that sounded like someone trying to gargle small river stones. Charlotte guessed it was laughter. "I told you, *I* didn't work for the mob."

Charlotte squinted at her. "So when you say *I* didn't work for the mob…"

"Time for you to go, missy." She stood and gave her arm a gentle shove.

"Fine. You're a tough nut to crack."

"I'm a regular walnut."

"Well…thanks again. I really appreciate the help."

"No problem."

Charlotte moved toward the front door and found Declan there, leaning against the interior wall.

"We're going," she said.

"Okay. Thank you, Mrs…" he faltered.

"Call me Tilly."

"Right, Tilly. Thank you for your help."

"No problem. Felt good to flex my legal muscle again."

Declan and Charlotte returned to his car.

"I think I need to return to my houseguest," she said.

He nodded and put the car into drive. They were only a few blocks from her house.

"I think I need to find a new job."

"Aw…" Charlotte placed her hand on his, which rested on the shifter. "Every time I think my problems are piling up, you've got even worse things going on."

"I love being the best. What can I say?"

"We'll figure things out. Maybe you can just talk to her."

He sighed. "I'm supposed to meet her."

Charlotte felt a pang in her chest.

Was that jealousy?

"When?" she asked, trying to sound as unconcerned as possible.

"I'm not sure. I don't want to. It's going to be a nightmare."

"Well…we'll prepare for it. We'll go through every option and possible scenario."

He pulled up in front of her house.

"Okay," he said. He offered her a weak smile and she leaned forward to kiss him goodbye. His hand slid forward to cup her face as their lips touched. He lingered a moment before pulling away to stare at her, his eyebrows in the shape of a squiggle that spelled *worry*.

"It will be okay," she said.

He nodded. "Sure. Worst case scenario I'll become a detective. Everybody's doing it."

She slapped his shoulder, slipped out of the car and waved as he drove away.

As he passed by Orchid Lane, which ran perpendicular to her own street, a car pulled out and followed him toward the exit of the neighborhood. The streetlamps were bright enough for her to see the car was red and sporty, very much like the one she'd seen while waiting for Declan.

She wished she knew more about cars. Maybe she could find a flashcard set to practice identifying makes and models. Maybe they had those for training police? She'd have to ask Seamus.

Abby greeted her just inside the door, tail wagging. At least her furry baby had avoided Gloria's petty wrath for the evening.

She dropped her purse on the living room table and walked to her chalkboard wall to add *Trey Oakford-flat tire* to the never-ending list of Gloria's victims.

Heading for bed, she returned to the wall a moment

later to add *red car?* to the list.

CHAPTER ELEVEN

Charlotte awoke to the sound of a toilet flushing and her heart raced before she remembered her new roommate. The one with a target on her back. A flushing toilet at six in the morning was a nerve-racking way to wake a girl who'd lived on her own nearly her entire life. She could attribute most odd noises to Abby, but knew the dog hadn't figured out how to flush. As cool as that would be.

She stood, stretched, and peeked through her curtains. Darla was already up and walking the path to Mariska's front door. Darla often went to Mariska's to have coffee after Frank left in the morning. With it being so close to the community bake sale, they probably had plans to make jelly or some other canned good they could sell.

Perfect. She'd get them together while they were hip deep cutting strawberries and unable to run.

She found her phone and discovered Tilly had sent her a video. She watched a loop of Mariska scooping up gnomes as Darla stood nearby in her incriminating tee shirt. There would be *no* denying their involvement in the great lawn-decoration-switching caper. She was the only *Sea Hag* in the neighborhood.

Nearly giggly with her plans to confront Darla and Mariska, she moved to the kitchen to make coffee. A few minutes later Gloria shuffled in wearing a ruby-colored housecoat with black lace trim and a black hair turban with a clear glass jewel in the center.

"My goodness, look at you," said Charlotte. "Maybe

people are out to get you because you're the missing Princess Anastasia."

Gloria lifted a hand to her turban and smiled.

"No, I just don't like anyone to see my hair before I have time to make something of it, but I need coffee to even attempt the transformation."

"I wasn't sure if you were looking for coffee or here to tell my fortune."

"I see coffee in your future."

"Ooh, you're *good*. I'm making coffee."

"Wonderful. I'm useless until I've had my coffee in the morning. Cream?"

"Creamer. On the fridge door. It's brown butter pecan flavor."

"Oh yum. I haven't tried that one."

Charlotte glanced at her chalkboard wall. "So I've been making a list of people who might want to hurt you..."

"A list? Surely there aren't enough for a list."

"You gave me four names yesterday."

"I did? Who?"

"The people who bought the snake house. The husband you falsely claimed *sold* the snake house. The sister of the husband you asked to climb onto a roof during a lightning storm. Any number of people at the food store who don't appreciate dead lizards in their fruit salad..."

Gloria laughed. "No one is going to kill me over a dead lizard."

"What about Trey Oakford?"

Gloria looked up from stirring her coffee, eyes even more doe-like than usual.

"Who?"

"Trey. You play bingo with him."

"Do I?"

"You do. Well you did at least once. That would be the time you knifed his tires."

"I did what now?"

"Gloria. You have to be honest with me if I'm going to figure this out."

She sighed. "Fine. How did you know about that?"

"I'm a detective, remember?"

"You're excellent at it, too."

"Thank you."

"Does *he* know?"

"That you're the one who popped his tire? No. I mean, I don't know; I didn't tell him if that's what you mean. Why would you do something like that?"

"I was one number away and way ahead of everyone else, I'm sure of it. All I needed was B17. Then he screams out *BINGO!* and pumps his fists in the air like the big oaf that he is."

"That isn't a reason to pop his tire."

"Oh you should have seen him. *Gloating.* I couldn't help myself."

Charlotte dropped her chin to her chest.

"Gloria, the mystery here isn't who is trying to kill you, it's how you've survived this long. You have to promise me you'll work on your unquenchable lust for revenge."

Gloria twisted her lips into a knot. "Fine. Sometimes karma's just too slow."

"Karma moves just fine without your help. Now, is there anyone else you can think of who's felt your wrath?"

"Felt my wrap?" her hand fluttered to her turban.

"*Wrath.* Anyone else who has experienced your revenge."

"Oh." Gloria tapped her fingers against her chest as she pondered. "I took the tennis balls off the front of

Dottie's walker. Does that count?"

"Yes that counts. Why?"

"She told me my cake was dry. No—*dry as a teetotaler's wine glass*. That's what she said."

"Fine." Charlotte wrote *Dottie* on her ever-growing list of suspects; though with Dottie's arms, if she'd really wanted to get at Gloria, she'd just put her in a headlock. Plus, Dottie, no shrinking violet, would have told her Gloria stole her tennis balls if she'd known.

"It's going to take me the rest of my life to look into all these leads. Anything else?"

"No… Oh." Gloria stopped the cup from touching her lips so abruptly she sloshed a little on the counter. "I don't know if this counts, but I cheated at Random Santa."

Random Santa was Pineapple Port's version of Secret Santa. Everyone brought a gift to the Christmas party, all their names went into a bowl, and then each fished to see which gift he or she would receive. Gloria won the opportunity to organize the Random Santa name bowl during her first holiday in Pineapple Port. The locals liked to *honor* new neighbors with important jobs they knew were a hassle. Gloria was lucky Jackie hadn't pushed her to take over water aerobics the way *she'd* been duped into the dubious honor.

"How do you cheat at Random Santa?"

"I peeked at all the gifts. If the gift was a good one, I wrote the name on cream paper. If it was a cheap piece of junk, I wrote it on white. You could hardly tell the difference in the bowl unless you knew what to look for."

"Really? What color did I get?"

Gloria took a sip of her coffee. "I like this cheery yellow paint in here. Did you paint it yourself?"

"I gifted a nice hardback book last year."

"I'm not much of a reader."

"Jeeze. A book is better than what I got last year: a spider plant seedling someone clearly pulled from their own plant and threw into a cheap plastic pot. I don't think it even had roots. It was a leaf in dirt."

"Oh I remember that one. Definitely a white paper."

Charlotte recalled the pathetic spider plant and mulled on how nice it would have been to get something useful or pretty. If she ended up with one more crocheted coaster set, she'd have to move into a bigger house. She squinted at Gloria.

"Are you going to do it again next year?"

"I don't know…am I?"

Charlotte thought for a moment. "Tell you what. We'll keep that little confession between us."

Gloria grinned. "Deal."

They clinked coffee mugs.

Charlotte looked out her front window. She was anxious to confront Darla and Mariska about their lawn decoration caper.

"I have to go over to Mariska's. I'll be back in a bit. You keep thinking about people you've…uh…*assisted with their karma*."

"Okay."

Charlotte headed toward the front door as Gloria strolled behind her.

"What's *red car*?"

She turned to find Gloria staring at her chalkboard.

"Oh, I meant to ask you. Do you know anyone with a red car? Kind of sporty? I'm not good with brands."

"No. Not that I can think of…"

"Okay. No biggie. Might be nothing."

Charlotte put a leash on Abby and started across the

road. She didn't know why she bothered to bring the dog. Miss Izzy didn't want a playmate. Mariska's little white witch hated other dogs and pretended they didn't exist. Poor Abby tried to get her attention, but Miss Izzy looked through her as if she were made of cellophane. The whole process was causing irreparable harm to Abby's self-esteem.

She knocked on the door and entered.

"Hey ladies."

"Hey girl, what are you doing here?" asked Darla. She was sitting at the island drinking coffee while Mariska peeled tomatoes at the sink. Miss Izzy flew around the corner on her stubby white legs, but came to a full halt in mid-bark upon recognizing her visitors.

"Oh you know, just switching up my routine. Don't you like to *switch* things once in a while?"

Charlotte unclipped Abby, who ran to stand nose-to-nose with Miss Izzy, tail wagging. Izzy showed no sign of noticing, turned and waddled back to the bedroom. Abby glanced at Charlotte for advice.

Charlotte shrugged. "Sorry girl. If I were you, I'd just ignore her back."

Abby trotted off after Izzy.

"She doesn't listen to a word I say."

"We're switching things up right now," said Mariska. "Instead of jam we're making fresh spaghetti sauce."

"Really. I thought I'd find you just *lying* here."

"What? Why would we be sleeping at nine o'clock in the morning?"

Charlotte crossed her arms over her chest and stared at Darla, whose smile began to fade.

"Uh oh. Mariska, Charlotte is looking at me funny."

Mariska shifted her attention from her peeling. "What's wrong?"

"Well…I was at Tilly's last night—"

"Tilly's? Why were you at that busybody's?" interrupted Darla.

"She had some interesting footage."

"Do you want to start on the onions?" asked Mariska.

"You know they make me cry," said Darla. "Why don't I do the peppers? You're tougher than I am."

Charlotte put her hands on her hips and tried to look as angry as possible. "I said, *she had some interesting videos…*"

"I saw a video last night about foxes," said Mariska.

Darla's eyes grew wide. "Oh, did you see that? We flipped past it but—"

"Aah! Shush it. I know it was you," Charlotte said, pointing to one and then the other. "Don't think I'm going to forget and get caught up in your fox stories and onion banter."

"What are you talking about?"

"*You* switched all the lawn decorations. There's no point in denying it. You're caught."

Charlotte waited for them to babble denials. Instead, Darla placed her hand on her chest and released a deep sigh.

"Oh thank goodness. It's such a relief you figured it out. We didn't know how to leave you clues."

"What?"

"We switched everything so you could practice being a detective but we were *too* good at it."

"Exactly. How were you ever going to catch us?" added Mariska. "That's what we were talking about before you showed up, about how we had no idea how to leave you clues."

"Well, this is less rewarding than I hoped," muttered Charlotte. "Turns out you had nothing to worry about. Tilly had you on video."

Darla grunted. "Busybody."

"Don't blame Tilly, you're the one who gave it away. The video was a little grainy, but I could still see your *Sea Hag* tee shirt easily enough."

"I knew I should have turned that inside out."

"What about me?" asked Mariska. "You didn't know it was me."

Charlotte rolled her eyes. "I knew it was you."

"How? I wore all black. I was practically invisible."

"First, you have a unique way of walking. Second, Darla was there. Third...well I don't need a third, I have video for crying out loud. I can see that it's you clearly enough."

She held up her phone and the two women watched themselves steal gnomes.

"Busybody," muttered Mariska, turning back to her tomatoes.

"Well, good job, sweetie," said Darla, patting Charlotte on the shoulder. "You're doin' real good."

"Well...you can put your witch back on your roof now. I know that must be driving you crazy."

"No." Darla's head jerked up and she nearly fell off her stool. "The witch really was stolen."

"Uh-huh. Whatever. Seriously, you don't have to keep this up."

"No, I'm not kidding. Someone took the witch while we were out taking everything else. I guess... I didn't notice it until I went to get the paper the next morning."

"Is someone in your house?" asked Mariska. She was staring out the window above her sink.

"Are you talking to me?" asked Charlotte.

"I think someone just peeked through your blinds."

"Is it Declan?" asked Darla.

"No."

"The fireman?"

"*Darla*," said Charlotte, feeling her face grow hot. "It's Gloria. She's hiding at my house until we figure out who threatened her."

"Why your house?"

"She hired me."

"With money?"

Charlotte nodded.

Darla, fished through her pockets. "Here." She thrust a crumpled five-dollar bill at her.

"What's this?"

"I'm hiring you to find my witch."

Charlotte smirked. "Gloria gave me a hundred."

"A hundred dollars."

"A *day*?" asked Mariska.

"No…I mean, she just gave me a hundred last night as a retainer."

"You can't even stay at a Motel 6 for a hundred dollars."

Darla nodded. "Sounds to me like you're the cheapest hotel in town. Are you feeding her too?"

Charlotte pictured her precious brown butter pecan creamer pouring into Gloria's coffee. "I—"

"You have to up your prices."

Charlotte looked at the five-dollar bill in her hand and then back at Darla, who huffed.

"Not with *me*. I'm not asking to stay at your house."

"Right."

Mariska clucked her tongue. "Gloria is so sweet. Who would want to hurt her?"

"She's got you two bamboozled…"

"What?"

"Nothing." Charlotte held up the five-dollar bill. "I'll keep looking for the witch."

"Thank you dear. Oh, I almost forgot. I have some bad news."

"What?"

"I can't be your tail-end on Friday."

Charlotte's jaw dropped. Mariska had been working on a unicorn costume for her and Darla to wear to the Charity Halloween Bonanza for months. Finally, Pineapple Port would beat the Silver Lake community, which had dominated the costume contest for as long as she could remember. The plan was for Charlotte to be the front end and Darla the back.

"Why not?"

"I pulled my back movin' around the lawn decorations. Tried to pick up that giant stone crane Bubbles has over there on Driftwood. I can't bend over for any length of time or I lock that way."

"Can't we just make you the front and I'll be the back?"

"I made the front to fit *you*," said Mariska. "It's too much work at this point to expand it for her."

Darla put her hands on her hips. "I don't think I like the way you said that."

Charlotte tilted her head back. "This is terrible. We should have made you the front in the first place."

"What about Declan? Could you ask him?" asked Mariska.

Charlotte sighed. She'd hardly been dating Declan a month and felt weird pushing him into a retirement community costume party dressed as a horse's butt.

"I'll think about it," she said. "I have to get back to work."

She found Abby lying on the carpet in Mariska's room, staring forlornly at Miss Izzy, who slept on the bed with her back turned to her.

"Come on Abby, let's hit the road. Stop being so needy."

Abby stood and with one last glance at Izzy's back, padded out of the room. Charlotte needed to get back home and cross a mystery off the chalkboard. Then, she had to concentrate on Gloria's case and get her out of her house before she drank all the creamer.

CHAPTER TWELVE

"Ding a ling a ling."

Declan looked away from his customer and saw Stephanie standing inside his shop's door shaking an imaginary bell.

He offered his customer an uncomfortable smile. "I used to have a bell."

The woman stared back at him, blankly, and he offered what final thoughts he could on the quality of the sofa they'd been discussing. He omitted how the previous owner had passed away on that very sofa, dead of a heart attack at age eighty-eight.

Stephanie wandered to the opposite side of the store. She was turning on and off an unplugged lamp when he approached her.

"Does this work?" she asked.

"With electricity. And a bulb. It's pretty high maintenance that way."

"I'll take it."

"That'll be forty dollars."

"No, I mean I'll *take* it." She pulled it closer to her.

Declan sighed. "What are you doing here?"

"We need to talk."

"I *know*. You told me to pick a time and I haven't picked one yet."

"You're taking too long."

"It's barely been twenty-four hours."

"I saw your girlfriend."

"What?"

"I've been in town for weeks. I didn't just drive straight to your door, you know. I've been watching. And I know about your girl who lives with the old people. I'll tell you one thing… She's not *me*."

Declan felt his anger rising. "That's one of the things I like *most* about her."

"I'm going to need you to dump her."

"What?"

"Uh oh." Stephanie reached out and tapped the tip of his nose with her finger. "You look like you're about to lose your temper."

"Sir?" called the sofa shopper.

Thank you.

He spun away from Stephanie and slapped a smile on his face as he crossed the shop.

"I'm going to bring my husband back a little later, but I think I'm going to take the sofa," said the woman.

"No problem. It will be here when you get back."

The woman shook his hand and left, corralling two young children through the door like a border collie herding sheep. Declan felt a wave of dread wash over him.

Now he was alone.

With *her.*

He glanced where he'd last seen Stephanie, hoping she'd left. She hadn't. She waved at him. He closed his eyes and took a deep breath before returning to her.

"Okay, let's get this over with. What do you want?"

"The shop."

"No, you don't. I know you don't. Sitting in this shop full of used furniture and knick-knacks, talking to customers is about as close to hell as you can imagine."

"That's true…" She wandered a few feet away before turning back to him. "I could sell it…"

"It's hardly worth more than the items around us. That isn't much."

"What about the building?"

"You want my mortgage? You can have it."

"So you don't own it?"

"No. I make enough to pay the mortgage by working long hours."

"That sounds so depressing."

"It's how most people live."

"That's what I mean. *Depressing.*"

"So imagine how depressing it would be for *you* to own it."

"I might be doing you a favor."

"You might."

"Okay…well…" She traced her upper lip with her tongue and stared at him. "Have you been working out?" She reached out and squeezed his bicep. "I don't remember you being so buff."

He jerked his arm away from her touch.

"Do you hate me so much?" Her bottom lip began to quiver. Her expression shifted from defiant brat to abandoned orphan in a matter of seconds. Declan felt a flash of sympathy.

No. Stop it. I've seen this play before.

He took a moment to steel himself against her emotional performance.

"Don't even try it."

Stephanie's eyes glistened and she turned away from him, though not far enough to hide her tears. He watched as a single drop rolled down her cheek, leaving a snail's trail of moisture in her apricot-colored foundation.

Her mascara didn't run.

She wasn't an *amateur.*

"You hate me," she whispered as a sob racked her

body and she dropped her face into her hands.

"Stephanie, can we skip the histrionics?"

She balled a fist and threw back her head. "Why? Why do you hate me?"

"Seriously, there's no point. I'm not going to send my security footage to the Academy for Oscar consideration."

"I can't bear the thought of you hating me."

He sighed. It looked like he'd have to play along for a bit if he was ever going to get her out of his store.

"Fine. I don't *hate* you. Not that you didn't give me a reason to."

She turned to him, her eyes two crystal blue lakes spilling onto the impossibly smooth terrain of her pink cheeks, the sudden flush making her appear even more beautiful. She didn't belong in a pawn shop. She belonged on a bluff, looking out over the moors, a defiant heroine, broken but not defeated, filled with the fiery resolve to survive through any hardship.

Boy, she's good.

Declan felt drawn to the pain in her eyes and began to feel…*guilty*? Could their failed relationship somehow have been his fault? What had he done to make her run to the arms of another man? He couldn't remember now.

What did I—

Wait a second.

"No," he shook a finger at her, scolding.

"What?" she asked, her voice filled with the sadness of a thousand broken dreams.

"No, no, no." He turned and walked clear across the store to his office door.

"Declan."

He pivoted again and walked back.

"Do you know for a split second I thought I was the

villain here?"

She looked as if she would laugh. "*Really?*"

"You cheated on me, once for sure, in hindsight I'm going to guess more than once. There was that guy with the hair…" He made a swooping motion over his head.

She closed her eyes and smiled as if remembering the scent of her favorite flower. "Marcos."

"Right. *Him.*"

"He was a polo player."

"*Whatever.* The point is you disappeared every time you thought someone wealthier might be available."

"He was from Argentina."

"What does that have to do with anything?"

"He was a polo player from Argentina."

"Why do you keep saying that?"

"If only he had loved me the way he loved that damn horse of his…"

"Forget the damn polo player. Forget my friend—"

"The one with daddy money or the financial investor?"

"You—wait, Peter, too?"

She shrugged.

Declan tried another deep breath. "Forget all of them. Now, you're trying to take my store from me. And for a minute there you had me questioning if *I'd* done something to *you.*"

Stephanie smirked, her eyes glinting like the sun reflected on a polished knife blade. She reached into her purse, retrieved a compact and proceeded to fix her makeup.

"I was starting to think I'd lost it," she said as she powered her nose.

"You're a snake."

Stephanie slipped her compact back into her purse and

stared at him. The corner of her mouth began to twitch. She licked her lips and hissed like a snake, playfully at first, but as she grinned, her lips began to quiver. She raised her chin, but her eyes again glazed with tears.

She sobbed. She expelled one loud blubber, and then slapped her hand to her mouth, eyes wide, as if shocked by the noise.

"You're not seriously going to try this again, are you?" asked Declan.

She shook her head and turned away. This time spinning all the way around; he couldn't see a single tear. Her shoulders bobbed.

"Stephanie?"

She shook her head and held up a finger, asking him to wait.

This time her pain seemed real. Was that possible? He reached out to touch her, thought twice about it, and then laid his fingers on her shoulder.

"Are you okay?"

"I'm so sorry," she said, gasping for breath between sobs.

Declan pursed his lips and tried to remain as unmoved as possible, but as her body began to shake, he felt something inside of him give.

"Come on. Don't cry. I don't hate you. I said I didn't hate you…"

She continued to cry, lowering herself to a sofa as if she might fall.

"Stephanie…"

"I'm so lonely," she said. He could barely make out the words.

"What are you talking about?"

"I don't have *anyone.*"

He sat beside her on the sofa, careful to keep a foot of

space between them.

"What are you talking about? You can get anyone you want."

"My last man dumped me for a Russian model. She didn't even speak English."

"Maybe that was the draw… I'm going to go out on a limb and guess he was a little on the shallow side…"

She glared at him, her eyes rimmed with red.

"Sorry." He reached out and patted her knee lightly with the tips of his fingers. "It's okay. You'll be fine."

"You were always so sweet to me."

"Well, I tried…"

"You didn't deserve the way I treated you."

"I didn't think so, no…"

"Oh Declan."

Stephanie fell forward and threw her arms around him, using his rigid resistance to pull herself closer to him. He tried to pull away but she slid along with him, her tight dress offering little resistance against the smooth cushions. She clung to him like a terrified baby monkey, and he wondered if he'd have to spend the rest of his life dragging her from one room to another.

Wrestling one arm free, he loosely encircled her body to pat her on the back.

"There there…" he said, attempting to free his other arm. "It's okay. You'll be f—"

She grabbed his face and kissed him, pushing hard against him. Her tongue poked against his lips like a Viking siege, battling to gain entry to his mouth. He sealed his lips together and tried to pull away.

When did she get so strong?

He heard a gasp and realized there was no way Stephanie could have gasped with her face pressed against his.

Stephanie jerked away from him.

"Oh no…" she said, her gaze turning toward the front door. "You must be Charlotte. Oh, I'm so sorry…"

Declan snapped his head so hard to the left he worried he'd unscrewed his skull from his spine.

"Charlotte!"

Charlotte stood staring at the two of them. Seamus stood beside her, a strange smirk on his face.

"We didn't mean for you to see this…" said Stephanie standing. Her eyes were still red and her makeup streaked with tears. Even a bit of her mascara had abandoned duty.

"No. I mean… *No.*" Declan stood and glared at Stephanie. During their tussle, most of her right breast had climbed the wall of her dress in what appeared to be an attempt to escape, so he quickly looked away. "She's making it sound like we're hiding something."

"It doesn't look like you're hiding much of anything," said Seamus.

Stephanie smirked and adjusted her dress.

"Don't you start," snapped Declan, pointing at Seamus. "Charlotte—"

Charlotte held up a hand to cut him short. She walked toward them and, seeing her approach, Stephanie stepped back, the sofa clipping her legs from beneath her. She fell back into the seated position, eyes never leaving Charlotte.

"Don't let her touch me," she said, tugging the bottom of Declan's shorts. He leaned down to jerk the fabric from her fingers and stepped away from her.

Charlotte smiled and reached out her hand. "Nice to meet you. I'm Charlotte."

Stephanie shot a look at Declan and then gingerly took her hand. "Stephanie."

Charlotte turned to Declan. "You've got a little *thing* here," she said, pointing at her own lower lip.

Declan wiped the back of his hand across his mouth and saw bright pink lipstick. He opened his mouth again to speak but Charlotte slipped her arm around his waist and stood beside him, hip to hip.

"How's work?" she asked, staring up at him.

Declan pulled her closer to him.

I think I love this girl.

"I'm going to use your bathroom," said Stephanie, standing again. In her heels, she was as tall as Charlotte. She lifted her chin before walking past them to the back of the shop.

"Ha!" said Seamus, slapping his thigh the moment Stephanie left the room. "I would have paid money to see that. The only way it could have gotten better is with a giant vat of Jello."

They looked at him.

"You know, for girl wrestling," he added.

"Yeah, I got it," said Charlotte.

"That was *amazing*," said Declan, spinning Charlotte to face him, his hands on her shoulders. "You knew *just* how to shut her down."

"I'm glad one of us does," she muttered.

"You know I wasn't—"

"I know. I saw her spot us across the parking lot and then launch into her attack. It was all for our benefit."

"Really?" Declan turned and looked where Stephanie had disappeared into the bathroom.

"Yup. But even if I hadn't, it looked less like you were kissing and more like she was trying to steal your tonsils."

"It kind of felt like that. Want me to show you a real kiss?"

He leaned in to kiss her and she stopped him by

placing all four fingers across his lips.

"Not until you soak in alcohol or something."

Declan snickered. "Fair enough. So what are you two doing here?"

"We thought we'd take you to lunch," said Seamus. "Thought maybe we could brainstorm a little about our leggy problem there and Charlotte's case—"

Seamus' phone rang and he pulled it from his pocket. He repeated *what?* several times, his voice growing louder with each word.

"Jackie? Jackie?"

"What is it?" asked Declan as Seamus lowered the phone.

"It went dead. I heard Jackie, she said something about a guy and then she sort of yelped and then the phone went dead."

"That doesn't sound good," said Stephanie approaching them. All signs of her previous emotional distress had evaporated.

Seamus was already half way out the door.

"I should go, too," said Declan.

"Me too," said Charlotte.

Stephanie shot her a look and headed for the door.

Seamus was in his car before Declan could lock the door. He ran to his car and jumped into the driver seat just as Stephanie eased into the passenger side.

"What are you doing?" he asked.

"I want to go, too."

"Why? No."

"She might need a lawyer. And anyway this all seems pretty exciting, don't you think?"

"Get out of my car."

Charlotte slid into the back seat. "We don't have time for this. Just go."

Declan glared at Stephanie and started his engine.

CHAPTER THIRTEEN

Declan pulled up to Jackie's house.

"Do you recognize that car?" he asked nodding his head toward a Mercedes parked against the curb in front of him.

"No, why would I?" asked Stephanie.

"I was talking to Charlotte," he said through gritted teeth.

"Oh, right," she mumbled. "I forgot *it* was there."

Declan glanced at his rearview mirror and found Charlotte glaring at the back of Stephanie's head.

"I don't recognize the car," she said. "Though I've been a little distracted by *him*."

She pointed toward Jackie's house where a large man in a white tee shirt and black jeans stood outside the door talking to Seamus. Declan wasn't sure how he'd missed the hulking figure, though he might have been distracted by the sound of Stephanie's nails clicking on the window as she ran the gauntlet from pinky to index finger over and over again. The drive had been five minutes long and she was already bored.

"I guess I better get up there." He stepped out of the car and approached Seamus. "What's going on?"

Seamus' face resembled a clogged steam engine ready to blow. "This bastard won't get out of my way and I'm about to show him my ugly side."

Declan eyed the man, whose arms looked like pythons that had swallowed pigs. He noticed the right was visibly larger than the left.

"You play tennis?" he asked.

The man smiled and pulled off his sunglasses to look at Declan. With the glasses lowered, he could see the *man* was more of an oversized boy in his early twenties, which was probably why Seamus hadn't already head-butted him.

"Yeah, I do, how'd you know that?"

"I noticed your right arm was larger than your left."

"Huh," the man looked at his right bicep and flexed it, the veins bulging. "You know I didn't think it was that obvious any more. I played a lot more when I was in college—"

"Are you daft?" Seamus screamed at Declan. "Whataya talkin' about tennis fer?"

Seamus' accent grew stronger whenever he was upset.

Declan shrugged. "I just thought—"

"Well stop tinkin'. You're terrible at it."

Seamus turned his attention back to the man-boy. "You, get outta me way."

The man slid his glasses back on and peeked through the door into Jackie's home. "I don't think I'm supposed to let you in there."

Seamus reached for the door and the man grabbed his wrist. Seamus swung at him with his other hand, his knuckles breezing across the tennis player's chin.

Declan grabbed the man's other hand to prevent him from hurting his uncle. Behind him, he heard Charlotte's voice.

"Stop, or I'll call the police."

Declan deflected the man's hand from Seamus' face, but as he did so, he redirected it towards his own chin. Before he could dodge, he felt knuckles connect with his cheekbone and his teeth rattled. He fell behind Seamus and slammed against the side of the house.

"Stop!" screamed a new voice.

Another man appeared in the doorway, his head nearly grazing the top of the doorframe. Though he stood five inches taller than his beefy companion, he looked as though he weighed a hundred pounds less. He wore thick, black-rimmed glasses, jeans and a dark suit jacket over a gray tee shirt with a dragon and a sexy woman holding a sword emblazoned across the front. Declan looked up from massaging his jaw and decided the man looked as though someone had built a computer programmer out of noodles.

"What's going on, Ashley?" he asked.

"Who's Ashley?" asked Seamus.

"I am."

Seamus looked up at the man still holding his wrist. "Your name is *Ashley*?"

He shrugged. "Mom was a big *Gone with the Wind* fan. My sister's name is Scarlett and my other brother is Rhett."

"That's ridiculous."

Ashley shrugged again.

Seamus turned his attention back to the short guy. "Where's Jackie?"

"She's inside. Can I tell her whose calling?"

"Can you tell her—? Get out of my way."

Seamus resumed wrestling to free himself from the grip of the goon.

"That's my boyfriend," said Jackie's voice from inside.

"Let him in, Ash," said the tall man.

Ashley stepped out of Seamus' way and the Irishman entered. Declan peeled himself off the wall, his cheekbone radiating pain. He held it as Charlotte approached.

"Are you okay?" she asked.

He nodded and looked up the stairs at the hulking man blocking his way. "I need to see what's up."

"The other ones want to come in," Ashley called into the house.

"That's fine."

The behemoth stepped aside and Declan and the girls entered Jackie's house. Inside, Seamus stood next to Jackie, his arm around her shoulders. She appeared upset but unharmed.

"This is Rocky," she said, motioning to the tall man.

"Rocky Conrad." He thrust a gangly arm towards Seamus. "You've probably heard of me."

Seamus remained motionless except to raise the corner of his upper lip and utter, "No."

Rocky dropped his untouched hand and cleared his throat. "Eh, I think we started off on the wrong foot. Let me start by saying I apologize for scaring the lady. I can be a little rough around the edges sometimes." He chuckled to himself as if he'd just told a joke.

Declan squinted at Rocky, wondering why the noodle-nerd talked like some tough guy from a cheesy gangster film, but looked like the runt from a litter of Vikings. His blond hair was slicked back from his forehead and matching gold chains encircled his neck and his wrist. But for the stubble on his jaw and the crinkles around his eyes that put his age at about thirty, Declan would have guessed he was a teenager dressed as a gangster for Halloween.

"He scared me a little so I called you," said Jackie. "He's missing a box."

"A box?" said Declan and Charlotte in unison.

"A box?" echoed Stephanie a second later in a breathy purr.

Rocky's gaze locked on her and she stared back at him

as if he were a cookie she'd been dying to eat. She blinked at him and his face spasmed as if it had considered bolting from his skull but then decided to stay.

"Hello, I don't think we've met," he said. "I'm Rocky."

Stephanie shook his hand. "Stephanie. Is that your car out front?"

"The Mercedes? Yes…"

Seamus pointed at the tennis goon who had followed them inside and now stood guarding the exit. "Who's the guy who ate John McEnroe over there?"

"Ashley? He's my…uh…driver… er… *bodyguard*."

"Yeah. I'm his driver slash bodyguard," said Ashley, looking as though he was trying not to laugh.

"You must be awfully important to have a bodyguard…" said Stephanie.

"You've got to be kidding me," mumbled Declan.

Rocky blushed. "No. I mean, yeah…I mean, I don't get my hands dirty, if you know what I mean."

Stephanie reached into her purse and pulled out a business card. "I'm a criminal lawyer. If you ever need *anything*…"

"Alright," said Seamus, snatching the card out of her hand and tearing it in half. "Enough of this nonsense. Can we get on with it?"

Rocky frowned as the pieces of Stephanie's card fluttered to the ground. "What's that? Oh. The *box*." He scowled at Seamus, which made his glasses slide down his nose. He adjusted them and tried scowling again with his head slightly tilted back. "I… I want the box now before things get *ugly*."

"Oh shut up," said Jackie.

Rocky blanched.

Stephanie pulled a second card and Rocky took it,

thrusting it in his pocket before turning to Seamus with a self-satisfied grin. "I came for the box. I told her all about it." He threw a finger in Jackie's direction.

"What kind of box?" Seamus glowered at him. "Tell *me*."

Rocky tilted his head and nodded. "Okay. Sure. It's rosewood, about so big." He held his hands about a foot apart. "It has a wooden flower embedded in the lid. A lily."

"Do you have it, Jackie?"

"I don't. I *did*, but I sold it at a yard sale. He brought a clipping."

Jackie handed Seamus a square piece of newspaper and Declan leaned in to see it. It was a photo of Jackie, smiling and standing behind a table full of knickknacks, while another woman perused her wares. On the table sat a box with a flower in the center of the lid. The caption said, *Pineapple Port's yard sale offered a treasure trove of items.*

"That's how he knew I had it, but I sold it that day. That was weeks ago. I don't remember who bought it."

Seamus turned to Rocky. "So there you go. She doesn't have the box. Be off with you."

"I'm afraid that's unacceptable." Rocky looked at Stephanie, a grin curling at the corner of his mouth when he found her watching him. He straightened to his full height and pushed his glasses up his nose again. "Ay, oh…I'm a nice guy, but my father is a very powerful man. Things could get bad for you if you don't find me that box."

"Enough with the mobster accent. You sound about as Italian as I do," said Seamus.

Rocky looked crestfallen. "I'm half Italian on my father's side." His accent had disappeared.

"What was your mother? A giraffe?"

"Look here—"

"No you look *here*. Are you threatening us?" Seamus' voice boomed.

Rocky took a tiny step toward Ashley who seemed in no hurry to help him. "Just get me the box and I'll be out of your hair."

"And if we don't?"

"I can't be responsible for what happens. Like I said, I'm just doing a favor for my father. Who is one hundred percent Italian I might add and a direct descendent of some very scary people if you know what I'm saying."

"You've really got a death grip on that insulting Italian stereotype," said Charlotte.

"What? No, I mean, like, *real* gangsters. *Really* real. I come from a long line of real gangsters. I do."

"Who?"

"Dad won't tell me," he mumbled. "But we had to change our last name, I can tell you that."

"I'd like to meet your father," said Seamus.

"That won't be possible. He's a busy man."

"*I'm a busy man.*"

"It's okay, Seamus. I'll find it," said Jackie, placing her hand on Seamus' arm.

"You've got twenty-four hours," said Rocky.

"That's no time at all," said Charlotte.

"Okay, a week. Let's say a week. I can…uh…keep my father at bay that long."

Jackie nodded. "I'll figure it out. I'll get the box."

Seamus looked at her. "You've got to be kidding me. These guys can't just come in here and—"

"I'll find the box," said Jackie in a low, strained hiss.

Seamus huffed. "Fine. Where should we take it?"

"Just give me a call," said Rocky, pulling out his wallet and handing Seamus a card. He made a big show of sliding Stephanie's card in his wallet and she lipped the words *call me* to him. "You've got a week," he added, before Ashley led the way from the house, Rocky tight on his heels, his eyes never leaving Seamus.

"I'm going to break that stickman," muttered Seamus as the door shut. "Break him, build a fire out of him, and burn him down."

"Oh he's a *kid* with delusions," said Jackie. "I realized it about two seconds after I called you."

"Maybe," said Seamus. "But we haven't met his dad."

"So you remembered who bought the box?" asked Charlotte.

"No," admitted Jackie.

Seamus sat down beside her, wringing his hands in his lap. Declan turned and spotted Stephanie standing just outside the door, waving good-bye to Rocky. He glanced at Charlotte and found she, too, was staring at Stephanie, her lip slightly curled.

"Did she become a lawyer to *date* criminals?" she asked.

He stared at the ceiling and shook his head with disbelief. "I hadn't considered that, but she certainly threw herself at him like he was a dart board, didn't she?"

"You seem like an odd choice for her. Do you have a dark secret you want to share?"

He chuckled. "I'm an idiot."

"That's no secret," mumbled Seamus with a wink.

CHAPTER FOURTEEN

"This is ridiculous," said Charlotte sitting on Jackie's comfy chair. "They can't just come in here and threaten you."

"Should we call Frank?" asked Jackie.

"I don't know. What could he do? He can't arrest them for asking us to find a box. The threat was vague and it's he-said-she-said stuff anyway. He could offer us protection...maybe talk to them...it might be easier to find the box if you think there's any hope. Do you have *any* idea who bought it?"

"No...no..." Jackie closed her eyes and squinted. "I'm trying to remember. I know it was towards the end of the sale, but by then I was getting into my Margaritas... I'm pretty sure it was a woman...maybe with blonde hair? Like a bob cut? Maybe a little upscale. Had a big wedding ring, I remember that."

"What *is* the box?" Seamus asked her. "Why is it important?"

Jackie sighed. "I have no idea. It was just an empty wooden box when I got it."

"Probably drugs," said Stephanie reentering the room. Everyone looked at her and she shrugged. "What? It's always drugs."

"Who *is* this girl?" asked Jackie.

Seamus rested a hand on Jackie's knee and shook his head with his eyes closed, the international symbol for *we'll talk later*. "Was there something in the box?"

"No. I mean, nothing I didn't put it in myself. Jack

gave it to me for my birthday not long before he died."

"Your husband's name was Jack?"

She nodded.

"So you were Jack and Jackie? That's adorable."

"Don't even start, Seamus."

"So it was empty when he gave it to you…" mumbled Charlotte standing to pace. She tried to picture the box in her mind and imagine ways it could be useful. "There *must* have been something in it at some point. It doesn't make any sense why Rocky's dad would want it. Unless maybe it's some sort of rare antique?"

"It didn't look like much. Jack said it was for my jewelry, but it had no hooks inside for keeping jewelry straight. I told him if I put jewelry in it I'd end up with a giant gold and silver nest and he said, *whatever, it's your damn box.*"

"Sounds like a sweetie."

"Tell me about it."

"He never said where he got it?"

"No… Honestly, it looked like a kid made it. I figured Jack made an emergency stop at a rummage sale when he remembered it was my birthday. I considered myself lucky that I didn't get a gas station rose."

"And now Rocky is threatening to kill you for it," muttered Charlotte under her breath.

"I don't think Rocky would hurt a fly," said Stephanie. "I mean, I don't know, but that's the vibe I get from him. I know criminals. I think he's a puppy dog."

"I agree we need to be less worried about Rocky and more worried about his father," said Charlotte.

Stephanie offered her a smirk as if to show she'd won that point and Charlotte made a mental note to never agree with her again.

"Surely, Rocky has to know if there was something in

the box, it's long gone."

"Hmm…" Stephanie tilted back her head and looked at the ceiling. "If the box is *empty*, then it must be the box *itself* that's important, right?"

"Makes sense," said Seamus.

Stephanie tilted her head and glanced at Charlotte from the corner of her eye.

Charlotte felt her lip twitch and tried to remember if she'd ever hit a girl before.

"The box is made out of *cocaine*," said Stephanie.

"It was made out of *wood*," said Jackie. She looked at Seamus. "Seriously, why is she here again?"

"How could you make a box out of cocaine?" said Charlotte finding herself first annoyed and then intrigued by the notion. "Maybe…if you mixed it in with paper mâché…"

"Rocky *said* it was wood," Declan reminded her.

"Maybe that was to throw us off track," suggested Stephanie.

"'He's not that bright," said Charlotte with a glare she hoped implied that Stephanie wasn't either. "The cocaine box theory is full of holes. Literally. I mean, it would crumble one way or another, right? Maybe it was carved by a master craftsman or some famous artist?"

"It looked more like it was made in a high school wood shop," said Jackie. "Besides, even if it *was* made out of cocaine the street value would only be about four grand. That's not enough for a gangster to get riled up."

"How the heck do you know that?"

Jackie shrugged and exchanged a glance with Seamus. "I'm old. Who knows how I know half the things bouncing around in my head?"

"I need to be somewhere," said Stephanie looking at her watch before taking a step towards Declan and placing her hand on his arm. "Take me back to the store to get my car?"

Jackie looked at Charlotte, who rolled her eyes.

Declan brushed away Stephanie's hand and took a step back. His look of disgust telegraphed that no ride would be forthcoming.

"I'll take you back," said Seamus. Stephanie smiled, batting her eyelids at him.

Jackie frowned. "*You* will? Someone threatens to kill me and you're starting a taxi service for...for..." Jackie threw her hand in Stephanie's direction. "For *that?*"

Seamus nodded. "I have things to do. I want to look into Rocky's dad. Find out what we're up against."

"In the meantime I'll see if I can track down who bought the box," said Charlotte. "Okay boss? Put me on the internship clock."

"Done," said Seamus. He planted a kiss on Jackie's forehead.

"Be careful," she said.

"They're not coming after *me*."

"I didn't mean the gangly gangster," she mumbled, glaring at Stephanie.

Seamus chuckled and headed for the door. Stephanie turned to Declan but before she could hug him goodbye, he made a cross with his fingers as if to ward off a vampire. She shot Charlotte a sideward glance, betraying no emotion, and followed Seamus outside.

Once she'd gone, Declan visibly relaxed.

"I need to get back to the shop. You're not going to do anything stupid, are you?" he asked Charlotte.

"No. There's a license plate in this photo." She held up the newspaper and pointed to where a car sat parked on the corner, license plate in full view. "I'll go see Frank. Maybe I can talk him into pulling it for me and, who knows, I might get lucky."

Declan nodded. "Okay. I'll catch up with you later. Jackie, you take it easy. We'll figure this out." He paused and looked at Charlotte. "And thank *you* again for being so understanding about…" He crinkled his nose as if a foul odor had filled the room. "You know. *Her.*"

Charlotte nodded and offered a lackluster smile.

As soon as Declan left the room, Jackie grabbed Charlotte's hand.

"You *are* going to have a talk with him about that witch, aren't you?"

Charlotte raised her brows and tilted her head. "*Totally.*"

"Good. She's trouble on a stick."

"Don't worry about me. What about you? Are you okay?"

"Yes. Nice gift, huh? Nice then, and nice now. It's the gift that keeps on giving."

"Can you think of *any* reason someone would want that box so badly?"

"No. But who knows with Jack? It might have been filled with money or jewels or *anything* before he gave it to me. Nothing worth anything made it to me, though, I can promise you that."

"That's what has me worried. Say we bring back the box and it's what was *in* the box that he really wanted."

"So you're saying we could kill ourselves trying to find it and still end up dead."

"Oh jeeze, I hope not. We'll get it all worked out. Can you think of *anything* else that might help? What does the box look like exactly? This photo is a bit too grainy to tell."

"It's rosewood like Rocky said, sort of pinkish with lines of different shades, as if it was made from a lot of small layered pieces glued together."

"Hm. Maybe there's cocaine in the glue..."

"Now *you* think it is a box made of cocaine?"

"No. Sorry. Mind wandering. And he said it had a lily in the center?"

"Inlaid in the lid."

She sighed.

"What is it?"

"I don't even like lilies. They make me think of funerals. And now they're making me think of mine."

"Oh don't be silly. No one is going to die. We'll find the box and give it back and that will be the end of it."

Charlotte held up the newspaper article. "Do you mind if I take this?"

"No. But promise me you'll never get married."

"That seems like a lot to promise in exchange for a piece of newspaper."

"No, I mean it isn't worth it." She flopped back into her sofa. "Declan seems like a wonderful guy, but they *turn* on you. I'm telling you. One day you're in love and the next day he's setting you up to be killed by a gangster."

"What about Seamus? Are you saying you'll never marry him?"

"That man..." Jackie turned her head in a failed attempt to hide a growing smile. "I have a feeling he'll be the death of me either way."

Charlotte headed for the door. She needed to touch base with Gloria and check if Frank could help her with the license plate. As she reached for the latch of Jackie's storm door, she noticed a crumpled pile of fabric near the entrance. Something about it was familiar. She stooped and held it aloft for a better view, then realized it was the drinking parrot flag from outside Gloria's door.

"Is this your flag?" she asked.

"Yes. I had one with flip flops after everyone had their things switched. I found mine down the street, so I switched them."

"That was Darla and Mariska."

"No...I think it was Gloria's house."

"No, I mean it was Darla and Mariska who switched everything."

"What? Why would they do that?"

"To give me a case to work on."

"Aw...that's kind of cute. But you've got a real case now."

"I've got a few...but this flag has me wondering if they're the same case."

"What do you mean?"

"Gloria received a threatening note demanding she return an unmentioned item—"

"Like underwear? How creepy."

Charlotte squinted at Jackie. "*What?*"

"You said they demanded an unmentionable."

"An *unmentioned* item. I meant they didn't say *specifically* what they wanted, not underwear."

"Oh. That makes more sense."

"Uh, yeah... Nobody is asking for her underwear."

"Stranger things have happened. Remember when that kid had a crush on Tippy and started leaving baseball cards on her doorstep?"

"He was, like, eight years old."

"Still."

"*Anyway*... My point is, she got the note when *your* flag was flying outside her door."

"And you think they thought it was my house? You think they were demanding the box?"

"I don't know. Seems odd that people are demanding

things from two people in a week around here, and nothing has happened at Gloria's since the flag came down…"

"But who gives directions using flags? That seems odd, too."

"Maybe someone scoped out your house and then told someone else to put the note in the house with the parrot flag?"

"That was taking a risk in Florida."

"No kidding. I don't think I'll tell Gloria to go home just yet, but let's hang up your flag and see if that ends the attacks at Gloria's."

Charlotte opened the door and strained to hang the drunken parrot back on Jackie's flagpole.

"Wait… Didn't Gloria's house catch fire?"

"Someone lit a box of brush—" Charlotte paused. "Hm. A *box* of brush. I wonder if that was a hint…"

"My point is, someone *started a fire*. Was that a threat, too?"

"Maybe. Or just kids being little jerks."

"And now you want to draw those people to *my* house?"

"Well, when you put it that way…but…no—Rocky knows where you live. It was probably an early mix-up amongst his flunkies. At this point, I don't think the flag will make a difference either way."

Jackie put her hands on her hips. "Well if it does, I'll be sure *you're* the first to know."

CHAPTER FIFTEEN

Tammy wiped the counter of the TikiMon Beach Bar as the young man took his seat.

"What can I getcha?"

"Mojito."

She nodded. Mojitos were a pain in the neck. All the *muddling*.

Squeezing lime in a glass, she opened a plastic bin and pulled out fresh mint leaves. She mixed the lime juice with sugar and the leaves and began to crush it all with a well-worn wooden muddler.

He'd looked like a beer guy, too. It's never easy.

"What are you doing?" he asked.

"Muddling your drink."

"Really? See, I do it with a mortar and pestle. Get the leaves nice and broken."

"Instead of in the glass? That doesn't make any sense."

He sniffed. "*I* do it the right way."

The tone of his voice made her look up from her muddling and his expression said she'd crossed a line. The skin on the back of her neck prickled. She'd seen that look on other people and it never ended well. She decided to backtrack. "I dunno. This is how I was taught. Anyway, we don't have a mortar and pestle here."

His dazzling grin reappeared like a fast-forwarded sunrise and she realized she'd been holding her breath.

"I just bought a new set," he said. "Too bad I didn't know you needed one. I could have given you my old one."

He giggled.

Freak.

"They your cats?" he asked.

She followed his gaze to the bar strays, Frick and Frack, sitting in the corner of the tiki porch.

"They were unofficially adopted by the restaurant."

"They nice? Like, you can pet them and pick them up?"

She nodded, handing him his cocktail. "Real sweeties."

"Hey, could I get some of those fish bites too?"

She punched in his order and turned to a couple sitting on the other side of the bar.

Five minutes later, a runner from the kitchen brought her the fish bites and she handed Mr. Mojito the greasy basket of fried nuggets.

"You got a pen I could borrow?" he asked.

Pulling one from behind her ear she slid it across the bar. Other customers commanded her attention and by the time she returned, the freak had gone. She felt relieved.

Throwing his empty plastic basket in the bin behind the bar, she realized the wax paper inside was missing. Did he eat the paper, too? Something else was misplaced...*her tip.* Instead of dollars, she found a napkin covered in ink.

My tip to you is my mojito recipe it said along the top, all in caps. Beneath it was a list of ingredients and precise directions that wrapped to the other side of the napkin. He'd even listed the size of the mint leaves. Three inches long.

Weirdo.

She balled the napkin in her hand and tossed it in the trash.

A break in the bar action offered a moment to feed

the cats. The feline mascots took most of their food from the TikiMon patrons, but she liked to give them a can of wet food every day to be sure they didn't go hungry or want for vitamins. When they'd arrived at the restaurant they'd been scraggily things. Now they were fat, sleek and happy, and she intended on keeping them that way.

She popped a can of Fancy Feast and clanged the lid against the beer tap. They always came flying when they heard that can banging. It cracked her up.

When they didn't appear, she peered over the bar for her furry buddies.

Nothing.

She plopped the food into the cat bowl and it sat at the foot of the bar, untouched, for half an hour. Dave the bar runner set two baskets of chicken wings in front of her and turned to leave.

"Hey Dave, you seen the cats?"

He paused long enough to shake his head before disappearing into the kitchen.

"Huh. That's weird."

She grabbed the baskets and handed them to her customers.

CHAPTER SIXTEEN

Charlotte returned home to find Gloria on the sofa watching daytime television. She'd changed from her morning gown into a matching shorts and top outfit featuring large red roses on a cream background. She looked like a tiny floral sofa sitting on another sofa. Abby had her chin and one paw resting in her lap.

"Charlotte, you're back. Any luck finding my assailant?"

"They aren't really assailants unless they've assailed you."

"My *potential* assailants then."

"No."

"Oh." Gloria sulked. "I'm getting a little stir crazy."

"I apologize. I'm a little distracted by...*another case.*" Charlotte found it hard not to smile as she said the words. She'd gone from unemployed to swamped in the course of a day. "I just popped in to check on you. I need to investigate some leads."

The image of a man squeezed into a giant barrel flashed on the television screen and Charlotte stopped to watch.

"Um...What's this?"

"I'm not sure what it's called. It's a crime show about a woman who killed her husband and put him in a barrel full of chemicals to dissolve his body. She was doing really well until she forgot to throw out the acid bottles. Now the cops are on to her. Stupid mistake."

Hm. "Doing research?"

Gloria didn't respond to her joke, once again engrossed by her program. Charlotte's gaze drifted from the television to Gloria to her dog.

"Hey, I've been meaning to ask you. How come you don't have a dog? You like dogs, right?"

Gloria paused the show. "Oh I love dogs."

"You never…oh, I don't know…accidentally fed one to a snake or anything…"

She laughed. "Oh no. I love dogs more than people."

"And you don't mind Abby?"

"Oh, no. She's a joy."

"Good. If she ever bothers you, just let me know. *First*. I mean, don't let it build up inside of you or anything. Just tell me."

"Oh don't be silly. She's a doll."

Charlotte nodded. "I'll be back in a bit."

"Okay. I took some pork chops out of your freezer."

Charlotte paused with her hand on the doorknob.

Is she making room in the freezer for something?

"Why?"

"I thought we could have them for dinner. I'll cook."

"Oh. Yes. Sounds wonderful."

Whew.

Charlotte went to Mariska's to borrow her Volkswagen. Working from home, she rarely needed her own vehicle and always had access to Mariska's. But now, as an investigator, she'd need to consider getting a car. Who knew when she'd have to rush off to check on a lead? She was going to need an official vehicle. Something understated that blended in with traffic. She could drive her golf cart to the store, but she'd look ridiculous staked outside a suspect's home in a candy apple red golf cart with *Sweet Charlotte* stenciled in gold flake on the side. Although, Mariska's VW Bug, with the giant pink flower in the dash, wasn't much more subtle.

Charlotte drove to the Sheriff's office, plotting how she might sweet-talk Frank into running a license plate number for her. She wasn't sure it was legal for him to share information, and Frank hated blurry lines when it came to the law. In addition, she didn't want to tell him about Rocky and Jackie. Not yet. So far, Rocky's demands seemed straightforward and getting Frank in a kerfuffle over vague threats wouldn't help anything. Hopefully, Frank would find her request for license plate information reasonable and she could be on her way.

She didn't want to have to sic Darla on him. That would be a last resort.

The square, brick, government building that served as the Sheriff's office came into view and she parked in the asphalt driveway that surrounded it. Charlotte sat in the car taking deep breaths to calm her rapidly beating heart. She wasn't a fan of conflict or begging and suspected her request would involve both before the day was over. After a few minutes, she grabbed her purse and stormed into the building before her resolve could abandon her.

"Hey Miss Charlene," she said to the heavy-set woman sitting behind the front desk. "Frank around?"

The woman smiled, her hair coiled into a bun that sat high on her head like a black mamba waiting to strike. "Well, hey there Miss Charlotte, how are you?"

"I'm good. And yourself?"

"Oh you know me. Peachy. Frank's in his office. You want him?"

"Yes, please."

Charlene pressed a button on her phone.

"Frank, Miss Charlotte's here to see you."

There was a pause before Frank's gruff voice crackled

through the intercom.

"Send her back."

"Will do."

She nodded. "His majesty will see you now."

Charlotte grinned and walked down the cinderblock hallway, its fresh beige paint gleaming beneath harsh lighting. *Why do government buildings have to be so soul-sucking?* They'd recently renovated the place, but forgotten to soften the bulbs or add art or a plant or *anything* to make the building feel less like a prison. Of course, it also served as a jail so…maybe pleasantries weren't high on the government's list of priorities. Still, she felt bad for the people who had to work there every day. No wonder Frank was so cranky.

She rapped on the door labeled "Sheriff Frank Marshall" and entered at the sound of Frank grunting.

"Hello little lady, how can I help you today?" he asked without looking up from his paperwork.

She sat in the chair on the opposite side of the desk, careful to avoid a sharp tear in the vinyl seat. Apparently, the makeover hadn't included new furniture.

Charlotte could feel her resolve slipping. Sitting across from Frank she felt like a little girl. She cleared her throat and steeled herself.

"I need your help with a case."

"A case?" Frank looked up, a smirk on his face.

Oh good. The idea of her working a case was amusing enough to tear him from his work.

"You got your first case, huh?"

"It's actually my third, remember? My first was to find Witchy—er, your roof witch."

"Right. I forgot about her." Frank's gaze jerked past her to the back of the room before he sniffed and looked away.

What was that?

Charlotte twisted in her chair to look behind her, finding nothing but a dented file cabinet and a large cardboard box. Frank's expression had made her think someone had entered the room. Someone he didn't want to see.

"So what can I do for you?" he asked.

"Seamus gave me a job and it would *really* help me solve the case if you ran a license plate for me. I'd like to impress him with my skillz."

"Your skills, huh."

"My *skillz* with a z."

"Of course. And what about Seamus?"

"He's Declan's uncle. The Irish guy. You've met him, remember?"

"I know who he is. I mean, what does he have to do with anything? What sort of job did he give you and why?"

"In order to get my private investigator's license I have to intern with another investigator and it turns out he is one."

"I thought we established he wasn't a cop?"

"He's *not* a cop, he's a private investigator."

"Seamus is a licensed private investigator?"

"Yep."

"And he's training you?"

"Uh huh."

Frank leaned back in his chair, tapping his pen against the arm, his mouth hooked to one side.

"What about law enforcement?"

"What do you mean?"

"Can you intern with law enforcement to get your license?"

"Yes."

"Why didn't you ask me?"

"Oh…I…I just didn't think to bother you with it."

"Well, I can teach you anything he's teaching you, that's for sure."

Charlotte smirked. "Frank…are you *jealous?*"

"Jealous? No, I'm not jealous. I just thought I could help. But if you don't want my help—"

"No, I'd love it. I'm sure you could help. I could work with you both."

"I mean, I'm *actual law enforcement.* I don't know *what* he is."

"A licensed private eye."

"Yeah, but…what is that *really?*"

"I imagine it's a licensed private eye."

"But what has he *done?*"

She opened her mouth to share what she knew of Seamus' past, but decided against it. Reminding Frank that Declan's uncle had served as a confidential informant for the Miami police wouldn't impress him. Frank was old school. He'd picture Seamus as a bad guy breaking the law with impunity in exchange for information. Which was probably partially true…but it also meant years of experience solving crimes and thinking like a criminal. His training could be invaluable. Seamus could teach her how to think like a criminal and Frank could teach her how to think like a cop. How could she not succeed with such diverse coaching?

"I don't know what he's done *exactly,*" she said, which was the truth.

"So, what do I need to do? Think of a test for you? Come up with something to sharpen your skills as an investigator?"

"That would work. But—"

She stalled, desperate to steer their conversation back

to the license plate. She had to get Gloria safely out of her home *and* she had to find Jackie's box before the gangster's kid returned. The last thing she needed was a new project. "No hurry though."

"No hurry?"

"I mean, I have a few things I'm working on now, so don't feel like you have to come up with something *tomorrow*."

Frank grunted.

"But what I do need is a plate run. Could you do that for me?"

He shook his head. "You know I can't do that."

"Why not?"

"I can't go running plates for any yahoo who walks in the door."

"Did you just call me a yahoo?"

"You know what I mean. How do I know the plate I'm running isn't someone Seamus is trying to find."

"It's not."

"How do you know?"

"I mean, I don't *know*. But I'm sure it's the plate of a friend or something. He's using it to see if I can track down a person."

"Well...you'll have to find another way. Having me run a plate for you isn't teaching you anything."

"But it would speed things along and then I'd have more time to work on whatever project *you* have for me..."

"You just said you weren't in a hurry."

"I'm not, but... Boy, you would really help me show up Seamus if you could run that plate. He'd know I have more powerful friends than *him* when it came to law enforcement, wouldn't he?"

The expression on Frank's face changed from

dismissive to one of deep contemplation. She'd hit a nerve.

Bingo.

She could feel Frank about to agree, when a voice called from the doorway behind her.

"Sheriff, can I see you for a second?"

No! Charlotte turned. A female police officer stood in the hallway outside Frank's door holding an opened manila folder. It was the sour woman who had guarded her doorway the day she'd found Declan's mother's bones in her garden.

Figures.

The woman looked at her, a flash of recognition sweeping across her face.

We meet again…

"Just a sec…" Frank stood and stepped outside, closing the door behind him. Charlotte heard the low mumbling of conversation in the hall and busied herself scanning the office for anything useful, like she did whenever she was left alone in a doctor's examining room. No free cotton balls in Frank's office though. No wooden tongue depressors to paint and use as bookmarkers. Was there a *license plate machine* she could put the number into while he was out of the office?

Yes.

Duh.

It was called a computer.

She peeked at Frank's monitor and the Windows desktop stared back at her. The computer wasn't locked. But if movies were real, even if she found the license plate database, she'd find *that* locked.

Of course, if movies were real, she'd be able to guess the password in two or three tries…

She twisted in her chair and stared at the closed door.

The voices continued to drone in the hallway. She crinkled her nose. If Frank opened that door and found her on his computer, he would be furious. He might never trust her again. She had to find Jackie's box, but...

Her gaze fell on the large cardboard box tucked between the file cabinet and the wall. Was *that* what Frank looked at earlier with such discomfort? *Another mystery box.*

There wasn't anything wrong with taking a peek in there.

She stood, careful not to screech her chair across the floor, and took one sidestep toward the package. Closed but not sealed, each flap of the box folded beneath the next. A square hole remained open in the center.

She peered into it.

A white-rimmed pupil stared back at her.

I know that eye...

She pulled at one of the flaps and revealed a large green face, bent and folded at odd angles, glaring back at her from the carton.

Witchy-Poo! Darla's precious Witchy-Poo, deflated and folded into a box in *her husband's office.*

Charlotte's shocked expression melted into a grin.

Gotcha.

She closed the flap.

"Okay, we'll worry about that later," said Frank over his shoulder as he re-entered the room. He looked at the chair where Charlotte had been sitting and, finding it empty, soon spotted her standing in the corner.

"What are you doing over there?"

"Stretching my legs. Everything okay?"

"Yes, uh..." His gaze flitted to the box and then shot back to her as he hooked a thumb toward his door. "They like to bounce everything off me."

Frank sat down at his desk and Charlotte perched on

the edge of her chair.

"So...that license plate..."

"I just can't do it, Char, I'm sorry."

"Aw...I'm sorry to hear that," Charlotte looked at her toes. "And to think I *really* didn't want to tell Darla that Witchy-Poo was in a box in your office."

Frank sat up straight in his chair. "What?"

Charlotte smirked. "You heard me."

He looked at the box and then settled back into his seat. "Dang."

"Why would you steal your wife's Halloween decoration? She's losing her mind over that stupid witch."

Frank sighed. "I hate that thing. Every year I have to blow her up, haul her to the roof, secure her, worry about her every time the wind picks up... When I found out she and Mariska were swapping all the decorations in the neighborhood to create a case for you, I figured it was a good time to give her a taste of her own medicine and do myself a favor in the process."

"So you knew it was those two who switched the decorations and didn't tell me."

"Yeah. Sorry. I almost told on them when I saw they took Lil' Frankie."

"You can't keep the witch in here forever, you know."

"No, but I can keep it in the trash forever as soon as I work up the nerve to take it out there."

"She'll just buy another."

"I don't think so. They don't make that one anymore and she's partial to Witchy. Something about the nose to chin ratio."

"Uh huh. So, anyway, here's that license plate number I need run." Charlotte pulled a piece of paper from her pocket and held it out.

Frank grimaced. "You know blackmail is a felony,

right?"

"I've already committed a federal offense by putting flyers in people's mailboxes. I'm an outlaw. I'll be robbing banks by the end of the week."

"Let's hope not."

"And you know, it's bad enough you've played this trick on Darla, but on top of that you admitted that you *knew* I was on a wild goose chase with the mixed-up lawn art. I'm pretty sure you owe me."

"Come on, Charlotte. I couldn't tell you Darla did it. She would have killed me."

"So imagine what she's going to do to you if she finds out *you* stole Witchy-Poo."

Frank rested both hands on top of his balding head and then snatched the paper from her fingers.

"Fine. Give me a second."

He stood and walked out of the room. A few minutes later he returned with a white sheet of paper in his hand.

"Here you go," he said, handing it to her. "Some lady out on Swallow Drive. It's probably his girlfriend. You're probably doing his dirty work or something."

"Seamus'? No, he's dating Jackie."

"Jackie Blankenship?"

She nodded.

"Well, how 'bout that. Doesn't he move fast."

"Don't worry, nothing bad will come of this, I promise."

"And you promise to keep my secret?"

She grinned. "For now. Let's see how the rest of my case goes."

CHAPTER SEVENTEEN

Seamus pulled to the curb outside South Tampa's swanky Harbour Island neighborhood and turned off his engine. It hadn't been hard to find where Rocky's dad lived. Rich people always have their faces splashed all over the Internet, attending this fundraiser or that party. In addition, there weren't that many rich kids named Rocky. A few searches and he found Rocky's name and after that it was almost impossible to avoid his father, who was also named Rocky, but went by Rock.

Poor Sam Spade. Born too early. Life as a detective in the nineteen forties must have been a drag. By the time Seamus had done fifteen minutes' research, he even knew the layout of the Conrad home thanks to Realtor photos posted the last time the house was for sale. The article that he found about redecorating the Conrad pool house was *fascinating*.

Seamus had everything he needed to drive right to the Conrads' door except a pass to circumvent the community guard. Naturally, the Conrads lived in a gated community. Nothing could ever be easy. The moment the guard laid eyes on his ten-year-old car, he'd be sent packing.

This job would have to be done on foot and incognito.

He pulled his car to the curb a few blocks from the neighborhood entrance and cut the engine. Pulling a gardening trowel from his backseat, he hopped out of the car and secured a floppy sun hat to his head. He wore a pair of canvas khakis and a thin white tee. He hoped these extra props would allow him to pass as a landscaper out to keep the neighborhood manicured.

He walked the perimeter of the cement and stucco wall that surrounded the community until he found an unmonitored spot that seemed easy to climb. He jumped and grabbed the iron bars embedded at the top of the wall and hoisted himself to the cement shelf, cursing under his breath for not thinking to bring Declan. He was getting too old to hop fences and his strapping nephew could have shoved him over the wall without so much as a grunt.

After a litany of his own grunts, he scrabbled over the fence, found himself unable to hold his own weight, and fell to the mulch behind a large bush, scratching his arm and knocking the wind out of his lungs. He lay there for a few minutes, gasping, but grinning.

I still got it.

At fifty-five years old, he still had a little pep in his step, no doubt thanks to his strict diet of junk food and alcohol.

Genes are wonderful things when they're your friends.

Seamus strolled to Rocky's address, stopping occasionally to dig an imaginary weed from the perfectly weed-less grounds. He recognized the large stucco-covered mansion on Seddon Channel from the pictures he'd found on the Internet. A landscaper's truck sat outside the house and the side gate was open.

Jackpot.

He strolled in, snatched a pair of shears lying near an unnaturally round bush, and did his best to blend in with the other four men engaged in various stages of maintenance. One of them looked at him, squinted, and then nodded hello. He nodded back and the man returned to his work, unconcerned that he'd never laid eyes on the Irishman before.

Not a tight-knit group. Good.

Seamus continued toward the back yard of the home, where he spotted a man he guessed to be in his late sixties pacing a first floor porch overlooking the Conrads' pool. He wore a polo and shorts that accentuated his knobby knees. The man's voice echoed across the water as he engaged in an animated conversation via cell phone. The longer he paced the porch, the more certain Seamus became that he was Rock Conrad himself. He had the bored demeanor of a man who never did anything he couldn't pay someone else to do for him.

Seamus moved closer to the porch and nipped at the leaves of a rose bush, straining to listen to Rock's conversation. He wasn't sure what he was looking for or even hoping to hear, but he trusted his gut. He needed to get a feel for the man threatening a woman over an empty wooden box. As a tactic, confrontation was his favorite option in situations like these, but years of experience and bloody noses had taught him it was best to gather information *before* charging into the fray.

"Oh, it was terrible," said Rock, his booming laugh echoing across the pool. "Right. Right. I know…"

Seamus clipped a rose and it fell to the ground, bouncing off his toes.

Whoops.

He stooped down and stuffed it in his pocket as Rock walked towards him and sat in a chair just feet from where he pretended to work.

"Roger, I *had* to kill Artie," he said.

Wait, what?

Seamus leaned into the bush, thorns scratching his face.

"What else could I do? I told him what to do and he

totally ignored me. I tried to be kind for as long as I could, but he *had* to learn there are consequences…"

Seamus heard a branch crack. By the time he'd scrambled away from the bush, Rock was peering down at him from the porch, phone still pressed to his ear.

"Roger, I've got a situation here. I'll catch up with you later. Okay? Okay. Bye."

Rock lowered the phone as Seamus tried to clip his way down the line of bushes away from the porch.

"*You*. Who are you?"

Seamus pretended not to hear and walked away.

"You. With the hat."

Seamus stopped.

Shoot.

He turned and pointed to his chest. "Me?"

"Yes. Who are you?"

"I'm, uh, Ivan."

Seamus had no idea how the name *Ivan* popped into his brain. Maybe because it didn't hurt to use a scary Russian name when making a first impression with a potential gangster?

No. He suspected his choice had more to do with the name *Rocky*. He'd seen *Rocky IV* more times than he cared to admit and Ivan Drago had been a worthy opponent.

"I've never seen you before."

"I'm fillink in." Seamus said the sentence in his best Russian accent, which he realized was not good. Why had he started in Russian? Now he was going to have to continue his cartoonish accent for the rest of the conversation. He was much better at Spanish and…

Idiot.

Irish. I actually have *an Irish accent.*

Of course, he couldn't sound like himself, could he?

Wait. Why do I need an accent at all? This guy doesn't know anything about—

"Hey, are you listening to me?"

Seamus looked at Rocky.

"Vat?"

"I said are you listening to me?"

He nodded.

"Who are you filling in for?" Rock's gaze swept over the workers. "Oh, Edwardo?"

Seamus grunted and nodded again.

"You haven't worked for us long, huh?"

Us? Seamus winced. He'd read somewhere that Rock owned a landscaping firm, but he'd figured it was a front to make it easier to bury bodies. He glanced across the yard at one of the men and saw *Conrad Landscape Construction* emblazoned across the back of the man's shirt.

I'm trying to hide as one of the man's own employees. Brilliant.

He shook his head and plucked at the front of his plain white tee.

"No shirt yet."

"Well when you get some time have Javier show you how to work with roses. He's a real pro."

He nodded.

"In the meantime, you be careful with these bushes. Too much roughhousing and you'll kill them."

Seamus turned his head and mumbled. "Whatever."

"What's that?" Rock's voice grew sharp.

"Vat?"

"What did you just say?"

"Vat? Who?"

"You."

"I say sometink? No. I don't think so. Wodka."

Doing a Russian accent wasn't any fun unless you got

159

to say vodka as *wodka* at least once.

"What?"

"I cut flowers now. Potatoes."

"Did you say potatoes?"

"Vat?"

"Look, you—"

"Dad."

Conrad cut short and turned to the sound of the voice calling for him. Rocky stepped out on to the porch followed by a blonde in white bikini. Seamus looked her up and down and then felt his chest grow hollow as a strange feeling of dread washed over him. He *knew* that girl.

Stephanie.

Stephanie laughed and touched Rocky's arm as she surveyed the pool. She caught sight of Rock and turned her full attention to the older man, her hand outstretched as she introduced herself.

Seamus crouched to hide his face and clipped at the lower leaves of the healthiest rose bush he'd ever seen.

"Nice to meet you, Stephanie," said Rock. "Rocky. Could you feed the lady for me?"

"Oh come *on*, Dad."

"*Now.* I'll keep your friend company."

Rocky huffed and stepped off the porch on his way to a small greenhouse building in the corner of the yard.

Seamus did his best to keep his face hidden as he watched Rocky cross the yard. *Feed the lady? What was a lady doing in a greenhouse?*

He glanced at Stephanie. Rock was talking to her and she stared into his eyes as if he was the most fascinating man on the planet.

Seamus moved in a crab-like motion toward the greenhouse. He tucked himself behind an azalea bush and watched Rocky enter the glass building. He could see his form moving through the foggy glass. A few seconds later, he reemerged walking with bravado, no doubt to make up for the way his father had demanded his help.

"Dad, they already moved her."

Rocky headed for the porch and Seamus swept wide around the perimeter of the yard until he was once again near the exit, out of view of Stephanie and the Conrads.

Was Rock keeping a lady in his greenhouse?

No. He wouldn't be so blatant about a kidnapping in front of his son's new girlfriend. Would he? That would be a king-sized ego.

What about the conversation he'd overheard on the phone...*He'd killed Artie for not listening.*

He peeked around the corner of the home and peered at Rock, who stood chatting on the porch with his son and Stephanie. There was a lot to consider. He didn't know about the "lady" in the greenhouse, the man Rock might have had killed, or what game Stephanie was playing. But none of it mattered; he had to keep his attention on the problem at hand.

Rock was rich, powerful, apparently ruthless...

And he wants to hurt my girlfriend.

His lip curled. "I must break you," he mumbled, snapping the "r" off the roof of his mouth to sound as Russian as possible.

One of the landscapers opened the fence door and flinched, startled to find Seamus hiding near the bush just inside the yard.

"Qué estás haciendo?" asked the man.

Seamus handed the man the shears. "I quit." He walked past the man through the fence door.

"Hey!"

Seamus turned.

Pineapple Mystery Box

The man motioned to his lower back.

Seamus felt his own back and found his gardening trowel tucked in the back of his pants. He pulled it out and held it in front of him.

"This?"

The man nodded.

"This is *mine*."

The man shook his head.

Seamus pointed to the shovel and then his own chest. "Esto es mío." Working in Miami for all those years was coming in handy.

The man shook his head again. "No." He launched into a verbal scolding that went way beyond Seamus' ability to follow.

"Whatever. Here. Take it."

The man took the shovel and held it in the air as if he had pulled Excalibur from a stone.

"Yeah, you win." Seamus turned to make his way back to his car.

He couldn't spend all day arguing over a gardening shovel. He didn't know what Rock was up to, but all signs pointed to him being a rich, powerful and possibly deadly man. In his experience, men like that always got what they wanted.

He had to find that box before they *all* ended up in the greenhouse.

CHAPTER EIGHTEEN

Charlotte drove directly to the address provided by Frank. "Tomasa Molina" lived in a rancher on one of the older streets in town. With Charity's large influx of planned communities, not many original homes remained, but Tomasa had one. Charlotte pulled in front of a powder blue, cement block rancher, small but well kept. Flowering bougainvillea climbed the posts flanking the front door.

She knocked, and a short, caramel-skinned woman answered.

"Hi, Tomasa?"

"Si."

Oh no. Charlotte had been meaning to learn Spanish but she was *terrible* at languages. She'd tried several different self-teaching programs, but nothing ever stuck in her head except some numbers, colors and a smattering of random words with no way to properly string them together into sentences. Rocky's box could be sitting inside Tomasa's home and she wouldn't be able to *ask* for it. She closed her eyes, trying to recall if she'd ever known the Spanish word for box.

"Do you...speak English? Uh... Habla Inglés?"

The woman nodded. "Si."

"Oh. Great. I'm so sorry to bother you, but I...*accidentally* sold something at a yard sale that I didn't mean to sell...um...vendido." Charlotte grinned, thrilled she'd recalled the Spanish word for *sold*: *vendido*. She remembered it because it sounded a little like *Vin Diesel*, so to remember it, she'd imagined herself selling the actor. Too bad her mnemonic device hadn't inspired her to look into the Spanish word for *box* while she was at it. Surely, anyone buying Vin Diesel would want him boxed and shipped.

She fished the newspaper clipping from her pocket and unfolded it for the woman to see. "We, uh…remembered seeing you at the yard sale. You were at this yard sale last month? In Pineapple Port?"

The woman peered at the paper.

"I like yard sales," she said in a heavy accent.

"Great. So, this box…you can see it in the picture…did you buy this box?"

"Me? La caja?"

"Caja? Is that *box*?"

The woman nodded.

Well there we go. Caja.

"Yes. La caja. I want to buy it back. Did you buy it? Do you have it?"

The woman looked confused. "No. No, I didn't buy the box."

"You didn't?"

"No."

She held up a finger and slipped back into the house, leaving the door ajar. She returned a moment later with a large, orange plate.

"Compré el plato," she said, holding it aloft with one hand and pointing at it with the other.

"Oh. You bought a plate. But no caja."

"Si. El plato pero sin caja."

Charlotte sighed and refolded her newspaper clipping. "Okay. I'm sorry to have bothered you. Lo siento. Gracias."

Lo siento. Guess a little of the Spanish language CD did stick in my head.

She'd also recognized *plato*, but only because so many Spanish words resembled their English counterparts. If only the woman had said she was going to the *azul biblioteca* for *cervezas* she could have used all the Spanish she knew. Why language programs were obsessed with libraries, she had no idea. Who traveled to another country and went to the local library? Still, it was sad how infrequently Spanish speakers asked her to have beers at the blue library.

Charlotte returned to her car and rolled to the stop light at the end of Tomasa's street feeling dejected. She'd used her one lead. She'd even resorted to blackmail to pry the address from Frank.

What a waste.

She snatched the newspaper clipping from where she'd tossed it on her passenger seat and peered at the black and white photo until the objects in the image blurred into each other. The light turned green and red again, but there were no cars behind her so she let it go. There *had* to be something useful in the photo. She closed her eyes to rest them a moment and then again peered at the clipping photo. There stood Jackie behind her foldout table talking to a woman, but there was no way to identify the woman from the back of her shirt and shorts. She didn't look like anyone Charlotte knew from Pineapple Port. She supposed she could take the clipping around the neighborhood to see if anyone recognized the back of the mystery woman, but really, the figure could have been anyone. Shorts weren't an uncommon article of clothing in Florida. Anyway, the woman wasn't holding the box in her hand; she probably wasn't even the purchaser.

Charlotte tossed the paper into the passenger seat and hit the gas as the light turned green for a third time.

Solving mysteries was an adrenaline rush, but *trying* to solve mysteries was frustrating.

The next red light stopped her a block away from her turn into Pineapple Port. She knew the light would be long. In the picture beside her, the box sat on the corner of the foldout table, taunting her, daring her to find it.

She grabbed the photo and stared at it again, eye jumping from one newsprint pixel to the next.

One of these stupid dots will tell me something...

There were two cars in the photo, or more correctly, *parts* of two cars. While she was able to read the license plate on Tomisa's, the other vehicle had little showing but a bumper, part of the right rear light and the edge of a bumper sticker.

Bumper sticker...

Charlotte squinted at the second car. There *was* something familiar about that bumper sticker. It appeared to be white with a swirly pattern...perhaps a cursive letter *e*? Where had she seen an *e* like that before...?

She looked up to check the light. Still red. Looking down the road in front of her, she spotted the entrance sign for another one of Charity's famous planned retirement communities: Silver Lake.

Silver Lake...written in scripty font...

Silver Lake...that ended in an *e*...

She looked back at the bumper sticker and then up at the sign, a tendon in her neck twinging with the speed of her movement.

Silver Lake.

"Whoo-hoo!"

Charlotte threw her hands in the air in celebration as the driver behind her leaned on the horn. She jumped and hit the gas, nearly plowing into the divider as she struggled to grip the wheel without crumpling the newspaper clipping. She glanced in her rearview mirror and saw Tilly scowling at her. She waved an apology and made a mental note to find a cooler way to celebrate discoveries. Sherlock Holmes never yelped *whoo-hoo!* How embarrassing.

Once in the neighborhood Tilly turned left and Charlotte continued straight.

She smiled.

The investigation wasn't cold yet.

I have a lead.

Silver Lake residents slapped bumper stickers to their cars to make sure everyone knew *they* lived in the community with the *multiple pools.* Silver Lake lots were larger than Pineapple Port's and their modular homes were slightly bigger. Some of them had porches, a luxury rarely seen in the Port. The communities each harbored a quiet dislike for the other. They were like high school sports teams doomed to be each other's rivals in everything. Their residents battled in citywide bowling, shuffleboard and bocce ball tournaments and their crafty people tried to out-bake, knit, crochet and paint each other at every church bazaar. The upcoming Halloween costume contest was the biggest battle of them all.

The Port occasionally lost people to Silver Lake and Silver Lake lost people to Pineapple Port.

Neither spoke of those people anymore.

Traitors.

Charlotte rolled her eyes.

They had to have the box. Who else, if not miserable ol' Silver Lake?

She checked her car's clock. She had time.

Charlotte made a u-turn and headed into Silver Lake.

Silver Lake had a three-by-four-foot gatehouse that

made Silver Lake residents feel superior to *gateless* communities like Pineapple Port, even if it was protected by a seventy-year-old man. But what they didn't know, was that their precious gate wasn't protected by just anyone.

He was a Pineapple Portian.

Pete, known as Parking Pass Pete around the Port, was their man on the inside.

She lowered her window and gave Pete her cheeriest smile.

"Hey Triple P."

"Charlotte! How are you? What brings you over to the dark side?"

"I'm good, and I need to talk to a lady in here. I'm on a case. Okay if I go in?"

"I saw your detective flyer. Sounds exciting. Heard Arnie Caslin got a pie out of it. Can I threaten to turn you in for sneaking into Silver Lake for a plate of brownies?"

Charlotte laughed. "I'll see what I can do."

Pete chuckled, picked up his clipboard and slid a pencil from behind his ear. "Hm…I need to put something on the sheet. What should I say?"

"Maybe say I'm someone's granddaughter?"

He nodded. "Sounds good. How about Victoria…I know she has a granddaughter who comes through here from time to time…" He looked up from his scribbling. "But you're much better lookin' than her."

"Aw, thanks Pete. Keep up the good work."

He tipped his imaginary cap to her. "Keeping the world safe for mankind. Take it easy."

The gate arm opened and Charlotte drove into enemy territory searching for the bumper sticker. Several of the visible cars had stickers, but none had them in the right spot or with taillights that matched the news photo until she crept down Magnolia Court. There, parked in a driveway in front of what appeared to be a triple-wide home was an older model Audi with the right sticker in the right place. She pulled to the curb and parked.

Charlotte walked to the front door of the Audi home and stood on the porch for a few seconds before knocking. She admired the wooden railing and the small umbrella-covered outdoor dining set.

Gosh. This is a nice porch.

She wanted to build a porch behind her home, but after finding Declan's mother there, she was terrified to dig.

She knocked. A moment later a woman answered. She had a sharp nose and a steel-gray bob.

"Yes?"

Charlotte smiled. "Hi…I hate to bother you but I have a sort of silly question for you."

"I'm not buying magazines, I don't need my driveway repaved and our roof is fine," said the woman, closing her door.

"No, no. It's nothing like that." Charlotte put her hand on the door to stop it from shutting.

Panic flashed across the woman's face. "There's no soliciting."

Charlotte removed her hand from the door and held both up to show she meant no harm. "I'm not soliciting, I'm sorry, I just need to ask you a quick question."

"I'm not joining your church."

"I'm not here to ask you to join my church. My friend had a yard sale in Pineapple Port a few weeks ago. You were there."

"I was not."

"You—you weren't?"

"No."

Charlotte could tell the woman was lying, but she didn't want the door closed on her again.

"Is that your car?" she asked, pointing at the Audi. "That car was at the yard sale, but maybe it wasn't you?"

"Yes. I—well…yard sale you say? Maybe I drove by. Accidentally. My friend likes yard sales. I *told* her she wouldn't find anything."

Charlotte knew the comment was a shot at Pineapple Port but did her best not to appear offended. If the woman knew she lived there, she'd be even less friendly.

"Okay…well…my friend did something accidentally, too. She sold a box she didn't mean to sell. I'm just trying to find it."

"A box?"

Charlotte nodded.

The woman closed the door a little tighter. "Why?"

"Why do we want it back?"

"Yes. Is it worth more money than you thought?"

"No, nothing like that. There's not an original copy of the Declaration of Independence in it or anything. It just has sentimental value."

The woman's lips twisted into a knot. She clearly didn't like what she was hearing, but Charlotte wasn't sure which part of the story disagreed with her. She guessed the woman still thought the box was worth money.

"So…did you buy the box?"

The woman's gaze darted past her and Charlotte turned to see where she was looking. All she saw were more houses. Houses where her friends probably lived…

She didn't buy the box. The friend did.

The woman stood a little straighter and put her hand on her hip. "What did it look like?"

"It was rosewood with a flower in the center of the lid. A lily. About twelve inches long, maybe five inches wide?"

"No, doesn't ring a bell. Sorry." She began to close the door.

"What about your neighbor?"

Again the woman's eyes shot across the street and she shook her head.

"She didn't buy it either."

Ah ha!

Charlotte smiled. The woman never said her yard-sale-shopping friend was a *neighbor*, but she didn't correct the reference to the friend *as* a neighbor.

The woman who bought the box lived nearby.

"You're sure she didn't buy the box? Maybe you two were separated for a bit?"

"No. She doesn't have it."

"Are you sure? Could you point her out to me so I could ask?"

Again, the woman's gaze fluttered past Charlotte and she felt confident the friend lived on the other side of the cul-de-sac.

"I wouldn't feel comfortable. I'm sure she didn't buy it. I have to go. I'm very busy. Good luck finding your box."

The woman closed the door.

Shoot.

Charlotte walked down the porch steps toward her car. She peeked down the side of the woman's house as she strolled, but found no easy way to eavesdrop. She suspected the woman was on the phone with her bargain hunting buddy, but there was no way to hear the conversation.

I know that friend has the box.

She could feel it in her toes.

She stopped to look back at the other houses in the

cul-de-sac. There were three houses across from the woman's home. Judging by the angle of her gaze during their conversation, Charlotte felt confident she could narrow the friend's house down to the two farthest to the left.

If only I could hear the conversation. Right now, the woman was probably telling her friend to get the box appraised.

An idea flashed through Charlotte's mind and she slapped her hip.

Maybe Declan could appraise it.

But she needed to find a way to get the box to *him.* *How?*

She could knock on the neighbors' doors… *No.* The lady with the pointy nose probably already warned her friend. She'd never answer her door now.

Wait.

She might not be planning to answer her door, but she *will* be on the lookout.

She'll suspect I'm coming. She'll want to know what I look like so she can avoid me in the future.

Charlotte stepped behind a street lamp, taking a moment to admire the fact that Silver Lake had impressive antique-style street lamps. Maybe if Pineapple Port had such lovely street lamps she'd want to slap a bumper sticker on her car, too.

Hm.

Back to the case.

She stared at the three other houses, mumbling to herself. "Come on…peek…you know you want to…"

After a few minutes, the door of the center house opened and a woman peered out. She looked around the cul-de-sac as if searching for someone. Charlotte stepped out from behind the lamp and the woman spotted her. She froze for a moment, and then squatted to adjust her doormat as if that had always been her intention.

Yep, sometime a person just can't sleep, worrying their doormat might be crooked.

Gotcha.

The woman slipped back inside and closed her door.

Charlotte walked to the house and rang the bell. No one answered. She tried knocking. Still no answer.

So that's how we're going to play it.

She gave up and headed back to her car. Just as she stepped inside, a golf cart with a light on top came wheeling into the cul-de-sac.

Parking Pass Pete.

She closed her door and slid down her window.

"I'm supposed to kick you out for soliciting," said Pete.

"I'm not soliciting, but that's okay, I'm leaving anyway."

He grinned. "That'll make me look good. It would be better if I threw you over the hood and cuffed you though."

"Not a chance."

"Ah well."

"Do you know who lives in that house there?" she asked, trying to point as discreetly as possible.

He looked. "Diana. Diana Fassbender. Thick as thieves with the one in this house here, though she's twice as miserable." He gestured toward pointy-nose's house. "Her name's Poppy."

Charlotte nodded. "You know, Pete, I don't think I'd want to live here even with all the fancy street lamps."

"Nope. Now get out of here, you snake oil salesman." He made a big show pointing her toward the exit of the neighborhood and she laughed as she closed her window and left the neighborhood.

She didn't have the box.
But she sure knew where it was.

CHAPTER NINETEEN

Charlotte pulled into her driveway and saw Declan's car parked on the curb. She smiled and felt a shimmy of giddiness run through her.

This day just gets better and better.

As she neared her door, Declan stepped outside to meet her.

She bowed. "How wonderful of you to greet me at my door, kind sir."

"My, you're in a good mood," he said, kissing her on the cheek.

She turned her head in time to catch him on the lips and he leaned into the kiss.

"A *very* good mood."

"I am. The license plate was a dead-end but I think the bumper sticker is a winner."

"I'll just pretend I know what all that means."

Charlotte opened the newspaper clipping and held it aloft for him to see. She pointed to the visible license plate. "I got Frank to run this plate and found a lady who had been to Jackie's yard sale, but she bought a plate, not the mystery box. But then…" She pointed to the partially visible bumper sticker. "I realized *this* is a bumper sticker for Silver Lake, across the street, and found the buyer."

"You did? So you have the box?"

"Well…no. That bit is a little more complicated. But I know where it is."

"That's great."

"Hopefully." Charlotte nodded towards the house. "So

I guess you met Gloria?"

"Yep. Interesting lady. Did you know she put fast drying cement in the finger holes of a woman's bowling ball?"

"What?"

Charlotte pushed past him to enter the house.

"Gloria!" she called.

Gloria's head popped around the corner from the kitchen.

"Charlotte! You're home. Perfect timing. I made pork chops. I even have enough for your handsome friend." She waggled her eyebrows in Declan's direction.

"Gloria, what's this about cementing bowling balls?"

Gloria's face fell and her gaze drifted back to Declan.

"Have you been telling tales out of school?"

He held up his hands. "Sorry. I didn't realize it was a secret."

Charlotte dropped her purse on the table next to the door. "You said you'd told me *everything*."

Gloria sighed. "I forgot. Sorry. A few weeks ago during bowling league, this woman kept stepping to the line when I was at the line. That makes me crazy. It is *so* rude. She should *wait* if she sees I'm ready to bowl. Then she did it again the week after that. I found out from some other people that she does it to everyone. So...I took care of it."

"You put cement in the holes of her bowling ball?"

"Gorilla Glue, to be exact. You only need a little bit and then it expands into this yellow foam that dries hard..."

Charlotte put her hand over her face and then looked at Declan.

"Do you see what I'm dealing with here?'

He chuckled. "I don't know. It's kind of nice when

people who deserve a comeuppance get theirs. She's like a prankster Robin Hood."

"See?" Gloria pointed at Declan and then walked over to give him a hug. "This one *gets* me."

"I can see I shouldn't leave you two alone."

Gloria released Declan and patted his chest. "That's a hunk of man, there."

Charlotte thought she saw Declan blush and to spare him further embarrassment she looked away and picked up her chalk. "Do you know the bowling lady's name?"

"Loretta. Loretta Rutter. I remembered because I always liked Loretta Lynn and this woman is no Loretta Lynn."

Charlotte wrote *Loretta Rutter—bowler* on her chalkboard.

"Okay," said Gloria, clapping her hands together and trotting back into the kitchen. "Pork chop time. You two sit down."

As soon as Gloria disappeared back into the kitchen, Declan turned to Charlotte and, pulling her into his arms, kissed her hard on the lips. Charlotte felt her body give into the kiss and hoped the muscular arms around her body would prevent her from melting into a puddle at his feet.

Just as quickly, he snatched away his lips with a smack and whispered in her ear, "Tag, you're it," before spinning her toward the kitchen table.

As she stumbled into the kitchen, mouth ajar, Gloria glared at her.

"What are you doing? Sit down."

Charlotte, in turn, glared at Declan, who was already pulling out his chair and acting as though nothing had happened.

"You're going to pay," she hissed in his ear as they sat.

"I'm sure I don't know what you mean," he said, snapping out his napkin and placing it on his lap.

"Are you kids ready to eat?"

"I am," he said, refusing to acknowledge his terror as Charlotte gave him her scariest squint.

Gloria delivered a plate of pork chops and a bowl of mashed yams to the table.

"Nothing green I'm afraid," she said, sitting at the end of the table across from Charlotte.

"Here here," said Declan. "It looks great. Thank you so much for making room for me, unannounced."

"Oh, my pleasure," said Gloria. "I'm a guest as well. Thank *you* Charlotte."

"If you're willing to cook, you can stay as long as you like. I'm afraid my ever-changing line-up of hobbies hasn't hit cooking yet, probably because Mariska is always foisting food upon me."

They passed around the dishes and dug in.

"Whoops, dropped my napkin," said Charlotte a few bites into the meal. She leaned over and, with her head hidden from Gloria's view, kissed Declan on his elbow.

He jumped and she sat up, napkin in hand.

"Here it is," she said and then coughed the word "Tag."

The corner of Declan's mouth twisted and he nodded his head slowly.

"Okay. I see how you are," he mumbled.

"So *nothing* new on my case?" asked Gloria.

"My lead turned out to be nothing," said Charlotte, hoping that if she remained vague Gloria would assume the lead was for *her* case. She'd been so involved with Jackie's imminent-death-by-gangster problem she hadn't had time to hunt for her houseguest's harasser.

Gloria stared at her.

Gloria.

The last thing she wanted to do was piss off Gloria.

Charlotte paused, the fork an inch from her lips.

She wouldn't do something to the food because her case isn't solved, would she?

She took a quick inventory.

Did I choose my own pork chop, or did she put it on my plate?

She studied the chop.

Is that an injection mark?

No…pepper.

She looked at Declan.

Does he look pale? I know we're eating the same yams…

"How do you feel?" she asked him.

"How do I feel?" Declan knitted his brow. "Fine. Great. Why wouldn't I?"

"Nothing. You…looked a little pale. It must have been the light."

He shrugged. "You said you ran a license plate?"

"Frank did, yes. But it was a lady who knew nothing about the box."

"What box?" asked Gloria.

Shoot. Cover blown.

"Different case."

"Can you tell me about it?"

"I can't. Client privilege."

Gloria's expression soured.

"I mean I will," Charlotte added. "I just can't quite *yet.*"

Gloria nodded.

"Hey, what kind of bird is that Gloria?" asked Declan, standing and pointing past her face to the backyard.

"Where?"

Gloria twisted to see where he pointed. As she did, Declan leaned over and pecked Charlotte on the forehead, whispering 'tag' in her ear before standing and heading into the kitchen.

Charlotte had looked for the mystery bird as well and felt like an idiot for falling for the oldest trick in the book. On the upside, he'd walked across the kitchen without frothing from the mouth and collapsing, so it was probably safe to eat more yams.

"Anyone need more iced tea?" he asked.

"What bird?" asked Gloria.

"I guess it flew away," said Declan returning with the pitcher. "It was sort of blue."

"Blue jay?"

"Probably."

After dinner, Charlotte waved Gloria away from the kitchen and began work on the dishes. Declan cleared the table while she fed the dishwasher and Gloria headed down the hallway to "put on her comfy clothes." As soon as she disappeared around the corner, Charlotte caught Declan's eye and crouched like a leopard, preparing to spring.

"Oh no you don't," said Declan taking two quick strides into the living room.

Charlotte jumped forward and tackled him as he neared the sofa, her face puckered in an exaggerated kissy-face. He turned and caught her, holding her body away from his as he flopped back onto the cushions, laughing.

"You're it," said Charlotte.

"There was no contact."

"I brushed your nose. You felt it, don't lie."

He ceased resisting and she fell on him. "Fine, I give up."

She felt his hand slide across her back as he leaned up

for a kiss.

"This doesn't count as a tag back, FYI," she said, avoiding his lips for a moment longer.

"Nope. Scout's honor."

They kissed. She felt her body rise and fall as his breathing grew deeper and faster.

"You know what's funny?" she asked in her sexiest whisper.

"What's that?"

"You think if you're super charming and cute tonight that somehow I'll forget all that nonsense with Stephanie today."

Declan opened his eyes wide and made an "O" with his mouth, before one side pinched into a smirk. "I never thought any such thing."

"Right. You—"

Before she could finish her sentence, there was a knock on the door.

"Whew," said Declan. "That was close."

Charlotte stood. "Did you plan this?"

He shrugged and sat up. "I can't tell you all my secrets."

Charlotte answered the door to find Mariska's husband, Bob, standing outside. In her driveway, Bob's golf cart sat adorned with the official *Neighborhood Watch* flag, hanging limp in the breezeless night.

"Hi Bob, are you here on an official matter?"

"What's that?"

She pointed. "The flag. It's your turn for neighborhood watch?"

Bob scratched his head and nodded. "Yeah...Frank got hung up at work and I saw Declan's car here, so I thought maybe he'd like to take a spin with me?"

Night watch duties circulated throughout the

neighborhood, pairing two or three people each evening to patrol via golf cart. Frank and Bob usually shared duty and, more often than not, returned an hour later smelling of bourbon thanks to the flask they smuggled to the golf cart for the evening's festivities. Neither Darla nor Mariska liked them drinking, so an evening away from the ladies made a great excuse for swig or two. Or four.

Bob always left for night watch as mild-mannered Bob, and returned as Lance, his snockered alter ego, a nickname he'd earned as a former Lance Corporal in the Marines. Lance was a hellcat.

Charlotte glanced at Declan. He was sitting on her sofa with no idea what awaited him.

"Declan, Bob has neighborhood night watch duty and he's wondering if you'd like to join him. His usual partner, Frank, couldn't make it and *nobody* wants to roam these dangerous streets alone."

"Night watch?" Declan jumped to his feet looking like a child who'd just received a Red Ryder carbine action 200-range-shot model air rifle for Christmas. "Sure. Do I need to bring anything?"

"You have a gun?" asked Bob.

Declan's expression clouded. "No…"

"Do you have any sort of martial arts training?"

"I took a kickboxing class for a while…"

"Do you have any bourbon on you?"

Declan's mouth opened but words failed him.

"He's just kidding," said Charlotte.

"About everything except the last bit," said Bob.

"You know I can't give you bourbon. Mariska would kill me. And we both know you already have some stashed in the cart."

Bob rolled his eyes. "I don't know what you're talking about. I should sue you for defamation of character."

Declan pecked Charlotte on the cheek. "I'll see you when I get back. Assuming I survive."

Charlotte felt herself blush as Declan walked outside to join Bob.

He kissed me in front of Bob.

Declan was halfway to the golf cart when he turned and jogged back to the porch.

"Oh, by the way…"

Charlotte had been about to close the door and she cracked it open again. "Yes?"

"Tag. You're it."

"Ooh." She shook a fist at him as he scampered back to the cart. "We're going to talk when you get back."

Declan waved.

"Hit the gas, hurry," she heard him say.

CHAPTER TWENTY

"I'm honored to accompany you on this terrifying mission," said Declan.

"It *is* quite an honor, and it comes with its own rewards. Open that glove compartment."

Declan opened it and pulled out a pint of Woodford Reserve bourbon. He held it up and admired it.

"Good stuff," he said.

"Not really. I thought I'd be sharing it with Frank so I filled a good bottle with cheap stuff, but it'll do."

"I'm not picky."

"Open it. Take a swig. Don't tell Mariska."

"What about Charlotte?"

"She doesn't care. Sometimes she sneaks me and Frank drinks when the ladies aren't lookin'."

Declan took a nip and grimaced as the booze burned his throat.

"Smooth," he said in a hoarse whisper, handing Bob the bottle. "I've heard about your infamous Bourbon Club. Is Charlotte an honorary member?"

"Nope. No two-legged, non-furry ladies allowed in the Bourbon Club."

"Please tell me you mean the dog."

"Huh? Oh, yep. Miss Izzy. But Charlotte never follows the rules anyway." He took a hit from the bottle.

Declan smiled. "I think that's what I like about her."

Bob handed him the bourbon and winked. "Me too."

They made two complete circles of the entire neighborhood and sped by Charlotte's house to begin their third patrol. The required minimum was three rotations.

Bob held up the bottle to judge how much remained.

"Heck, we might want to do four go-rounds tonight."

"For safety."

"Absolutely. For the good of the neighborhood."

"Here's to safety."

"Here's to safety," said Bob, taking another drink.

Declan took the bottle from Bob and was about to take a sip when he thought he saw orange sparks ahead of them. He squinted.

This stuff is stronger than I thought.

The lights resembled orange fairies circling an object he couldn't quite identify in the dark. They hovered about four feet off the ground, bursting into existence and then disappearing just as quickly.

"Do you see those sparkles up ahead?" he asked.

"I was afraid to ask you the same thing."

"What do you think—"

A deafening *boom!* cut Declan short. Where they had been watching the sparks fall, a ball of light expanded, blinding them. Something metal hit the front of the cart and Bob screeched to a stop.

"What the Sam Hill was that?" said Bob, holding his hands over his eyes.

"I think…" Declan looked over the side of the cart and found the metal object he'd heard strike the front of the golf cart. His vision still had a large round dark spot in the middle of it from the brightness of the blast, so he looked just right of the object to identify it. "It looks like…a mailbox?"

"Someone blew up a mailbox." Bob reached under his seat and pulled out the longest flashlight Declan had ever seen. He turned it on and flashed the beam on the smoking wooden stump where a mailbox once sat. The post was split, half of it leaning at a thirty-degree angle to create a vee shape. He flashed the light on the house.

"That's Gloria's house."

His light swept to the side of the house and Declan saw shadows jump into the brush behind the home.

"I see them," he said half-jumping and half-stumbling out of the cart. He set off on foot to catch them. He felt like a superhero, out to save the day, stronger and faster than he ever remembered feeling, ready to tackle the vandals and hold them until the police arrived.

I will be the best night watch buddy ever.

He could hear rustling just beyond the tree line. He blinked, his vision still marred by the flash of the explosion. He could hear them. The perpetrators hadn't gotten very far. He plunged through the bushes, slapping palm fronds from his face. Why should Charlotte and Seamus get to have all the fun while he sat in the pawnshop worrying about his fate at Stephanie's hands? Why did they get to be cool detectives while he played shopkeeper?

He stumbled and narrowly avoided falling head first by catching his balance against a tree. A thought ping-ponged through his head.

I might be a little drunk. Maybe this isn't the greatest idea—

The sound of a twig snapping dismissed all his anxieties. He was close. He could hear them just past the next bush. He could hear—

A loud squeal pierced his ears. The sound wasn't human. He hadn't touched anyone—why would they scream in such a horrible…

Someone is being eaten by an alligator.

He stopped and looked around him, trying to dodge the black hole in his vision.

Are there alligators in here? What am I doing in the woods at night?

Another squeal echoed, followed by a loud snorting noise and Declan pushed forward.

Wait. That's familiar. Not an alligator...no...that sounds like...

Declan burst through the brush into a large field.

The field was...*empty?*

He heard breathing in the darkness. Short, hard pants.

The field was *not* empty.

He saw movement, low to the ground. Black on black.

The moon slipped from behind a cloud and illuminated the largest, most angry, black *pig* Declan had ever seen. Maybe *pig* was the wrong word. It was much more. He wasn't sure *boar* even did the demon justice.

The word *tusks* hissed in his brain.

Tusssssssksssss...

That wasn't a word that came up very often.

The pig snorted as its eyes locked on him.

Oh no.

It charged.

If Declan had *felt* particularly athletic before, he *knew* the turn he made plunging back into the brush was the fastest he'd ever moved in his life. He flailed with his arms, swimming through the fronds and sticker bushes. Flesh tore from his body, leaving bloody dots and dashes on his skin like some grotesque Morse code.

He knew what the code said:

Don't run after wild boars, idiot.

As he burst back into Gloria's yard, he headed straight for the thin, marshy runoff pond next to her home. He could hear the beast hot on his trail and didn't feel confident that he could outrun it anymore.

Please tell me boars don't swim.

He plunged into the water and heard a grunt as the creature applied its cloven-hooved brakes behind him. A loud crack filled the air and he instinctively covered his ears.

Now what was exploding?

The pig reared up on its hind legs and spun before sprinting back into the brush.

Declan was still frozen when Bob walked into his field of vision and motioned for him to uncover his ears. He dropped his hands.

"What the heck were you thinkin'?"

Bob stood at the edge of the pond, a gun in his hands.

"You have a gun?"

"Of course I have a gun. I'm a retired Marine. It's a dang *law*," said Bob, slipping it back into his holster. "Not to mention, this is Florida. Heck, what *can't* kill you around here."

"That was a pig," said Declan. "I didn't expect to run into crazed, bloodthirsty pigs on patrol."

"You'd rather an alligator?"

"Well, no I—" Declan looked down and realized he was up to his waist in a swamp. "I've got to get out of here."

"That's my point. Watch for the snakes."

"What?"

Declan waded to the edge as quickly as he could and Bob offered him a hand. He climbed out and stood on the bank, soaked and out of breath.

"Did you shoot it?"

"The pig? No. Gun's loaded with blanks."

"Oh so it's not like a *real* gun."

"Bullets are under the seat, just in case."

"Oh." He looked down at his one soggy shoe. The other was missing, sucked off by the mud and lost to him at the bottom of the swamp. "So stupid."

"In the future I wouldn't go running into the brush like that. But if it makes you feel any better, you looked really brave."

"I thought I saw the person who blew up the mailbox trying to get away."

"But it was a pig."

"I guess. Did you see anything?"

"Nope. I'm going to take you back to Charlotte to get fixed up and pick up Frank. I gave him a call and he's home now. He can look into this mailbox mess."

Declan nodded and Bob slapped him on the back.

"Good job. That was the most exciting night watch since Minnie Gaston got caught skinny dipping."

Declan sighed. "Thanks."

He took a closer look at what remained of Gloria's mailbox and then stepped into the golf cart, doing his best not to track too much mud in with him. Before they drove again, Bob handed him the bourbon.

"You might need to finish this."

Declan took it. "Don't you want to save it for Frank?"

Bob laughed. "He'll bring his own. Don't worry about that. He knows I always try and sneak him the cheap stuff."

As they neared Charlotte's, Declan spotted a red sports car parked across the street, two houses past her home. There were still several car lengths behind when the car's lights came on and it drove away from them.

Stephanie.

What was she up to now?

Declan sighed.

He still had to deal with that disaster as well. He looked down at his sock and wiggled his muddy toes.

And now he had to do it with one shoe.

CHAPTER TWENTY-ONE

Charlotte had just said goodbye to Declan and Bob when another knock on her door had her spinning to return to the front of the house. She grinned, thinking it was Declan back to taunt her, and lunged for the door, narrowly avoiding Abby as the dog jostled for position.

"Hey sweetie," said Mariska. Darla stood behind her, waving.

"It's like Grand Central Station around here."

"Why's that?"

"Bob was just here picking up Declan for night watch...as if you two didn't know that."

"Why would we know that?" said Darla as they entered.

"Oh *please*. I knew Mariska pushed him to ask Declan out the second I saw his face in the door."

Mariska gasped. "Now why would I do that?"

"In the hopes they'd bond...or, more than likely, just to spy on him. Find out if he's *worthy* of me."

"She's good," said Darla, offering Mariska a sideward glance.

Mariska grimaced. "I'm a little worried we're getting predictable."

"Could be. I knew you were going to say that."

Gloria stepped into the front room.

"Hello ladies."

"Gloria, what are you doing here?" said Mariska.

Charlotte looked at Mariska, stunned by the ease with which she could pretend she didn't know Gloria was staying at her house.

"Someone's trying to kill me, and Charlotte said I could stay here until she figures out who."

"Oh my. Who would want to kill you?" said Darla.

Another little faker. She shut the door behind the ladies. "That's what we're trying to find out."

"Right, so keep it on the low down that I'm here," said Gloria.

"Down low," corrected Charlotte.

"What?"

"It's *down low.*"

Gloria looked at her toes. "What is?"

"Never mind."

"So you're helping Gloria *and* you're trying to find Witchy-Poo. You *are* busy," said Darla with enough sarcasm to imply that Witchy-Poo should be top priority.

"And I have a third case. A missing box."

"A box?" asked Mariska.

She looked at Gloria. At dinner she'd been strong and told her she couldn't divulge the particulars of Jackie's case, but now she was *itching* to share.

Ah well. Gloria already knew she was working on another case, no sense hiding the details.

I'm weak. Admitting it is the first step.

She revealed the threats on Jackie's life and the box she needed to find.

"Heavens, is everyone in this neighborhood being threatened?" said Mariska.

"Who's this gangster?" asked Darla. "Since when do we have gangsters?"

"He's from Tampa."

"Oh," said all three at once. That was the big city.

"Seamus is trying to find more about him so we know what we're up against."

"Do you have any leads?"

"I think I've located the box, but the lady is pretending she doesn't have it."

"Why would she do that?"

"She's from Silver Lake."

Again, all three sang "Oooh…" in unison, their lips curling in disgust.

"We need to get in there and *take* that box back," said Darla.

"I'm thinking it might come to that, but I need to think it out. See if there's any other way."

"But you said you only have a week to get it."

Charlotte nodded.

"You need *revenge* on that selfish woman," muttered Gloria.

"Revenge? For what?"

"For being rude. She could have just given you the box, maybe asked for their money back. Instead, they had to be jerks. They should pay for that."

"I don't know…I don't think it's a revenge thing," said Mariska.

"You'd be surprised what turns out to be a revenge thing," mumbled Charlotte, glancing at the chalkboard. "You're going to end up staying at my house for life if you don't cool your jets."

Gloria sniffed. "Well I already thought of an idea. If you want to hear it and solve all your problems…"

Charlotte shook her head and then realized Darla and Mariska were staring holes through her.

"Tell us," said Mariska.

"We should at least hear what she has to say," said Darla.

"It couldn't hurt," added Mariska.

Charlotte sighed. "Fine. What would you do, Gloria?"

"Me?" Gloria put her hand on her chest as if she was shocked someone would ask. "Well... It's easy, really. What do the snotty little cowbells in that neighborhood like more than anything?"

"Snotty little cowbells?" echoed Charlotte.

"Bragging about how big their houses and lots are," said Darla.

Gloria pointed at her. "Yes. But we can't make their houses smaller...I guess...I mean, without burning them down."

"Gloria, can you stay off the crazy train for ten minutes please?" asked Charlotte.

"I wasn't suggesting we burn down their houses. I was just saying that would be the only way to make their houses smaller. That's all. It was perfectly logical."

"What about that extra pool?" asked Mariska. "They're always yapping about how they have two pools."

"Yes, but...say...filling the pool with roadkill or something wouldn't help us get back the box."

Charlotte put her head in her hands. Asking Gloria for help planning revenge was like opening Pandora's box. She'd never be able to stuff all the crazy back in there.

Mariska and Darla looked at each other.

"What about their landscaping?" asked Gloria.

"Oh they're always going on about the landscaping," said Mariska, changing her voice to imply she was mimicking the Silver Lake women. *"The service came by today and did such a fabulous job on the garden..."*

"They picked all the blades of grass that didn't match out with tweezers..." added Darla in the same snooty voice.

Gloria laughed and clapped her hands. "Yes."

Charlotte looked up. "First off, Gloria, I've never seen you *so* giddy as here, now, hatching an evil plan, and that worries me for your long-term wellbeing."

Gloria's eyes sparkled. Seeing that her first comment hadn't made a dent in the evil genius' happiness, Charlotte continued.

"Second, how can Silver Lake's passion for landscaping help me get the box?"

Gloria slapped her thigh, closed her eyes and threw back her head. "Landscaping…grass…dogs."

"I don't get it," said Darla.

"I think she's channeling some vengeful demon…" said Charlotte.

Mariska scowled. "Did she say *dogs*? How can dogs help? Miss Izzy won't even go out to pee in the rain unless I hold an umbrella over her."

"Miss Izzy is scared of the dark," said Darla.

Mariska nodded. "It's true."

Having experienced her moment of inspiration, Gloria refocused on the group.

"Here's the plan. We get as many people and their dogs as you can. We go into Silver Lake, en masse, and let the dogs do their business on all the lawns near the person who has the box. Her, the friend who warned her about Charlotte…*all* the other nearby lawns. Before you can say pooper-scooper, everyone will be out in a rage."

"So?" asked Charlotte.

"So that's when you sneak in and take the box."

"Couldn't I just wait until she leaves?"

"How are you going to know when she leaves? How are you going to stake out the house in Silver Lake?"

"Pete will let me in."

"But there are two ladies there who would recognize you now."

"I could send Seamus…"

"To wait for what? Maybe days? Someone will see him

in a tiny cul-de-sac, that handsome man and his accent."

Charlotte scowled. "Gloria, when was the last time you were on a date?"

She tilted her head and looked at the ceiling. "Maybe a year ago?"

"I think you might be due. I don't think we've met a man in the last few days you didn't think was handsome or try and feel up."

Gloria tittered. "You might be right."

"Get back to the plan," said Mariska.

"Maybe we could just ask Parking Pass Pete to give us a call when she leaves?" suggested Darla.

"I don't want to get him fired…"

"And her door would be locked if she left," said Gloria.

Darla chuckled. "That's usually where I come in."

Gloria's brow knit with confusion but Charlotte opted not to share Darla's expertise in lock picking. Who knew what the little nut might ask her to do in the future if she knew? Darla didn't need to know Gloria had her first husband sent to jail and her second struck by lightning, and Gloria didn't need to know Darla's ex was a thief who'd taught her how to pick locks.

She sighed. *What was wrong with these people?* If by a certain age everyone had a checkered past, she really needed to start cultivating hers or someday she would be the most boring person in the Port.

"That's breaking and entering," said Mariska. "If we sneak in when the door is open, then it is just *entering*. That's got to be half the jail time, don't you think?"

"Jail time. This is all going too far," said Charlotte.

"You said you have a week," said Gloria. "What choice do you have?"

"There has to be a better way. But I will take it under

advisement."

"It's kind of a terrible idea," said Mariska.

"No, I like it," said Darla.

"You would."

Gloria shrugged. "It's what I would do. And I *always* win."

"Do I need to remind you that someone is trying to kill you?" asked Charlotte.

The front door opened and Bob walked in.

"Sorry to come in without knocking but we could see you all through the front window," he said. "We need some antiseptic. A *lot* of antiseptic. And a hose. Not necessarily in that order."

"I have the hose," called a voice from outside.

"What?" Mariska stood. "Are you okay?"

"Where's Declan?" asked Charlotte.

As she moved towards Bob, she could see Declan standing at the threshold of her door beneath the porch light, hose in his hand. Black mud soaked his legs, khaki shorts and the bottom of his shirt. Every visible inch of his flesh had a cut or was caked with blood.

"Holy swamp thing!"

The other three women stood and trotted over to see what Charlotte saw. They all gasped in unison.

"Great. An audience," muttered Declan.

What happened to you?"

"It's a long story."

"Short version is Gloria's mailbox blew up and he chased a pig into the brush thinking it was the bomber and ended up in the pond next to the house," said Bob.

"Thanks, Bob," said Declan hosing his legs. "You told that like pulling off a Band-Aid."

"My mailbox blew up?" screeched Gloria.

"You chased a *pig*?" asked Darla.

"Why do you smell like booze?" asked Mariska, sniffing at Bob.

"I gotta go get Frank," said Bob, pulling away from the group and heading back to his golf cart.

"We're going to talk, mister." Mariska called after him.

"I should go, too," said Declan.

"Hold on, I'll get you something to change into," said Charlotte.

"Don't. I'll just go home—"

"You can't get into your car like that," said Mariska as Charlotte ran to her bedroom to look for clothes. "You stink like swamp mud."

Charlotte searched her drawers and closets and found two things that might work. She looked back and forth from her fuzzy robe to her largest pair of sweatpants and knew Declan would feel equally ridiculous in either. She decided on the fuzzy robe. At least it wouldn't be quite as…*candid*…about his physical bits as her sweatpants. She foraged for medical supplies and found only rubbing alcohol, a few Band-Aids and a nearly empty tube of Neosporin.

As she walked back down the hall, she heard the bathroom door open as she passed it.

"*Charlotte*," hissed a voice.

She stopped. It was Declan.

"Are you okay?" she asked. "I got you something to wear and some medical stuff."

"The ladies insisted I take off my socks out there and come in here to get a shower. They pretty much pushed me down the hall. They said I might get some sort of jungle rot from being in the swampy water."

"I can neither confirm nor deny jungle rot."

"I feel like an idiot."

"Don't feel bad. You were trying to stop a perp."

"That's nice of you to say, but it was a pig, not a perp. And a little bit of me suspects you only said that because you thought it would be fun to say *perp*."

She grinned. "You already know me too well. Can I give you a kiss or will it hurt?"

"Go ahead. I think my lips are largely unscathed."

She kissed him.

"Oh, just a second…" She ran to the hall closet and grabbed a towel, placing it strategically on top of the robe, and returned to him. "Here, take these things. If you want help with the cuts just let me know. You look like someone filled a shotgun with thumbtacks and shot you."

"Thanks."

He took the items. The door opened enough that she could see he was already down to his boxer briefs. Her eyes locked on his abs. They looked like someone had neatly stacked six charcoal briquettes beneath his skin.

Does he spend all his downtime at the shop doing sit-ups?

They hadn't been dating very long and with all the distractions she really hadn't had a chance to…

She searched for the words.

… read his body braille.

She chuckled at the phrase.

His gaze snapped up to meet hers and he held the towel and robe up to cover himself.

"What are you laughing at?" he asked.

"Just remind me never to write romance novels," she said.

"I—you know…I'm not even going to *ask*. I'm going to get a shower before I get leprosy. I'll see you in a bit."

"Bye," she said, offering him a little wave before shutting the door. Once safely on the other side of it, she remained a moment longer and then snorted like a pig, twice, as loud as she could.

"That's not funny," he called from inside.

CHAPTER TWENTY-TWO

"Oh you look so much better," said Mariska.

They all turned to see. Declan stood at the end of the hall, Charlotte's fuzzy pink robe hanging to the top of his knees.

Darla snorted a laugh and covered her mouth with her hand.

Declan pointed at the group. "If any of you ever breathe a word of this…"

Gloria's hand was also over her mouth, her shoulders shaking with laughter, her eyes teary.

"It's all I had…" said Charlotte.

"Oh you're going to pay for this," he said, visibly struggling to squelch a smirk as he walked into the living room and sat in the corner chair. He sat with his knees together but they naturally fell open, so he crossed his legs and tucked the robe under his thighs.

"Such a lady," said Darla.

Declan shook his head. "I hope you're all enjoying yourselves."

"You have no idea," said Gloria.

He looked at Charlotte. "Can I go home now?"

"Like that?"

He sighed. "Oh. My clothes. Do you have something I can put them in?"

"Like a Hazmat bag?"

Laughter started anew from the ladies.

"Like a garbage bag."

"I already threw them in the laundry. Tell us about your evening."

"Please," said Gloria. "What happened to my mailbox?"

Declan told them the story of the exploding mailbox, the wild boar and trying to save his skin by jumping into the pond.

"Someone is still after you," said Charlotte to Gloria.

Gloria nodded. "Seems like it. I just bought that darn mailbox."

"Blowing up a mailbox is childish, isn't it?" asked Mariska.

"It is," said Charlotte, realizing that the continued vandalism at Gloria's house ruined her theory that Jackie's flag at her door had confused the gangsters. "I think I'm still leaning with Frank and the kids-playing-pranks theory."

"But why just me?" asked Gloria.

"Have you…uh…exacted your unique form of justice upon any children lately?"

"No…um…no."

"What was the *um* about?"

"Nothing. The person I was thinking about had to be in her mid-twenties."

"Is she one of the names on the chalkboard?"

Gloria glanced at the chalkboard wall. "Um…"

Charlotte sighed. "Spit it out."

"The girl cut me off in the food store. Just pushed her cart right in front of mine as if I was invisible. She knew it too, but she didn't apologize."

"And how was she made to pay for this heinous

transgression?"

"I saw that she had bananas in her cart, so I followed her until she left her cart unattended and then scratched *you're rude* on one."

"What do you mean you scratched it?" asked Darla.

"I had a nail file in my pocketbook, so I scratched it into the peel. The scratch turns brown in about an hour so shortly after she got home the message would have been clear as day."

"Do you think she saw you?"

"She was on her way back as I was doing the third, but I think I got away before she could tell."

"The third?"

Gloria nodded.

"You wrote *you're rude* on *three* bananas?"

"No. I wrote that on one, *your skirt is ugly* on the second and just *you're* on the last one. I ran out of time."

"You're like a petty revenge savant."

Gloria smiled. "Thank you."

Mariska shook her head and turned to Charlotte. "Did you ask Declan about your rear-end yet?"

Charlotte looked at Declan, whose eyes grew wide.

"I'm sorry?" he asked.

Charlotte chuckled. "The big cross-retirement-community Halloween party is coming up and there's a costume competition. Silver Lake almost always wins."

"So I made a costume for Charlotte we thought would win for sure," said Mariska.

"I did the head."

"Darla did the head."

"But there's a problem with the tush," added Darla. "I was going to be it, but my back just can't take the bending over."

Declan looked at Charlotte. "You're still losing me."

"It's a unicorn," she said.

"What is?"

"The costume. You know, like the old-timey horse costumes, but with a horn and sparkles. It's a two person costume but the front end is fit for me, and Darla can't bend over to be the back end because she pulled her back out shuffling gnomes."

"Shuffling gnomes..."

"Yep."

"So we were thinking you could be her backend," said Mariska.

Declan nodded. "So it's true. You all *do* think I'm an ass."

The women tittered.

"I wasn't going to drag you into this," said Charlotte. "But I'm running out of options."

"No, I'm honored," he said. "And a little relieved. I didn't know where this was going."

"You will?"

"Of course I'll be your bum. When is it?"

"Tomorrow night."

"Tomorrow. Normally I'd need weeks to prepare for something like this..."

"I know. I'm *so* sorry. I only just found out myself."

"No problem."

"Thank you. And I only need *one* other little favor."

He huffed. "Jeeze. Remind me never to borrow a robe from you again. The payment plan is *brutal*."

"It's not a big deal. I need you to call the lady with the box. I'll get her telephone number for you from Parking Pass Pete; he has the neighborhood address book."

"Should I ask who Parking Pass Pete is?"

"No."

"Whew."

"I need you to tell her you're offering free appraisals for used objects. Antiques and whatnot. She's got to be wondering why we want the box back and I bet she wants to know if it's valuable. Maybe if you offer a free appraisal, then she can bring it by the shop and we could buy it from her or at least assure her it isn't worth anything."

"I can do that."

Gloria let loose an exaggerated yawn. "Well, if you'll excuse me I think I'm going to go to bed. Being hunted like an animal is exhausting."

"We should head back, too," said Mariska, standing.

Darla stood with her. "So, just to be clear...no word on Witchy-Poo?"

Charlotte shook her head. "No. But I think I might have a lead. I'm working on it."

"Oh good. A lead. That sounds official. It's almost Halloween. I'm running out of time. Unless I throw her in a sleigh and slap eight reindeer on it."

"Nine if you count Rudolph," said Mariska.

The two of them let themselves out.

"I should be heading back as well," said Declan. "Mind if I wear the robe home?"

"Mind? Not at all. Of course I'll have to call Frank and make sure one of his officers pulls you over or it won't be half the fun it could be."

"Ha ha. I think I can drive a mile without being pulled over."

"You better hope so."

Declan and Charlotte both stood. He walked over to her and hugged her. It felt *very* snuggly.

"I hope you know there's nothing left between Stephanie and me," he said.

"I know. You said so."

"I'm just treating her with kid gloves until I figure out what's going to happen with her claim on the store."

"How is that going?"

"It isn't, so far. She hasn't really made her move."

"Have you seen it?"

"What?"

"The will she claims to have. Have you actually seen it?"

"No."

"I'm thinking that should be the first step. Maybe she's bluffing. She seems to have a thing for you still. This could all be a ploy just to get you to pay her some attention."

Declan shook his head. "That's crazy."

"It's not that crazy. People do nutty things when they're in love. Or lonely. Or confused. And if you don't mind me saying so, in the little time I've spent with her she's managed to convey a bit of all three."

"You're really trying hard to give her the benefit of the doubt."

"I know. And it's super hard. Someone should probably nominate me for sainthood."

He laughed and then sobered. "In all seriousness, don't drop your guard while trying to be the bigger person. She was sitting outside your house tonight."

"*What?*"

"In her car. She was staking out the place."

"Red? Sporty?"

"Yep."

"Ah. I saw it a few days ago. I thought it might have something to do with Gloria's case. That's good to know."

"Good to know it's my crazy ex?"

"Good it wasn't someone after Gloria and she was

probably there because your car was in the driveway."

"I hope so. I hope she isn't casting an evil eye toward you."

"Don't worry about me. I have an attack dog."

She motioned toward Abby, who lay snoring on the sofa.

"Hm. Terrifying. She told me I had to dump you, you know."

"What? Stephanie said that?"

He nodded.

"Boy, she's got a lot of nerve. What have I ever done to her?"

"That's my point. She's thinking about you, and you don't want to be on her radar."

"I know some people like that," she said, glancing back at the house where Gloria slept. "So...I guess I should probably dump you?"

He grinned. "Probably, though it has nothing to do with her."

She put her arms around his waist. "You be careful, too. Don't get pulled over. I'll work on getting you that lady's phone number and you'll call her for me in the morning?"

"Will do. Actually, it's a good marketing idea. I should start calling around with promises of free appraisals." He kissed her on the forehead. "I'll see you tomorrow."

"See ya."

She watched him get into his car, where he lowered the window and called out to her.

"Remind me if we ever start a band, we should call ourselves The Shuffling Gnomes..."

"Definitely." She laughed and waved as he drove off in all his fuzzy pink glory.

CHAPTER TWENTY-THREE

"Okay, I'll let you know how it goes. And I'll tell him, don't worry. I wouldn't miss it." Seamus put down the phone as Declan walked into the kitchen, bags beneath his eyes and tiny cuts peppering his face, arms and legs.

"Rough night? You look like you were attacked by angry squirrels."

Declan rolled his eyes as he pulled a coffee filter from the cupboard. "Don't ask. Who were you talking to? You'll tell me what?"

"How do you know we were talking about you?"

"Who else do you know?"

"It was Charlotte."

"Why'd you call her?"

"I didn't. She called me. She had an idea for getting the box and needs my help."

"So it must be a last resort."

"Funny."

"It sounded like she gave you a message for me?"

"To remind you the costume party is tonight. And that you're an ass."

Declan paused, the scooper of coffee in his fingers held suspended over the can. "That I'm a—oh. Right. I'm the ass of the unicorn. Gotcha. I might have been a little drunk when I agreed to that."

"I can't wait to see it."

"You're going?"

"Jackie invited me."

"What are you going as?"

"I thought I'd go as a charming Irishman."

"Good luck with that."

"Speaking of charming, did I tell you Stephanie was at Rocky's house?"

"*What?* When?"

"I slipped myself on to his daddy's compound to see what he was about and there *she* was, in all her glory, side by side with our pal Rocky."

Declan sniffed, head shaking. "Unbelievable. Chasing the money, no doubt."

"Oh, and Charlotte also said to remind you about the lady you were going to call. The one with the box. You have to try your bit before I try mine."

"She was going to get a number from Party-time Pete or something..."

"She did. I wrote it here." Seamus pushed a junk mail envelope toward him with a number scrawled on the back.

"Okay. I'll do that in a little bit. It's still a little early to call. Hey..." Declan flipped on the coffee maker and turned to Seamus. "At any point during your chat with Charlotte did she ask to talk to *me*?"

"Never came up."

"Hm."

"Of course, I have that effect on the ladies."

"Of course."

Declan went to work and Seamus did more research on Rock Conrad. The man had a lot of money, but all his dealings seemed above-board. He owned a dozen businesses around Tampa but Seamus couldn't find a single article where his name or his companies were linked to scandal. It worried him. If Rock was a gangster, he was *really* good at it. However, he did find a few articles where Conrad's name appeared in conjunction with antique auctions, which led him to believe the box might be worth more than Jackie thought.

The only mentions of his goofy son, Rocky, involved local social gatherings and his mediocre standing in the local tennis circuit.

What kind of gangster played tennis? They certainly made criminals different up north. In Miami, the only time a gangster had for tennis was putting someone's head in a ball machine.

His phone rang, and he answered it to find Declan on the line.

"Didn't work," said his nephew.

"You called the box lady?"

"Yep, and she didn't bite. Said she didn't have anything to appraise. I didn't want to be too obvious, but I tried to prompt her by listing a bunch of things she might want to check out; china, lamps, jewelry, jewelry *boxes*, blah blah blah. She just said no thank you and hung up on me."

"Looks like it's my turn."

"Don't do anything too stupid."

"Why would I do that?"

Seamus knocked a third time on the Silver Lake address Charlotte had given him. She'd been right about Parking Pass Pete; he let him into the community, no problem. Unfortunately, it looked as if her target, Diana Fassbender, wasn't home.

The leather tool belt he'd found in Declan's garage rubbed against his hip bone and he tugged at it. The boy didn't own any decent tools, just the belt, but it worked for his handyman costume. The plan had been to talk the woman into letting him in to check the cable...or electric...he hadn't decided yet. He didn't know much about either. Once in, he'd planned to scan the house for the box.

He tried the door, but found it locked.

Give up or break in? That was always the question. He couldn't count the times he'd been in the same predicament and *still* the answer was never clear. Sometimes he walked away and regretted it. Other times he broke in and things turned out worse. He was thinking on it when he heard a woman's voice.

"Hello?"

He stepped back from the door to check the home's windows.

"Hello?" he called back, seeing no one.

"Over here."

Seamus turned. A woman stood at the railing of the porch next door, waving her hand. She was a handsome woman, probably in her early sixties, trim and tall, wearing a black spaghetti-strapped top that displayed her ample cleavage.

"Hello," he answered, trying to look as non-threatening as possible.

"Are you looking for Diana?"

"I am; is she about?"

"I—why don't you come on over so I don't have to scream? I'll tell you everything you need to know."

Seamus felt a grin slither across his face. The woman had almost sung her last sentence, and if he didn't know better, he would have guessed she was flirting.

Sometimes I forget what a handsome old devil I am.

He started down the stairs, hoping by the time he finished talking up the neighbor, Diana would have returned. There were worse ways to spend an hour.

He climbed the woman's porch steps as she moved

from the rail to greet him with an outstretched hand.

"I'm Simone."

He shook her hand. "Seamus."

"Oh. Irish, yes?"

"Aye." He offered her a half-wink. More of a squint than an actual wink, with emphasis on his right eye. It was a move he'd trademarked in his own head back in nineteen seventy-nine.

"And Simone...French?" She had raven hair cut in a clean bob that grazed the alabaster skin of her delicate shoulders.

She smiled. "Yes, but by way of Canada."

"Little warmer here?"

"For both of us," she purred.

Oh my.

"Can I offer you a drink? Beer? Wine—"

He shook his head. "No thank you. I'm—"

"Whiskey?"

"What's that now?"

"Bushmills?"

"You've got Bushmills?"

"I've got a little Black Bush you might like."

Seamus swallowed. She held his stunned gaze without so much as a twitch of her cheek. Either she didn't realize her double entendre, or she was a force of nature. Either way, he knew he was going to have to stay for a glass and figure it out.

"I'll uh...I'll have a nip of the Bushmills."

"Ice?"

He raised his eyebrows in mock horror.

She tried again. "*Neat.*"

He nodded.

She slipped inside and returned a moment later with a drink for herself that looked like orange juice and smelled like scotch, and a healthy pour of whiskey for him, both in crystal rocks glasses.

"You're much too kind," he said, taking a sip.

"So," she said, settling into a cushioned chair. "You're looking for Diana?"

He let the whiskey coat his tongue and then nodded. "I am."

"She's out. I saw her drive away about half an hour ago."

"Oh. Maybe her husband?"

"She says he's out of town but he's been *out of town* for nearly a year. She still takes every opportunity to show you the rock on her finger." She held up a hand and wiggled her long fingers in the air.

"Ah. Well, divorce is hard."

"You are divorced?"

"No. Never been married. But…that's what I hear."

She looked over the railing of her porch at his old car parked down the street.

"Who are you with?"

He finished his glass. "What's that?"

"You don't have a company truck."

"Oh…Silver Lake hired me to check on some electrical issues. I'm more of a…freelance handyman."

"A handyman…" She traced her finger around the rim of her own glass. "I have something I'd like you to see. Would you mind?"

"Sure."

She stood and entered her home, holding the door open for him to follow. Once in, she walked towards the kitchen of the open concept home and then made a left down a hallway. He followed her into a room that stood empty, but for a shiny silver metal bar along the wall. Behind the bar, a mirror ran from floor to ceiling. A dark red paint covered the other three walls. Dark shutters kept any light from entering the one window.

"There is a strange vibration in this room," she said, walking toward the chrome bar and placing her hand on it. He followed and did the same.

"I don't feel anything," he said. "Hey, what is this place?"

She ignored him. "Sit on the floor and reach your hands up to touch the bar. I think maybe you have to be grounded."

He snickered. "I don't think grounding my bum is going to make a difference, but I'll give it a go." He eased himself to the floor and pushed his back up against the wall beneath the bar. She stepped toward him as he reached up and grasped the metal.

"Can you feel it?" she asked. "It's subtle. Close your eyes and concentrate."

He closed his eyes. "I don't feel—"

An all-too-familiar sensation grazed both wrists and he heard simultaneous clicks. His eyes opened as the sound of a third snap reached his ears.

"What the—"

Simone stepped away as he tried to pull down his arms, only to find his wrists in handcuffs. A third bracelet secured him to the handrail.

He jerked on the cuffs and found them secure.

"Are you a cop?" he asked.

She smirked. "Are you a handyman?"

He pursed his lips, thinking on a way out of his situation. "Look—"

"Hush." She stepped forward and put a finger against his lips. She moved her finger to kiss him once, gently.

He stared at her, her face just inches from his own. "Lady, you've been reading way too much of that *Fifty*

215

Shades stuff. Why don't you unlock the cuffs and I'll be on my way…"

Simone straddled him and sat in his lap, facing him.

"Oh…" The groan escaped his lips before he could stop it. "Oh boy…"

"Are you sure?" she asked, leaning in to kiss his neck.

He swallowed. "You people around here are crazy."

"What do you want with Diana?" she asked, her tongue tracing the edges of his ear.

"Nothing."

She bit his lobe.

"Ow!"

"Don't lie to me."

"Fine." He tilted his head to keep her teeth as far away as possible from his ear. "She bought a box at a yard sale that my girlfriend wishes she hadn't sold. I'm trying to get it back."

"So you're going to try and steal it dressed up in this way?"

Seamus sighed. "Something like that."

"Why is this thing so important? It is valuable?"

"I don't know. It belongs to this guy Rock Conrad and he wants it back."

"Rock Conrad?" She sat up straight. "Why does *he* want it?"

"I don't know. Hey—" Seamus realized Simone's heavy accent had disappeared. Her last sentence had sounded very much American. "What happened to your accent?"

"My accent? I do not know of what you speak—"

"Lady, you can't just start talking all Frenchy again. I *heard* you lose the accent."

"Fine. Who's this girlfriend of yours?" she said without a tinge of French.

Seamus grimaced. "Look, I don't need to sit here and answer all your loony questions. You're obviously mental. Let me go. I have things to do."

She slapped him on the cheek. Hard.

"Hey!"

She shook a finger in his face. "You *do* have to answer my questions or the next one will be a punch somewhere much more tender."

"Fine. *Jackie.* Jackie Blankenship is her name. Okay?"

Simone stood. "Hm. She isn't one of mine. Does she live in Tampa?"

"One of yours? What are you talking about?"

She raised her foot over his crotch. *"Does she live in Tampa?"*

"No. She lives in Pineapple Port."

"Pineapple Port? Oh no…no, no, no…"

He sniffed. "You know, you Silver Lake people are really snobs, you know that?"

She scowled at him. "It's not *that.* Why does he want the box?"

"I have no idea. But he's threatening her so we're trying to get it back. Can I go now?"

She nodded, slowly, as if still deep in thought as she reached into her pocket and retrieved the key to unlock him.

"There is someplace I need to be. If I let you go; you'll be good, yes?" she asked.

"So now you're French again?"

"Just answer me."

"*Yes.* I'll be good."

She unlocked the cuffs and he stood, rubbing his wrists.

"You are off your nut."

She shrugged, a coy smile on her lips. Seamus placed

his hands together in front of him, as if he were praying.

"Look. I don't need to know all your secrets, Simone, but you seem to know something about Rock that I don't. Tell me, long story short, is my girlfriend safe?"

Simone sighed. "I don't know. That's why I must end our play date."

"That's what you call kidnapping a man? A play date?"

She smiled. "If I feel you need to worry about your Jackie, I will let you know."

"Do you want my number?" he asked, reaching for his phone.

"No. I'll find you. And my door is always open, Monsieur Seamus, should you choose to visit of your own volition."

"Volition," he echoed, unsure what the word meant but understanding the gist of her suggestion. "So you really *are* into this stuff? I was starting to think it was just a way to interrogate me."

She walked to the closet and slid open the door, revealing a collection of whips and other items Seamus couldn't identify. "You thought maybe I was a ballerina?" she asked.

He shook his head. "Lady, I don't know *what* you are."

Seamus walked out of the red room and made his way to the front door, where he paused and turned to take one last lingering look at Simone.

"I'll admit, you have me intrigued."

She smirked. "I could feel that."

"But I think I prefer playing quarterback, if you know what I mean."

She nodded once and blew him a kiss.

Seamus headed back to his car. Stopping at the guard booth on the way out of Silver Lake, he lowered his window.

"Get what you needed?" Pete asked.

Seamus shook his head. "No…" He rubbed his wrists. "I might have missed something, too."

Pete leaned closer to him. "Simone?"

Seamus shot him a look and Pete nodded, settling back on to his stool and raising his newspaper to continue reading.

"You missed something all right," he muttered.

CHAPTER TWENTY-FOUR

"It's been going on for days, Ma'am, on and off."

The officer's gaze wandered to the roadside sign that read *Casa Siesta* in faded paint. Once a motel, the shabby building now served as an assisted living home for a handful of unlucky patrons. The doors were feet from the road. A telephone pole beside the sign had a black and white photo of a black cat's face with *Missing!* written beneath it and a phone number. Keeping elderly people so close to the road didn't seem like a good idea to her, and she suspected things wouldn't turn out well for the cat either.

She sighed. *If my kids throw me into one of these places when I'm old, I'm going to hunt them down from the afterlife.*

Opening her notebook, she returned her attention to a young man wearing baggy shorts and a stained tank top. "So, you heard screaming?"

He scratched at his moppy hair and thought for a moment. "Not *screaming* really. Mr. Sutherland—he's next door—he said he heard more like a moaning. I listened and heard somethin' kinda screechy. Sutherland is half deaf so it must get pretty loud sometimes."

"And you are?"

"Mark."

"And what do you do here, Mark?"

"I'm like a general helper. Clean up the yard and stuff. My mom owns the place."

"Uh huh. And why isn't Mr. Sutherland calling in this complaint himself?"

"I told you; he doesn't hear so good. He asked me to do it."

"Mm hm."

She jotted down a few notes and then squinted at the kid. This wouldn't be the first time an older person *or* a kid had sent her on a wild goose chase, but she had to check every complaint. You never knew.

"Your mom name the place?" she asked, motioning at the sign. "*Casa Siesta?*"

"Yeah, it means napping house. A place where they can rest? Right?"

She grunted. "How would I know?"

"Uh—" the boy shrugged and looked away.

Officer Castillo knew she *looked* like she knew Spanish and it *was* her first language, but it was fun to mess with the kid.

She knocked on the dingy door of room 202.

"Ma'am, if you're in there, I'm afraid I'm going to have to insist you open this door."

Nothing.

"I have it," said a voice behind her.

The owner of the assisted living hotel approached them, out of breath, holding a key in front of her. She started a coughing fit and Castillo snatched the key away before she could use it to cover her mouth. She soon realized she hadn't needed to act so quickly. The woman had no intention of covering her mouth.

"Have you heard anything from Miss..." She looked down at her notes. "Miss Bobbi Marie Boite, lately?"

The woman held up a finger and took a second to clear her throat before spitting. "No. Her grandson's been taking care of her. He told us he didn't need us checkin' in on her no more, so we didn't."

"Mm hm. And that just about broke your heart," she

mumbled before knocking again. "Miss Boite, I'm unlocking the door now to check on your safety. Please step away." She turned to the two beside her. "You both step way back over there. You never know what's going to come through this door once I open it."

"She's old," said the boy.

"You will be too one day. Remember that."

The kid snorted his disbelief and stepped a few feet back to stand beside his mother.

Officer Castillo slipped the key into the lock turned it, her hand on her weapon.

The door opened six inches before the first cat shot through. She turned to watch it skitter across the parking lot as two more slipped out and galloped after the first.

"How many cats does she have?" she asked.

The owner shrugged. "I thought she only had one."

Castillo noticed paw prints on the cement outside the door and stooped down to examine them.

They look almost like…

She tapped the liquid and found it thick and sticky.

Blood.

She stood. "We're coming in Ms. Boite."

Drawing her weapon, Castillo pushed open the door and peeked around the corner. She spotted a body twenty feet inside, lying on the ground in front of a boxy television on a metal stand. The woman lay on her side, her back to the door. There were bloody paw prints on the carpet and what little furniture she could see. Two more cats looked up from their position near the body, their faces slick with blood. That's when the stench of decay hit her nostrils and she recoiled as if someone had slapped her.

Castillo felt the blood drain from her face. She suffered a wave of nausea and took a step back from the doorway, re-sheathing her weapon and pulling her radio.

"I'm going to need an ambulance."

Though, no hurry.

The boy stepped forward and poked his head in the door. He looked inside and then back at her, his nose wrinkling at the smell.

"Get back," she snapped. "This is a potential crime scene."

He strolled back to his mother.

"What is it?" she asked.

He thrust his hands in his pockets.

"Well, good news and bad news."

"What's the bad news?"

"Bobbi's dead."

She hung her head. "Dang. That's too bad, she was a steady pay. What's the good news?"

He spat and wiped his mouth with the back of his hand.

"I think we found Mrs. Williams' cat..."

CHAPTER TWENTY-FIVE

Charlotte felt Declan's hands settle on her hips as they walked into the party tent.

Bonus.

"You're a superstar for doing this at the last second," she said from within the head of her unicorn costume. "Can you breathe?"

"Unicorn air; it's like rainbows and kitten kisses back here," she heard his muffled voice behind her.

She giggled. "Don't worry, we'll make a grand entrance and then we'll split the horse. Then we just have to combine again for the judging."

"We should have had a bunch of tiny people spill out of the costume. We could have been the Trojan Unicorn. That would have won for sure."

"Shoot; that's a great idea. But where would we get tiny people?"

"We'd fill it with dolls dressed like Trojan soldiers."

"Darn. *Really* good idea. Make a note of that for next year."

"Ha. Like I'm going to let you talk me into this again *next* year."

He pinched her right butt cheek and she jumped forward, smacking her unicorn nose against a man's shoulder. Luckily, he was wearing football pads and a helmet.

"Sorry."

Charlotte squinted through the screened eyes of her papier-mâché head. The costume party was already crowded. She counted the usual array of witches, vampires, pirates and zombies and spotted a few admiring gazes directed toward her own costume.

"People seem to like us," she said.

"We're huge, they're probably just trying to get around us to get to the punch. Assuming there is punch. I don't know. All I see is…well…it's not a *bad* view…"

She tried to reach back and smack him but found it difficult within the confines of the unicorn.

"We're not in front of the *punch*, smarty. But you're right, let's go ahead and disengage."

Declan took a few steps back and then stood, ruffling his hair and stretching his back. The tail end of the horse hung from him by suspenders.

"If Darla was ever thinking about being the back, I'd have to say this costume was ill-conceived," he said, pulling at the chest of his tee shirt to let some air beneath it. "It is *hot* under there."

"In our zeal to destroy Silver Lake we may have overestimated our abilities. Hey, have you heard any news from Seamus?"

"Nope. Last I heard he was going to dress up like a handyman and try and get into her house to look for the box, but he's been gone all day."

"Is he coming here?"

"I think so. He said Jackie invited him."

Charlotte scanned the crowd, hoping to see Seamus enter, box in hand. She spotted a bright green sweatshirt with the letter "e" on it and realized it housed Frank. Darla stood beside him wearing another sweatshirt with paper clips and paper pinned all over it.

"What the heck are you two?" asked Charlotte as they approached.

"He's email and I'm his attachment," said Darla,

pointing a thumb at Frank.

Charlotte laughed. "How did she get you to come this year?"

"She said all I had to do was wear a sweatshirt and I said, *I'm in.*"

"Finally," said Darla. "I told him he couldn't come as a sheriff anymore and that was the last I saw of him for four years."

"I almost didn't make it though, got a report another mailbox blew up."

Charlotte straightened. "Where?"

"Down the street from the first."

"Not Jackie's?"

"No, over in the older part of the Port. Why would it be Jackie's mailbox?"

Charlotte shrugged and shook her head, hoping Frank wouldn't press for an answer.

"Anyway, good news is this time we had a witness. I've got an officer picking up the kids now."

"So it *was* kids?"

"The Rutter boys."

"Rutter?" *Why did that name sound familiar...? Oh...Loretta Rutter.* The bowler with fingers full of Gorilla Glue, compliments of Gloria. They probably destroyed her mailbox to avenge their mother and had so much fun doing it they came back for mischief night.

"So it's safe for Gloria to go back home?"

Frank nodded. "I don't see why not. I never thought she had anything to worry about in the first place, but if you want, I can let you know if they 'fess to the letter and the fire, too."

"That'd be great. Thanks Frank."

Charlotte scanned the tent searching for other Pineapple Port residents and then blinked, certain her eyes were playing tricks on her.

"Is that woman naked?" she asked.

All heads turned.

"Oh no," said Declan.

The blonde in question wore a sheer, flesh-colored body suit with leaves pasted strategically over her nipples and crotch. In her hand, she held a bright red apple.

"*Is* she naked?" asked Darla, squinting.

Frank grinned, his eyes never leaving the woman's leaves. "Ours is not to question why...*oof!*"

Darla slapped him hard in the stomach and he ended his sentence.

"It's Stephanie," said Charlotte, her voice falling to a whisper. *Boy does she have a body on her...*

"Yep. Which is weird, because, *gosh*, normally she hates being the center of attention," drawled Declan.

Darla gasped. "*That's* the girl trying to steal—" Charlotte glared at her and she cut short before continuing. "I mean...trying to *steel* herself against the pain of losing Declan to a better woman?"

Charlotte dropped her head to her chest. "That might have been even worse."

Mariska approached their group wearing a shiny red bubble of fabric with black dots all over it. The sack-like costume gripped her loosely at the knees and black antennae bounced atop the headband nestled in her curls. She turned in Stephanie's direction, revealing her ladybug wings.

"Did you see that naked girl?" she asked, pointing.

"Yes," said Declan, Charlotte and Darla together.

Bob, standing behind Mariska, shot Frank a look and they smirked at one another. Bob wore no costume; only his usual tee shirt and shorts.

"What are you supposed to be?" Charlotte asked him.

"I'm the most interesting man in the world."

"Did you lose your beard?"

He shook his head. "I'm not the guy on the commercial; I just *am* the most interesting man in the world."

"Ah, gotcha."

"The less I make him dress up, the less he pretends to get a stomach ache before the party," said Mariska.

"Wait…" Declan touched Charlotte's arm. "Is that guy with Stephanie…"

Charlotte realized what she thought had been one of the tent poles was actually a very tall, thin man in a flesh-colored body suit. He wore boxers covered in leaves, his ribs and boney chest clearly visible beneath his giant leotard.

"Rocky. Looks like Eve brought Adam with her."

"Who's Rocky?' asked Mariska.

Charlotte waved her away. "I'll tell you later. Have you seen Jackie?"

Mariska shook her head. A woman behind her called her name and she, Darla, Frank and Bob wandered over to her to say hi.

"Are you sure Seamus said he was coming?" Charlotte asked Declan.

"Yes—in fact, there he is…Jackie is with him," Declan stood on his toes to peer over the heads in the crowd. "I'll go warn them Rocky's here."

"Okay. I'll stay put and keep an eye on him."

Declan touched her arm and then slipped into the crowd. She stood a moment longer, and was about to look for Mariska and Darla when she heard a voice beside her.

"Hey, I know you."

Charlotte turned to find Jason the fireman standing

beside her, dressed in his fire gear.

"Gosh, you look exactly the same."

He grinned. "Makes for an easy costume."

"What are you doing here? You seem a little young."

"I could say the same to you, but you're famous."

She laughed with nervous confusion. "Famous?"

"You're the girl who grew up in a retirement community."

"Did I tell you that?"

"No. I may have asked around a little."

"You did?"

"Just now. I saw you a little bit ago and figured you were somebody's granddaughter. I asked a lady over there who you were before I worked up the nerve to come over. So...decide if you have a boyfriend or not yet?"

She smiled, embarrassed. "I do. He's here actually. Somewhere..." She turned and looked in the direction she'd last seen Declan retreating, but couldn't find him.

"Sure he is. I'm starting to think he's one of those imaginary boyfriends."

"No, I swear."

He grinned. "I'm just kidding. I saw him. Anyone else with you?"

"Anyone else?"

"I mean...did you come with a fun group of people or something?"

"Oh, no. What brings you to the party? Do you know someone in the retirement communities?"

"Uh, yeah. And you know, I should probably get back to her. I gotta get going."

"Oh, okay. Well, it was nice to see you again."

"You too." He flashed a smile and wove his way through the crowd.

She wandered to the punch bowl and scooped a plastic

cupful. Declan found her there and Seamus and Jackie arrived beside him.

"Couldn't get the box, Char," said Seamus, clapping her on the back. His entire costume was composed of one empty tool belt wrapped loosely around his waist.

"And I thought for sure you had it," said Declan. "Where were you all day?"

Seamus rubbed his wrist and stared at his hand as if deep in thought. "I…er…I got tied up."

Charlotte sighed. "Gloria's idea for luring Diana out of her house with dogs is starting to sound like our best option, which is scary."

"One bit of good news—" said Seamus, perking. "Her husband left her, so we don't have to worry about two people watching over the box."

"How'd you find that out?"

"Uh…neighborhood gossip. The usual."

"Are you sure you should be here with Rocky lurking nearby?"

Seamus scoffed. "I'm not concerned about him."

"This is all so stressful," said Jackie, dressed as a flapper from the Roaring Twenties. "How's your other case going?"

Charlotte shrugged. "The only new clue is that I found out kids did blow up Gloria's mailbox, so if I take that out of the timeline…the threats could still fit my flag theory."

"My parrot flag?" asked Jackie. "So my trouble became her trouble after all."

"What are you talking about?" asked Seamus.

"Jackie and Gloria's flags were switched. I mentioned to Jackie it was possible someone meant to threaten *her* with that note, but ended up giving it to Gloria by accident. Same with the fire."

"So you think they confused Jackie and Gloria's houses because of the flags?"

"Maybe… Oh…no…" Charlotte's gaze turned to the door of the tent.

"What is it?" asked Jackie.

Charlotte closed her eyes. "It's a Pegacorn."

"It's a *what?*" asked Declan.

"A Pegacorn. It's a unicorn with wings, half unicorn, half Pegasus."

"Oh, no," said Jackie. "They stole your costume."

"And raised it. We can't beat a Pegacorn with a unicorn. That's like trying to beat a manticore with a plain old sphinx."

Declan nodded. "Right, I was *just* about to say that."

"You were?"

Declan peered down his nose at her and she realized he was teasing.

"Oh. Sorry. A manticore is like a sphinx but with a scorpion's tail."

"Duh."

"What are we going to do? We can't just trot up as a unicorn. It's an instant fail."

Charlotte swept her gaze across the room, her mind whirring as she searched for possible solutions. The Pegacorn had combined two creatures. Maybe she…

She spotted Stephanie standing beside Rocky with her oversized handbag in her hand and wondered why Declan's ex would lug such a ridiculous bag to a party.

That's when she had an idea.

"Seamus, you stole Declan's napkin contract out of Stephanie's bag, didn't you?"

"I did."

"Why do you think it was in there?"

He shrugged. "She wants to keep things close to her I

suppose."

"What about the will?"

"Oh that's in there too," said Declan. "She pulled it out and waved it at me."

Charlotte smiled. "I was hoping you'd say that." She stood on her toes and waved. "Hey Stephanie. Come here."

CHAPTER TWENTY-SIX

"Well, fancy meeting you here," said Stephanie approaching the group, trademark smirk on her lips. "Declan, you remember Rocky."

Rocky thrust out his hand and Declan scowled. "Really?"

The tall man scratched his cheek as if that had always been his intention and looked away.

Stephanie scowled at Charlotte. "Why are you looking at me like that?" She looked at Declan. "What's wrong with her?"

"How would you like to win the costume contest?"

Charlotte watched a parade of emotions cross Stephanie's face. Confusion, glee, triumph—yes! *She was enamored with the idea of winning.* Her eyes had lit beneath her knitted brow.

This just might work.

"Me?" said Stephanie, placing her hand on her chest. "I mean... I'm looking pretty good, but there are cleverer costumes here."

"But as a pair..."

She glanced at Rocky. "Adam and Eve? Still not enough. Maybe if we'd thought to bring a live snake..."

"No, I mean with *us*." Charlotte snapped the unicorn horn off her horse head and dropped it to the ground.

"What are you doing?" asked Declan. "You've downgraded us from unicorn to horse."

"Not *just* a horse. We're Lady Godiva's horse."

Declan followed her gaze to Stephanie and began to

shake his head. "Oh no... No, no, no. She is *not* sitting on my back."

"What's a horse have to do with chocolate?' asked Rocky.

"Not Godiva the *chocolate*, Godiva the lady who rode naked," said Stephanie, rolling her eyes at him.

He shrugged.

"So you want me to ride him?" asked Stephanie, her gaze never wavering from Declan. "Naked?"

Declan dropped his head into his hand. "Charlotte, please make this stop. We'll win next year."

Charlotte leaned towards him and hissed *"Go with it - Trust me"* in his ear.

Stephanie glanced at the competing Pegacorn costume and pursed her lips. "I *could* win this."

"How naked are you without the strategically placed leaves?" asked Charlotte.

"Believably so. I'm wearing a flesh thong and pasties."

Rocky's already large eyes bugged and he swallowed hard.

"Seriously?" asked Declan. "Who owns pasties? Do you jump out of cakes on the weekends?"

Stephanie glared at him. "It's a *costume*."

"Perfect," said Charlotte clapping them both on their shoulders to distract them from their quarrel. "Time to assume the position, Declan."

He set his jaw. "I hope you know I'm only doing this for you."

Charlotte grinned. "I know."

"And you..." he turned to Stephanie who had removed her leaves and now stood as close to naked as she could in a sheer bodysuit. "You're going to have to sit back toward the butt. I can't support your weight on my shoulders bent over."

"That's not how I remember it."

"That...that doesn't even make sense."

"I'm trying to picture it..." said Rocky.

Declan shot him a glance. "You are a *weird* dude."

He shrugged again.

Declan looked at Charlotte. "Are you sure you want to do this?"

She nodded. "This is a *winner*. Do it for Pineapple Port."

He huffed and bent over, pulling the covering over his head and resting his hands on Charlotte's hips. "Rocky, help her up."

Grunting, Rocky lifted Stephanie and placed her on Declan's lower back. She wrapped her legs around his waist.

"Ah, just like old times," she said.

"I'm going to pretend I didn't hear that," said Charlotte.

"You and me both," mumbled Rocky.

"You can't carry your bag with you," said Charlotte. "Lady Godiva didn't have a purse."

"Sure she did," said Stephanie, clutching it tighter.

"Come on. We have to do this right if we—I mean, if *you're* going to win."

Stephanie grimaced. "Fine." She thrust the bag at Rocky. "Hold this."

He took it.

Charlotte looked at Seamus and widened her eyes before using them to point toward the bag in Rocky's arms. Seamus returned with one almost imperceptible nod of his head.

"Last call for the costume contest," said a voice over the loudspeaker.

"Wait," said Stephanie, her eyes on her bag. "I—"

Charlotte pulled Declan toward center stage and put on her horse head. "Let's go."

They trotted toward the line of costume trophy hopefuls, nearly knocking over a woman dressed as a cat.

"Watch it, lady," snapped Stephanie. The woman glanced at her and scurried away.

"I'm not going to be able to walk for a week," said Declan, grunting.

"Usually, it was me saying that," said Stephanie. Her voice seemed louder, as if she'd leaned forward to be sure Charlotte heard the comment. In her horse head, Charlotte growled.

They found their place in line, careful not to stand too close to the Pegacorn. "I hope Pineapple Port appreciates what I'm doing for them here," said Charlotte.

"What *you're* doing?" said Declan. "I have a she-demon on my back and I don't even *live* in Pineapple Port."

"I'm having a wonderful time," said Stephanie, slapping her horse's rump and waving at the receptive crowd like a pageant queen.

"First we're going to narrow it down to six," said the contest announcer.

The three judges weeded out the weaker witches, pirates and other costumes. When they finished six contestants remained. An extremely scary spider-like alien, Darla and Frank as email and attachment, a convincing zombie, a seventy-year old French maid, the Pegacorn and Lady Godiva.

"What happened to your horn?" whispered Darla, shuffling toward Charlotte. "And don't look now but Declan's ex has mounted him."

Charlotte sighed. "The Pegacorn."

"Popping corn?"

"The *Pegacorn*. See down the other end? It's a unicorn

with wings. We didn't stand a chance as a unicorn; we had to improvise."

Darla gave Stephanie a dubious once over and grunted her disapproval. "By the looks of her you should have dressed like a pole."

"She's Lady Godiva."

"Oh that girl is no *lady* anything."

"It's time to announce the winners," said the announcer and Darla took a step back toward Frank to be judged.

"For scariest costume and the winner of a twenty-five dollar gift certificate to Chuckie's Grub Haus...*the alien*!"

The spider creature stepped forward and took the coupon, waving to the crowd as three fake arms followed in unison below his topmost.

"For funniest costume and winner of another twenty-five dollar gift certificate to Chuckie's Grub Haus...*email and attachment*!"

Darla whooped and ran forward to claim her prize.

"I'd like to thank the academy..." she said holding it over her head, and a ripple of laughter ran through the crowd.

"And for best overall costume and the winner of a *fifty* dollar gift certificate to Chuckie's Grub Haus..."

"Sounds like the real winner is Chuckie's Grub Haus," mumbled Declan.

"...Lady Godiva!"

Charlotte took a step toward the judge, but not before Stephanie slid from Declan's back and ran forward to snatch the gift certificate from the judge's hand. She held it aloft and raised her other fist in victory, bobbing on her toes enough to make her pasties bounce. The crowd exchanged glances with one another as they clapped; some sharing disapproval, some *other* thoughts.

Declan stood from beneath his drape and helped Charlotte pull off her horse head.

"Unbelievable," he said.

"I just hope it took long enough," Charlotte muttered. "I'm going to try and keep her tied up here a bit. Go check on Seamus."

"Seamus?"

"If he gives you a thumbs up, let me know."

"Wait—what?"

"The *purse*," she said from the side of her mouth.

"The—" Declan gasped. "The will!"

"Yes—Go!"

He grinned and nodded. "Going."

Darla walked over to Charlotte and turned to stare at the bouncing Godiva with her. "She took the prize?"

"Not for long."

As the dance music began and the crowd filled in, Charlotte stepped forward and yanked the gift certificate from Stephanie's hand.

Stephanie spun and put her hands on her hips. "Hey. They said the winner was Lady Godiva. That's *me*."

Charlotte shook her head. "Sorry. Mariska and Darla spent months on this costume. This is going to *them*."

Stephanie set her jaw. "We'll see about that." She tried to grab for the certificate and Charlotte jerked it away from her.

"Hey now ladies," said Seamus, stepping between them. "Am I going to have to get that vat of Jello after all?"

Stephanie glared at him. "Chuckie's Grub Haus is disgusting anyway," she spat before storming towards Rocky, who stood waving at her from fifteen feet away, a goofy grin on his face.

Charlotte sighed and leaned toward Seamus. "I take it

your presence means mission accomplished?"

He nodded. "Easy as a summer breeze. The boy never knew what hit him. Declan is already on his way to the car with the tube."

An angry scream echoed through the tent and Charlotte looked up in time to see Stephanie, her fists raised in the air. Rocky appeared even paler than usual.

"We better get out of here too," she suggested.

Seamus nodded.

They ducked and jogged from the tent until they found Declan just sliding into his car. Charlotte jumped in the passenger seat and Seamus slid into the back.

"You're a genius," Declan told her.

"Hey, I did all the hard work," said Seamus.

Charlotte couldn't hide her giddiness. "Let me see."

Declan slid the will out of the plastic tube and rolled it open. His face fell and Charlotte felt a rush of dread.

"It isn't the will?"

"It's the will," said Declan. "But a real will would be on file somewhere, wouldn't it? Stealing it doesn't do me any good. I was hoping it wouldn't be real at all."

"It looks real," said Seamus, peering over his shoulder.

"Let me see," said Charlotte.

He handed it to her and she flipped to the last page. She smiled.

"What is it?" asked Declan. "Did he forget to sign it?"

"Oh no, it's signed. But take a close look." She held up the sheet so both could see.

"What?" said Seamus. "It says Bonehead O'Malley…"

The corner of Declan's lips began to curl. "It says *Bonehead…*"

"Exactly. He wouldn't have signed a will with his nickname."

"She must have forgotten his real name."

She nodded. "Keep this. If she tries to make another it will be nice proof that she's up to no good."

"If she figures out you arranged the distraction, she's going to be furious," said Seamus.

"Oh I hope she figures out that I planned it," said Charlotte, grinning. "I *hope* so."

CHAPTER TWENTY-SEVEN

"Have you heard from Frank yet?" asked Gloria as they crossed the street heading for Silver Lake.

Charlotte shook her head. "His deputies haven't found the Rutter boys yet. They're going to try and grab them tonight. Looks like you should stay another night, just to be safe."

Gloria's case was coming to an end, but for a few loose ends. Charlotte wanted the Rutter boys to admit to the threatening letter and the fire. If they didn't, she'd have to ask Rocky if one of his people had confused the two houses. Either option would rule out someone actually trying to harm Gloria.

Unfortunately, the Rutter boys appeared to be seasoned punks who knew how to avoid the police. Frank had yet to locate them.

Gloria could stay another night or two. For now, she needed to concentrate on retrieving Jackie's box. The Pineapple Port dog owners were about to embark on their most dangerous mission yet.

Operation Doo-Doo.

"This is so exciting," said Gloria as they approached the entrance to Silver Lake.

"This is insane," mumbled Charlotte.

She stopped at the edge of the wall that surrounded the community and held out a hand to stop the ladies and dogs behind her. She threw a pebble at Pete's air-conditioned guardhouse box. He looked up and then returned to his book. She threw another. This time he slid open the door and stepped out, scanning the area.

"Psst! Pete! Don't look, it's Charlotte."

Pete's head twitched as he resisted the urge to look in her direction. He grunted.

"This is going to end with me fired, isn't it?"

"Not at all. We have you covered. All you have to do is respond to the commotion that is about to occur near the south pool."

"And leave the guard box unattended."

"Yes. That way when the camera records us entering, you won't be there."

"You tell Mariska she owes me three dozen pierogies for this one."

"Will do."

As if on cue, fireworks shot into the sky behind him, and Pete strolled to his golf cart to investigate. "How long do you need me gone?"

"Maybe twenty minutes? And don't go anywhere near Magnolia Court if you can help it."

"Gotcha."

Pete wheeled off, the battery-operated police light on his canopy flashing blue.

Charlotte motioned and a sea of Pineapple Portians swarmed the gate, most with dogs in tow.

"Follow me, it's about two blocks this way."

Declan jogged up beside her with Abby leading the way.

"Are you sure you want to do this? You said the whole *lure her out of her house with dogs* idea was nuts."

"It is, but we're out of options at this point."

Declan sighed. "I've never dated a jailbird before, but don't worry; I'll wait for you. Twenty, thirty years, whatever it takes."

"Very funny. No one is going to jail. I'll be in and out

of there before anyone has any idea what's going on."

"Uh huh."

Charlotte turned and found Darla in the crowd.

"Darla! You and I are going to circle wide and approach the house from the other side."

"Ten-four." Darla handed Oscar's leash to Gloria and scurried to Charlotte.

"Oh no."

Charlotte heard Mariska wail and turned to see Miss Izzy had hunched to relieve herself before the allotted time.

"Don't worry. I brought doggie bags. We can scoop it up and move it to the right lawn," said Charlotte pulling a string of plastic bags from her pocket. "Darla and I are going to split off. I'm leaving you in charge of the troops."

Mariska saluted. "I won't let you down."

Behind her Jackie raised a fist. "Okay ladies this is it."

Darla and Charlotte slipped down Sea Turtle Drive, which wrapped behind Magnolia Court.

"Do you have your kit?" asked Charlotte, picking up the pace.

Darla tapped her fanny pack. "Yep. You?"

Charlotte patted her pocket where her lock picking set awaited its inaugural run. Darla had bought it for her after she'd announced her new career as a private eye. The leather case contained pointy metal picks that looked like a dental hygienist's dream kit, brimming with tools for scraping even the most offensive teeth. She'd spent hours picking her own door lock and was eager to try her *skillz* on someone else's.

They scurried through the neighbor's yard and set up behind a small shed in Diana Fassbender's back yard.

Charlotte pulled a pair of surgical gloves from her pocket and slipped them on as Darla watched and pouted. She pulled out another pair.

"Don't worry. I have some for you too," she said.

Darla grinned and put them on. "Now we wait."

A light went on in Diana's home. Somewhere a dog barked. A woman yelled. After another minute, they could hear voices yelling back and forth. Charlotte's phone vibrated announcing the arrival of a text from Jackie. It said *The chicken has left the coop.*

"She's out."

Darla's face animated with excitement. "Good. Let's go."

"I can't believe this is working."

"Never underestimate snooty Silver Lake witches."

They scurried to the back of the house and Charlotte realized Diana's back door didn't fit the picture she'd built in her head.

"It's a slider. Can you pick a sliding door?"

"Can't pick it; we'll have to pry it open and pop the lock and hope she doesn't have a bar on it."

Charlotte stared at her. "It's still a little disturbing to me that you know these things."

Darla shrugged. "I can't change my past, I can only improve my future."

"Is that a saying you learned in prison?"

"Oprah."

Darla scowled and took a few steps to the right to peek around the house. She called back to Charlotte.

"She's got a side garage door."

Charlotte jogged to Darla, who swept her hand toward the lock with an accompanying bow. "After you."

She glanced to the front yard, where she could see some of the ladies from her covert dog walking group.

Diana's neighbor to the left, pointy-nosed Poppy, was pounding down her porch steps to assist her friend against the interlopers. Charlotte squatted behind the bushes lining the side of the garage and looked at Darla. "We don't have the time for amateur hour. You'd better take this one."

Darla knelt and removed her pack. Tilting her head to better see through the bifocals of her glasses, she had the lock picked within twenty seconds. She pushed open the door to reveal her prowess.

"No alarm," said Charlotte.

"None we can hear, anyway. Let's go."

Charlotte touched Darla's arm. "No, you stay here. I'll find the box. If something goes wrong there's no sense in both of us getting caught inside. First sign of trouble, run."

"Char—"

"I'm not arguing about this. *Stay.*"

Darla grimaced. "Fine. I'll keep watch. Hurry."

Charlotte slipped into the dark garage and discovered the inner door to the house open. She gave Darla the thumbs up and slipped inside.

The garage entrance to the house led into an empty area splitting the kitchen and living room. Peeking out the front window, she spotted Diana and Poppy screaming at Gloria, who stood coldly assessing them, her arms crossed against her chest.

"That isn't going to end well for them," she mumbled.

Jackie and a few other Pineapple Port ladies hovered nearby. Mariska was chatting with a glamorous dark-haired woman who lived to Diana's right.

Leave it to Mariska to make friends during war.

Jackie had Abby's leash now. Declan and Bob were nowhere to be seen.

Turning back to her mission, Charlotte scanned Diana's living room.

No box.

She glanced in the kitchen.

Nothing.

Trotting down the hallway, she poked her head into two more bedrooms and a bathroom before finding the master bedroom at the end of the hall. On the bedroom dresser sat a familiar wooden box with a lily inlaid in the center of the lid.

Ah ha!

Fishing five dollars from her pocket, she placed it on the dresser. Jackie had given it to her in the hopes it would turn Charlotte's theft into a *refund*. The woman had only paid three for the box, so it was a payoff as well. Staring at the bill on the bureau, she couldn't imagine the last time three dollars had bought so much trouble.

Time to go. She grabbed the box, finding it heavier than she'd imagined. She set it on the bed to check for Diana's personal belongings inside. If caught, the police would never believe her story if she also trotted away with all Diana's jewelry. Even Frank would have trouble swallowing that one.

She unlocked the hook clasp and found a bag of what looked like medium gray sand. She scowled and hefted it from the box, bobbing it in her hand. She guessed it weighed about five pounds. The material inside didn't feel like sand. It felt finer. More like—

Her grimace of confusion slid into an open-mouthed stare.

Ash. Human ashes.

She gasped and bobbled the bag. It slid from her palm and in trying to catch it, she smacked the box and *it* began to slide from the corner of the bed. Attempting to catch both, she instead spiked the bag to the ground and it burst, spewing a cloud of dust across her shins and sneakers, like the aftermath of a tiny volcanic eruption.

"Dang."

She stared in horror, one hand steadying the box on the bed and the other hanging helplessly at her side. Crouching, she surveyed the mess, wondering if she could somehow gather the ashes and put him or her back into the bag.

Not a chance. Not without a Dust Buster.

She rubbed her hand over her eyes and then suffered a tiny freak out as she realized she might be rubbing an ex person into her eyes.

She stood and fished another twenty out of her pocket, placing it beside the five. Twenty wouldn't buy Diana a vacuum, but it *would* pay for a clean filter bag so her dead relative didn't end up mixed with the house lint.

Doing her best to avoid the ashes, she retrieved the now much lighter box. She'd taken one step into the hallway when the front door slammed.

"I can't believe those people. I'm calling the police," said a voice.

"I think Sally said she already did," said another.

Charlotte turned and leapt back inside the bedroom.

Trapped!

She moved to the window and peeked outside. The drop to the ground wasn't far. As quietly as possible, she unlocked the window and slid it open. The women were still expressing their outrage in the front of the house.

The window had a screen.

Muttering to herself, she unclipped the screen and began to push on it as steadily as she could. It refused to budge, so she increased pressure. When it gave way with a pop, she slipped forward and banged her forehead on the sash. She stopped breathing as the screen fell to the grass below, bounced on the corner of its frame, and clattered onto the nearby patio.

"Did you hear that?" said a voice in the kitchen.

Charlotte heard Darla gasp and swear from somewhere nearby before she appeared outside the window.

"What're you doin'?"

"They're in the house. Take it, quick," Charlotte dropped the box as Darla reached to catch it.

She failed.

Together they watched as the box danced in Darla's fingers before deflecting toward the patio, her reach shadowing it as it flew to her left like a released dove. The box cracked against the pavers and the side panel sprung at an odd angle, disconnected from its joint.

Darla uttered a strange whimpering noise and looked up at Charlotte, whose torso now hung from the window, her legs dangling in the bedroom. Diving from the window had seemed like a good idea, but now she'd lost her nerve.

Behind her, Charlotte heard a voice.

"I think there's someone in the bedroom."

"Get it and run," she hissed at Darla.

"What about *you*?"

"What are you going to do? Catch me? I saw how that worked out for the box."

"But—"

"Get the box and *run*."

Head nodding back and forth in a panic, Darla scooped the disjointed pieces of the box and clutched them to her chest before running from view.

"Momma."

Charlotte looked behind her and saw Diana standing

inside the bedroom doorway, staring in horror where she knew the ashes lay splayed on the carpet. The moment Diana shifted her gaze to Charlotte she propelled herself through the window.

"Poppy! Call the police! There's someone in my window."

Charlotte did her best to tuck and roll. Her foot caught on the window frame and after hitting the grass, she smacked her forehead on the porch pavers, her hand partially cushioning what might have been a deadly blow to her temple. Stunned, she spun away from the house like a rolling pin, doing her best to hide her face until she hit a metal patio chair and found herself stuck.

"I see you!" screamed Diana from the window. "The police are on their way!"

Crawling to her hands and knees, Charlotte scurried away from the house on all fours like a mouse. Once she reached the shed, she stood, steadied herself against the wall, and sprinted across the yard. She could hear Diana wailing after her.

Fumbling for her phone, she hit redial, unsure of the last number she'd called.

Mariska answered. "Charlotte?"

"It's me. She saw me—"

"I know. She went back in the house. We tried to call and warn you."

"I'm okay but you need to abort mission. Everyone back to Pineapple Port."

"Darla told us. We're already headed home."

"Good. Hurry. The cops are coming." As she finished her sentence, she saw the group of women and dogs ahead of her. "I see you." She thrust the phone back into her pocket.

Charlotte caught the group and whipped off her dark

tee, revealing a bright yellow tank beneath it. Her head throbbed. "Give me one of those doggie bags."

Mariska handed one to her. She peeled off her thin gloves and thrust them into the bag with her tee, squeezing them small enough that the wad appeared to be nothing more than dog droppings. She looked around the group and found a few people missing. "Where's Darla?"

"She went streaking past us before you called," said Mariska. "She told us all to hightail it."

Charlotte found Jackie in the crowd.

"Jackie, you go on home. I'll get the box from Darla and bring it to you in a bit."

Jackie nodded and split off to head for home.

Mariska squinted at Charlotte. "Are you okay? What's that on your head?"

She felt the rising egg at her temple and winced.

"I'm fine. Out of breath. Did Darla have the box?"

"She had something. It was hard to tell. I haven't seen her move that fast since they put her favorite sandals on sale at Bealls."

"What about Declan? I saw Gloria had Abby."

"He disappeared somewhere with Bob. Gloria's up ahead and Abby's fine."

Even under duress, Charlotte could tell Mariska wasn't being completely honest with her. "Why aren't you looking at me?"

"Hmm?" asked Mariska, still refusing to turn her head.

"You're not looking at me. What part of what you said was a lie?"

"What?"

"Mariska…"

"I'm a little too out of breath to speak right now…I'll tell you when we get back to the house—"

"Nuh-uh. Nice try. *Now.*"

Mariska huffed. "Fine. I borrowed him, okay? But it was *really* important."

"What do you mean you borrowed him? Who?"

"Declan. I didn't like those terrible women and all the screaming and Miss Izzy already did her business, so after talking to the nice woman next door—her name was Simone. She's French. Isn't that exotic? Simone?"

"Very exotic. Go *on*."

"Oh. Well, anyway, I wandered down the street a bit, and that's when I saw her."

"Who?"

"Witchy-Poo. Someone *here* stole her."

"What are you talking about?"

"She was on a house around the corner from the street we were on, so I told Bob to go get her and Declan went to help."

Charlotte tried to let this new information percolate. She felt dizzy, though she didn't know if it was from her collision with the pavers or the stress of house-robbing and accidental grave-desecration. In the distance, a police siren blared to life. They'd be looking for her, but the group had reached the outskirts of Pineapple Port and in a moment she'd be home safe. The police wouldn't find her—

Oh no.

"Mariska, do you think Declan and Bob are still trying to get the witch?"

"I would think so...why?"

"Don't you see?" She turned and stared back at Silver Lake. "The police are on their way to find *me*, but they're going to find *them* instead."

CHAPTER TWENTY-EIGHT

"Okay ladies this is it." Jackie had said as Charlotte and Darla headed off to retrieve her box.

"Hey, wait a second," said Bob, patting his own chest.

Jackie acquiesced with a nod. "Sorry, I meant ladies and *gentlemen*... Fire at will."

The dog walkers scattered, allowing the straining pets to reach the grass in front of Diana "Box Buyer" Fassbender's home and the lawns of her neighbors. Gladys Underwood's Scottish terrier, Mac, was first to stake his claim on the neighbor's plot of manicured heaven. When no one in the houses seemed to notice, the Pineapple Portians chatted to their furry boys and girls using various euphemisms for bathroom breaks at top volume.

Abby eyed a particularly dark green patch of Bermuda grass and pulled Declan toward it.

He noticed a woman stepping onto her porch, her mouth agape as she surveyed the mob preparing to defile her lawn.

"Hey, what are you doing?" screamed the woman to no one in particular.

Abby hunched her back and lowered her hindquarters. Next door, Diana Fassbender stepped onto her porch, emboldened by her neighbor's bravado.

"Go away. What are you doing?" she called, catching the eye of her neighbor. They exchanged a look, cementing their solidarity against the dog-walkers.

Althea Jackson held up an empty doggie bag covered

in bright pink polka dots. "Don't worry, we have bags."

"No Althea, we don't have bags. That's the point," said Jackie.

"Oh. Right. Sorry." She looked back at Diana. "Never mind. We *don't* have bags."

"This is the dumbest idea," Declan muttered to Bob, who stood next to him with his hands in his pockets, doing his best not to make eye contact with the angry ladies.

"I don't even know why I'm here, except Mariska promised she'd get off my back about Bourbon Club for a bit if I helped, so here I am. And she's over there…"

Declan looked to his left and spotted Mariska chatting with a dark-haired woman who lived to the left of Diana. That woman seemed more amused than angry.

"You can't let them go all over our lawns. You'll kill the grass," said the first woman.

"It's a free world," said Gloria.

"But it burns the grass," echoed Diana. "Poppy, what's going on?"

"They're letting their dogs go all over our lawns, that's what's going on."

"I'm going to call security."

"I'm sorry, could you come down here? I'm a little hard of hearing," said Jackie to Diana.

Declan stared at the curb, worrying about Charlotte.

"I found Witchy-Poo!" screamed a voice to his left. He jumped and found Mariska directly behind him as Miss Izzy settled at his feet and panted.

"What are you talking about?" said Bob.

"Darla's witch. I found it. It's on a house around the corner. I was talking to that lovely woman over there, Simone, and I could see it between the houses."

"I know you people. You're from Pineapple Port. You

shouldn't even be in here," screeched a voice behind them.

"Is that why we're harassing these ladies?" asked Bob. "Because they stole Darla's witch?"

"No, but I found her. You have to go get her."

"On a roof?"

"Yes. You have to go get her back. *Now*, Bob."

Bob looked at Declan. "Am I supposed to sprout wings?"

Declan glanced at Diana and saw that Gloria and Jackie had drawn her off her porch and tied her in a heated conversation. The woman who first appeared on her porch, the one with the pointy nose, joined the group and all four screamed back and forth at each other. Most of the other Pineapple ladies had gathered behind Jackie and Gloria. It was like the Sharks versus the Jets, only with less dancing and more dogs.

It looked as though Gloria and Jackie had Diana distracted. Charlotte and Darla would have plenty of time to slip into Diana's home and find the box. He worried that if he moved to the shrieking group, as the only man, he might spook Diana. Plus he had zero urge to involve himself in *that* argument. He looked at Bob.

"I'll help."

"Thank you." said Mariska. "Hurry!"

Declan handed Abby's leash to Mariska and turned to head down the road.

"And she wonders why I drink," muttered Bob. "Do you have a ladder in your pocket?"

Declan chuckled.

They had no trouble finding the inflatable witch. Fifteen feet tall with a green face and orange hair, she sat perched atop a modest double-wide modular home. There was no car in the driveway and the house looked dark and empty.

"There're two papers in the driveway. I'm guessing they're gone for the weekend," said Declan as they approached. The sky had dimmed to dusk, which offered some cover from the neighbors' prying eyes.

"Great. Now what?" said Bob.

Declan tilted to his left and peered behind the home. "There's a porch in the back there... If I stand on the railing, I can hoist myself up and grab her. Then we can deflate her in the backyard and walk her home."

Bob scoffed. "Better you than me."

They made their way to the back porch. Declan climbed the railing and stood there, surveying the pitch of the roof. He put his hands on the asphalt shingles, did his best to avoid the gutter, and pulled himself onto the roof.

Staying low, he scrambled to the witch and found her tied with ropes threaded through eye screws embedded in the rafters. He scrambled back down to the roof's edge.

"She's tied. Do you have a knife with you?"

Bob sat in the homeowner's patio chair and knitted his fingers across his chest. "While I *usually* like to be prepared for witch-nappings, seems I forgot to bring my witch-napping knife."

Declan grimaced, crawled back to the witch, and began the slow task of picking free the knots. It took him nearly four minutes to undo the first and as he moved to the second, he heard Bob call up to him.

"Do you want a drink?"

"What?" Again he crawled to the edge of the roof and peered down. Bob stood on the porch holding aloft what looked like a bourbon on ice. "Where did you get that?"

"Porch door was open. He had a bottle of Knob Creek in there. Figured he wouldn't mind. Made one for you."

"Figured he wouldn't mind if you drank his booze while I stole his witch?"

Bob shrugged.

Declan leaned down and took the glass. "I suppose I shouldn't be sober for this."

"Just don't fall off the roof."

He drank the low pour in two gulps, handed back the glass, and returned to work on the remaining three knots. He was about to start the third when he heard sirens in the distance and froze. He scurried to the edge of the roof again. Bob sat on a patio chair with the bottle of Knob Creek sitting on the glass table beside him.

"Are those sirens getting closer?" Declan asked.

"Sounds like it."

"You think someone reported us?"

"Those ladies, more than likely."

"Hm."

"So you think they're after the dogs, not us?"

Bob shrugged. "You want another?"

Declan stared at the empty glass of ice next to Bob's pour. "Sure."

Bob poured another and stood to deliver it. "You almost done?"

"One more. Whoever installed this was a knot-tying genius."

Declan finished his drink and went back to work. Witch freed, he hauled her to the edge of the roof.

"Incoming." he called and dropped her to the porch beside Bob.

He dropped to the railing and then hopped onto the porch.

"We should celebrate," said Bob.

Declan looked at the witch and then back to Bob. He shrugged.

"I guess she's not going anywhere."

He sat as Bob freshened his drink.

"Howdy boys."

Declan jumped at the sound of the voice. Sheriff Frank peered at him through the railings of the porch. He walked around and climbed the stairs to join them.

"Hey Frank, what brings you here?" asked Bob.

"On my way home and got a call about a break-in on Magnolia Court around the corner."

"You don't say."

"As I was pulling up, I got another call about somebody on a roof over here."

"Huh. This neighborhood is a mess."

Frank nodded. "By then, my deputy had arrived at the other scene, so I thought I'd roll over here and check on things."

"You want a drink?"

"I'm still in uniform."

"So take it off."

Frank chuckled and eye-balled the witch. "So let me guess. You're stealing the witch? Darla thinks it's hers?"

"I'm acting on Mariska's orders."

"Darla know about it?"

"I don't think so. Darla was—" Bob stopped short. "Darla wasn't around."

"And you got sucked into helping?" Frank asked, looking at Declan.

He nodded.

"Well, I can tell you on good authority this isn't Darla's witch."

Bob took a sip of his bourbon. "No?"

"No. I have Darla's witch back in my office."

"*You* do?"

Frank nodded. "Got sick of putting her on the roof."

Bob laughed.

"That all being said, I'm afraid I'm going to have to ask you to put this witch back on her roof."

Both the older men looked at Declan and he sighed. "I guess that's my cue."

Frank unbuttoned his uniform and hung the shirt on the back of his chair. Standing in his undershirt, he pointed a finger at Declan's glass. "Gimmee that."

Bob freshened Declan's glass for Frank while Declan climbed back on the roof and Frank handed him the witch.

As Declan threaded the witch's ropes through the eyebolts and began to retie her, he heard Frank's voice.

"Wait…where'd you get this whiskey?"

CHAPTER TWENTY-NINE

Charlotte caught Darla and took the broken wooden box from her with one hand, while the other held her phone to her ear.

"It's seen better days," said Darla.

She nodded. "It'll have to do."

"I have a surprise coming for you," said Mariska, putting her hand on Darla's shoulder. Mariska winked at Charlotte.

Charlotte rolled her eyes as Declan's phone rang a third time. Finally, he answered.

"Oh! I thought you'd never answer," she said. "The police are on their way. You need to get out of there."

"Frank's already here," said Declan.

"He is? Did you steal the witch?"

"I'm tying her back to the roof as we speak. He says it isn't Darla's."

"It isn't."

"You knew?"

She nodded before realizing he couldn't hear her nod. "Yes. But I wasn't there to stop you."

"Speaking of which, did you get the box? Are you okay?"

"Bit of a bump on my head, but I'm fine and I do have the box. I'm about to walk it over to Jackie."

"Good. I'm going to stop by the store and then I'll be home. I've got a new kid watching over the place and I want to be there to close up."

"See you soon."

She hung up and turned to Gloria who stood in her driveway, Abby's leash still in hand.

"Gloria, I'm going to run this over to Jackie. I'll be back."

Gloria nodded. "That was exciting, wasn't it?" Abby began to weave her way around Gloria's legs and she tried to unwrap herself.

"Definitely. Here, I'll take Abby with me."

Gloria handed her the leash and waved before letting herself inside.

Charlotte pulled her black tee shirt from the plastic bag and wrapped it around the box to hide it, just in case the police came through the neighborhood looking for the mad poopers. She felt confident Diana would have noticed her box went missing, too. Her mother's ashes strewn across her bedroom carpet were a dead giveaway.

No pun intended.

She put the plastic bag and the gloves in the trash. Getting caught with gloves might be more incriminating than being caught with the box itself.

Tired from her ordeal, she still walked at a good clip, eager to hand the box to Jackie and return home. Tomorrow they'd call Rocky and another case would be solved. She didn't know what made the box special, but at this point, she wasn't sure she cared. But *maybe*...maybe she'd linger with Jackie for a little while and they could look it over. She felt the side of the box shift beneath her hand and hoped Rock wasn't too particular about the shape in which the box returned to him. At least she *had* the box.

Passing Gloria's house she noticed the lights were on inside. The porch door hung at an awkward angle, but she chalked that up to Mac's forceful entry during the fire.

Still...

A sporty older model red car sat parked in front of Gloria's neighbor's home. She suddenly had a bad feeling that the red car parked outside her own home wasn't necessarily Stephanie's. Not every time. What if someone had been spying on Gloria?

She stared at Gloria's glowing windows and knew in her gut the car and the open porch door were not a coincidence. Inside the home, she thought she saw a flutter of movement in the lamplight, and felt her stomach roll with nerves.

Someone is inside.

Charlotte took a deep breath, unsure whether what she'd seen was movement or her imagination running wild. She tucked the box under her arm and approached Gloria's house. Creeping onto the porch, she saw the inside door was also ajar. Mac *had* done some damage in his zeal, but Gloria told her he'd been kind enough to fix the door well enough that she could lock it in her absence. Granted, she'd only mentioned it as an excuse to gush about Mac's pecs, but still...the door should have been locked.

She eased open the inner door far enough to peek inside. Abby poked her face in below her own and she took comfort in the terrier's presence. The Wheaten could be very protective, sometimes embarrassingly so.

Charlotte's eyes grew wide with wonder at the scene inside Gloria's home. Drywall lay in piles, pieces strewn about the floor, dust covering furniture and rugs. Between wall joists and ceiling rafters lay only ruin, ragged holes replacing once seamless white paint. The floor was torn in strips, as if a giant gopher had run tunnels through the house. The skeleton of what was once the kitchen island sat in the middle of the room gutted of every pot and pan.

From the extensive damage, she could only guess someone had been furrowing for the copper pipes or that a gaggle of teens had vandalized the house, causing as much damage as possible. *Maybe this was where the Rutter boys were hiding in plain sight.* The desolation far exceeded any smash and grab robbery of convenience. Whoever was in the house was *angry*. It had to be the boys, but still…maybe…

Protecting Gloria might be beyond my pay grade.

Time to call in the cavalry; not only to investigate the damage to the house, but maybe to find Gloria a safer place to stay. If it wasn't kids, it meant the person threatening her was spending enough time in the neighborhood to destroy her home. Surely, he or she would soon find Gloria at *her* home, just a few blocks away.

She thought about the red car parked outside, *the car she'd seen outside her home.* Maybe the person after Gloria already knew where she was hiding.

She leaned against the door frame and fished in her pocket for her phone to call Frank. She'd tapped one digit before Abby lunged forward, yanking her arm and causing the phone to clatter to the porch floor. She stood, hoping to find some leverage against Abby's strong neck, but instead went stumbling into the kitchen. Dragged by one hand, she threw out her other, grasping for the edge of the island to break her fall. The box spun out from under her arm and skidded across the cluttered floor. She yelped as her elbow clipped the granite counter top and sent pins and needles through her arm.

The leash wrapped around her wrist jerked and she yanked back as Abby strained against it, barking in her lowest, most threatening tone.

"Abby!"

She pulled herself up and saw no one but Abby, barking at the end of her leash as she peered up the hallway. Charlotte's mouth felt dry as she wondered what Abby saw around that corner.

Time to leave.

"Abby, no one's here. Let's go," she said loudly, hoping that if someone was there, they would wait until she left to appear.

Then she could hide somewhere *safe* and call Frank.

She pulled the dog to her and shoved her onto the porch. She was about to follow when she realized she'd forgotten Jackie's box.

"Wait there a second," she said closing the door with her foot.

She took a few steps into the kitchen and retrieved the box. Turning back to the door, she felt a presence in the living room, just out of her field of vision. Startled, she paused for a second, but her stall was enough to alert the intruder that he'd been made.

"Put down that box."

Charlotte turned to face the voice.

A man stood at the end of the hallway leading to the back bedrooms.

Abby *had* seen someone.

The man was large, bare-chested and muscular. Even covered in drywall dust, she recognized him.

Jason, the hunky fireman.

He seemed much less hunky now.

She wanted to believe he'd come to check for fire damage, but the hammer in his hand implied otherwise.

"You're not a fireman," she said.

"No."

He stared at her, the smile so quick to jump to his handsome face the day of the fire nowhere to be found.

Sweat beaded his forehead and he raised his arm to wipe his brow, raising the hammer as he did so. He only stood two paces from her. Should he choose to bring down that hammer, she'd be hard pressed to get out of the way in the tight, messy kitchen. Her body tingled with nerves.

"Well I'm sure you have your reasons. I'll just be going—"

"Stay right there," he said, pointing the hammer at her.

She put down the foot she'd been swinging toward the door.

"I guess that's your car out front?"

He nodded.

"I saw it outside my house."

"I was keeping an eye on that lady. Making sure she wasn't back here."

"So *you* pasted together her threat note? Set the fire? Blew up her mailbox?"

"I had to get her out of the house—" he paused and knit his brows. "Wait, blew up her mailbox? I didn't blow up any mailbox. Is that what happened to that stump out there?"

Okay. We can officially chalk that up to the Rutter boys. Look at me solving Frank's cases while being threatened by a hammer-wielding nutjob.

"What do you have against Gloria?"

"Who's that?"

"The lady whose house you're destroying. You're the one threatening to kill her; shouldn't you know?"

"If I was trying to kill her she'd be dead. Believe me..." He shook his head and chuckled to himself. "Whether I meant to kill her or not."

"Then what are you doing here?"

"This was my grandmother's house."

"But...why destroy it now?"

"My dad left something with her and I think she forgot it. Or never knew where it was, exactly. I dunno. It's here though. I *know* it."

"Your dad...? You think he hid something in the walls?"

"A box. Probably full of money, he pulled a bank job not long before they caught him. They never found the money..." His gaze fell to the box in her hands. "Where'd you get *that* box? Did you find that here?"

"No, it's mine, I mean—"

"What's in it?"

"Nothing."

"It's kind of small, not how I pictured it, but maybe..." His expression grew hard. "*Give it to me.*"

Charlotte clutched the box to her chest. *What terrible luck that this psycho is looking for a box as well.*

"It isn't what you're looking for; I promise. It belongs to someone else."

He held out his free hand. *"Give it to me."*

Charlotte leaned toward the door. *So close.* If she could just inch closer to the door before—

Jason strode forward to block her escape. She threw the box at him and spun away, hand rising to cover her head as she fled. She never saw him raise the hammer, but she felt it slam against her shoulder, pain radiating in all directions. She fell to the ground and he collapsed on top of her, straddling her hips with his knees. He jerked her shoulder and tried to flip her to her back. She resisted the first tug and grabbed a handful of debris. On the second tug she allowed herself to be turned and threw the dust where she thought his face would be.

Sputtering, he waved the hammer wildly in front of his face as she slid out from under him. She slammed his head against the counter as hard as she could as she ran past him toward the door. He dropped the weapon to clutch his skull for a moment and then dove to grab her ankle. She screamed, falling again.

As she splayed forward, the front door burst open and Abby flew into the room, nails scrambling on the tile floor. She leapt into the air over Charlotte who heard snarling and rolled in time to see the Wheaton's teeth clamp onto Jason's forearm. He screamed at the dog and reached for the hammer with his other hand.

Charlotte scrambled to her feet and kicked Jason in the chin. His head snapped backwards and he flopped to his back.

He lay still on the ground, Abby's mouth still gripping his forearm.

Charlotte grabbed Abby's collar and pulled her off the man, dragging her outside where she took the dog's leash and ran as fast as she could away from the house, Abby galloping at her side. She wanted to stop at every house she passed but was too afraid Jason would see her enter and she'd endanger the people there. When she reached her own house she looked back and saw no sign of Jason. She passed her own home and knocked on Mariska's door.

"Charlotte, what's wrong with you?"

"Let me in, quick."

Charlotte pushed past her into the house and locked the door behind her. She grabbed Mariska's phone from the counter and called 911. "Do you know where Frank is?"

"No; what happened? You're scaring me. Why are you covered in white dust? You're filthy. Are you *bleeding?*"

"Jason was at—" The operator answered her call and she shifted her attention from Mariska. "I need to report a robbery and vandalism and an attack. Maybe attempted murder. A lot of stuff."

"Murder!" yelped Mariska. "Who's Jason?"

The woman on the phone told Charlotte to slow down and she took a deep breath, finally easing the death grip she had on Abby's leash. As she told the woman her story, Mariska's eyes grew wider and wider until she grabbed Bob's cell phone and moved to the other side of the room to make a call of her own.

The emergency operator assured Charlotte someone was on the way, both to her location and Gloria's home. The woman asked her to remain on the phone and she held it to her ear as she tried to pull Abby close to her.

"You saved me," she said, hugging her and whispering in the dog's ear. Abby pulled away, more interested in eating Miss Izzy's food than accolades for her bravery.

Mariska approached from her spot across the room. "That all just happened? The things you said on the phone?"

"Yes, and, *oh*, Gloria. I have to warn her. I have to get her somewhere safe. I think he only wanted her scared out of the house but I don't think he found his box and he might think *she* has it now. He knows she's at my house."

"Well you're not going anywhere. I called Frank; he was home and he's on his way over. We can send him to fetch Gloria."

"He's got to hurry."

They both straightened as the sound of sirens filled the air. A moment later someone pounded on the door.

"Mariska, it's Frank. Is Charlotte still in there?"

Charlotte opened the door. "I'm fine. We have to get Gloria out of my house to safety until we know they have Jason."

"I'm already on it. Jason's the man in Gloria's house?"

"If he's still there."

"What's he look like?"

"Dark brown hair, muscular, tall but not crazy tall—"

"What was he wearing?"

"He was shirtless last time I saw him. And...shorts I think. Tan? I...jeeze, I should have paid more attention. Everything happened so fast. I left him lying on the kitchen floor."

"Unconscious?"

She nodded, and her eye began to throb. She touched it gingerly with her fingers and groaned as the motion of lifting her arm made her shoulder ache.

"What's wrong?"

"He hit me on the back with a hammer."

"What did he hit you in the face with?"

"The floor hit me in the face."

"Eye *and* forehead? That's a heck of a lump."

Charlotte felt the knot she'd received falling out of Diana Fassbender's bedroom window. She offered Frank a subtle nod, not wanting to lie but not wanting to elaborate either.

"I'm fine. Go get Gloria."

"I already have an officer collecting her and three more at her house."

"Frank. Come in." A voice crackled on the sheriff's radio.

"Frank here."

"There's no one in the house. The place is torn apart, though. Looks like a tornado ripped through it."

"If you're sure it's clear, don't mess with anything. Just tape it off. One of you watch the dwelling and wait for CSI, the other two start a search. Call it in, get some more help out here looking for that bastard. Caucasian male, dark hair, muscular build, last seen shirtless and in shorts."

"And covered in drywall dust," said Charlotte.

"He looks like he just made that mess in the house," added Frank.

"Oh. And there was a red car that might have been his."

"What kind of car? Did you get a plate?"

"No. I should have. Arg." She shook her fists in the air.

"And as for make...I'm terrible at that. I don't know. It was sporty and kind of old-looking."

Frank grimaced. "Now I know what to teach you first, detective Charlotte." He relayed the information to the officer.

"Ten-four."

"Williams?"

Another voice came through the radio. "Williams here."

"You have Gloria Abernathy?"

"She put up a fight but we do. We're en route to the station."

"Keep her there 'til I get there."

He clipped the radio back to his belt.

"Charlotte, we have to get you to a hospital."

"I'm fine. Nothing's broken. Just scrapes and bruises."

"Let someone else be the judge of that. Your shoulder could be broken for all you know with the adrenalin you must have pumping. I'll go with you and see what other facts we might be able to shake from that lumpy head of yours."

Charlotte stuck her tongue out at him. "Mariska, will you watch Abby?"

"Of course."

Charlotte followed Frank to his cruiser, the scrapes on

her knees beginning to sting.

She flopped into the seat beside him and took a deep breath.

"I've decided life is too short, Frank. You have to give Darla back her witch."

He grunted. "I know. It's in the dang trunk."

While at the hospital, Charlotte received a text from Mariska letting her know everyone would be spending the night at Mariska's house. By the time she left the emergency room, all she wanted to do was go home and sleep, but Frank insisted she stay with Mariska. He had an officer stationed inside her own home, just in case Jason returned to look for her or Gloria.

He was still on the loose.

Entering Mariska's, she could see Gloria through the glass doors of the office, sleeping on the floor on an inflatable mattress. The guest room light was on and Abby was in the bed, waiting for her.

She undressed to her tee shirt, slipped under the sheets and fell asleep seconds later.

The next morning, she walked to Gloria's. The crime team had come and gone. She snuck under the crime tape and entered the kitchen through the broken front door.

Jackie's box was gone.

She dropped her head into her hand, flinching as her fingers touched her tender face.

CHAPTER THIRTY

It was after nine o'clock when Charlotte called and Declan couldn't hide his relief. He'd expected to hear from her again the night before, but by the time he'd finished retying the witch to the roof in Silver Lake, she was nowhere to be found. He'd tried to call her with no luck and told himself she'd been tired and gone to bed.

Or…she was in prison. One of those.

He'd planned to call her the moment he arrived at work, but found himself distracted by a grisly story in the newspaper about a woman in Tampa who'd died and been eaten by her cats. At least he hoped that was the order of things. As he read the last paragraph, his pocket rang and Charlotte's name popped on his phone as he retrieved it.

"Charlotte?"

"Hello."

"You didn't call. Are you okay? Did they haul you to jail?"

She laughed. "Nope. No jail. Things got a little crazy last night though."

Charlotte told him the story of Diana's mother's ashes, hitting her head and finally her confrontation with Jason.

Anger boiled beneath Declan's skin as he pictured a man striking Charlotte with a hammer. He was about to lose his mind when he heard a voice.

"Little help?"

Declan turned to see a customer standing at his checkout counter. He hadn't heard him enter. Squinting at his useless door bell, he made a mental note to retrieve the clapper from Stephanie.

"With you in a second," he said, holding up a finger.

"Thanks, I'm in a hurry."

"So are you okay?" Declan asked Charlotte as he walked toward the counter.

"I'm fine. The worst part is I lost the box."

"You think this guy took it?"

"I don't know why he would. It's obviously not his father's box; it isn't big enough to hold wads of bank money or other ill-gotten gains."

"So they took it as evidence, right? Ask Frank. He can probably get it for you."

"I will, but he's going to wonder why it's important, and then he's going to want to talk to Rocky…everything will get more complicated."

"At this point maybe that's not such a bad idea. Doing things on our own has been a little—"

Declan stopped mid-sentence, staring at his counter. His latest customer had brought in two items; a silver tea tray littered with silver place settings and a wooden box spilling over with jewelry.

The box had a lily inlaid in the center of its lid.

Declan made eye contact with the muscular young man. He had a large bruise on his chin and a split lip. The dark circles beneath his eyes said he hadn't slept.

Because he was hiding from the police.

This man had attacked Charlotte. He was sure of it. Then he'd taken Jackie's box to carry what was probably Gloria's jewelry.

What did Charlotte say his name was?

Jason.

He needed to tell Charlotte to send the police, but he'd strolled to the counter and now Jason, if it was him, would hear anything he said.

"I'll be right with you," he said, taking a step toward the office.

"Look, I don't have time for this," said the man. "I'll sell this stuff somewhere else." He began to scoop up the silverware.

"No. No, I'm sorry," said Declan. "I'm...I'm going to have to call you back," he said to Charlotte. He hung up the phone and smiled, holding out his hand. "I'm Declan. How can I help you?"

Jason eased the silverware back onto the tray and nodded.

"I want to sell this stuff."

Declan lowered his hand. He'd hoped the guy would introduce himself. It had to be him. And the box *had* to be Jackie's box. He could kill a lot of birds if he just had a stone...

"I didn't catch your name," he said, trying again.

"You don't need my name."

"I do for the paper work."

"Jason."

Declan's nerves came alive.

Stay cool.

"Okay Jason, sell or pawn?"

"I said sell."

"Right. Sorry. Well, let's see. Do you have receipts for any of it?"

He scowled. "No. It all belonged to my grandmother. She died."

"I'm sorry to hear that. Do you mind if I look through it?"

"No, just hurry. I don't have a lot of time."

"No problem."

Declan moved forward and stepped on the silent

alarm button on his floor. He'd never had to use it before; he hoped it worked.

He laid out a cloth and picked up one of the forks first, noting that each had an ornate *A* engraved on it.

"What was your grandmother's last name?"

"Why's that matter?"

He held up a fork. "Just wondering. The *A*."

"Oh. Uh… Apple."

"Her last name was Apple?"

"Yeah."

"That's an unusual—"

"Look, can you just cut to the chase? Just give me a ballpark. Check out the jewelry."

Jason flipped open the lid of the box and the side shifted as if the whole container was about to collapse.

Declan pulled a clump of jewelry and set it on the cloth. He looked past Jason through his front window, hoping to see police, but his parking lot remained empty with the exception of his own car and an old red Acura he assumed was Jason's.

"That box has seen better days," he said. "Know anything about it?"

Jason shook his head. "No. I just used it to carry the jewelry. Hey… Do I know you?"

Declan glanced up at Jason, who stared hard at him.

"I don't think so," he said.

"You have a girlfriend? In Pineapple Port?"

Declan felt his lip twitch and the anger he'd felt talking to Charlotte returned.

He looked at Jason and saw recognition wash across his face before he turned and bolted for the door.

Declan jumped over his counter and gave chase. Hampered by the furniture arrangement, Jason only made it half way to the door before Declan tackled him and the two of them plowed into a china cabinet. The glass doors shattered and the pair bounced away to the floor, fists flying, until they rolled up against a sofa with Declan on top. He straightened to punch his foe squarely in the face before Jason's foot entangled with a lamp cord and the light fell on Declan's back. The Tiffany-style glass shade crashed against his skull and he collapsed on Jason, who took the opportunity to slip out from under him and run for the door.

Declan shook his head to clear it and scrambled to his feet. That's when he spotted Stephanie standing inside his door, Jason barreling toward her. He wouldn't be able to catch him before he reached her.

"Get out of the way!" Jason screamed at her, waving her away.

"Watch out!" called Declan.

She looked at Declan, looked at Jason, and stepped outside, holding the door open for the approaching man.

Well you don't have to hold the door open for him...

Declan tripped over a fallen bowl and the world swam around him as he leaned against a chest of drawers. The lamp had hit him hard, but he *had* to hurry. If Jason reached his car he'd never catch him. He scrambled over a low banquet table and nearly fell again.

Catching his balance and standing, he watched as Jason reached the front door. At the last second, Stephanie threw out a stiff arm, catching him in the throat beneath his bruised chin. The muscular man flipped to his back as if he'd run into a clothesline, head slamming against the door threshold. He remained there, unmoving, as Declan stumbled to the door.

"I think you killed him," he said.

She grimaced and rubbed the inside of her elbow. "*You took my will.* I want it back. You don't need it, it's on file anyway."

"No, it's not." He looked at Jason, who remained unmoving. "Aren't you curious about this guy?"

"No. Give me the will."

"The will is fake. It's signed *Bonehead*. Pretty boneheaded maneuver, if you ask me."

"I'll make a new one with the right name. In fact I already have. I just hadn't switched them yet when you stole the tube."

"I have examples of Bonehead's real signature around here, you know. Your version won't match."

"Oh, I know you do," said Stephanie, seeming to regain some of her swagger. "I stole an example when I took the napkin, so that won't be a problem."

"Maybe not. But thanks to Charlotte using your own ego to separate you from your purse, I have an example of your first lame attempt, which will make them *really* study your next forgery. Better practice your penmanship. I imagine there's jail time for forgery?"

Declan had never seen Stephanie's nostrils flare before. She stomped her foot and ripped the clapper necklace from her neck.

"Here. I want you to *hear* me coming for you next time."

"I could have used this an hour ago. You're a little late."

She scoffed and pointed at Jason. "Um, *perfect* timing I'd say."

Nearby sirens wailed.

CHAPTER THIRTY-ONE

They were standing in front of Jackie's door when Declan began worrying again.

"What if the police ask for the security camera video? I could be arrested for obstruction of justice or something, couldn't I?"

Charlotte sighed. After capturing Jason at the Hock o' Bell, Declan had dumped Gloria's jewelry from the wooden box and slipped it under his desk to prevent it from falling into evidence. She praised him for the fast-thinking move, but he hadn't stopped agonizing about it since.

"Don't worry about the box. When you hid it, you'd just had your skull nearly crushed by a Tiffany lamp. You didn't know what you were doing."

"Faux Tiffany lamp," muttered Declan rubbing the back of his head. "Twice as heavy and ten times as cheap."

"Anyway, they don't care that Jason stole Gloria's jewelry as a consolation prize. Robbery is the *least* of his problems. Frank told me this morning that Tampa homicide thinks he might have killed his grandmother and filled her room with cats, hoping they'd eat the evidence."

Declan's eyes grew wide. "That was *him*? I just read about that. So…" He puffed out his chest. "I captured a *killer*…"

She chuckled. "Well, *Stephanie* did."

"Hey! I would have got him. And she took him out

278

after I roughed him up."

She balled her fist beneath her chin and fluttered her eyelashes at him. "My hero. Of course… I *did* rough him up for you first."

Declan grinned and knocked on Jackie's door.

"There you are," said Jackie, answering. She gasped. "Look at your face."

Charlotte's hand fluttered to hide her blackened eye. "Cripes, I hope that isn't how you greet all your guests…"

They walked inside, where Seamus awaited.

"Tilly get everything setup?" asked Charlotte.

Jackie nodded and pointed to a Christmas cactus hanging in the corner of the room. "She's got a camera hidden in the cactus and one outside. If anything goes bad, she'll call the police and hopefully they'll get here before we're all dead."

"Way to stay positive." Charlotte waved at the plant. "Hi Tilly. Thank you for doing this."

"Here's the box," said Declan, handing it to Jackie.

Jackie took it from him and sighed. "I can't believe how happy I am to see this piece of junk." She opened the lid and wiggled it. "It's in bad shape."

"It's had quite a week," said Charlotte.

There was a knock and Seamus moved to the door to peek outside.

"It's him. He's early."

"Rocky?' asked Charlotte.

"No. His father."

Seamus looked at Declan and they nodded to each other.

"Here we go…" Seamus opened the door.

The dapper, gray-haired gentleman on the step broke into a broad grin.

"Hi, I'm Rock Conrad. My son said..." He looked past Seamus. "You found it. You've got my box."

Seamus moved aside so Rock could step in.

"May I see it?" he asked Jackie, who stood with the box in her hands.

She handed it to him. As he took it the wood shifted, revealing the large crack along the joint.

"It's broken," he said.

"Yes. I needed to tell you about that..." began Charlotte.

Conrad shook his head and slid his thumb along the side of the box. A piece of wood slid out, jutting four inches past the corner.

He slid another piece and then another until a panel on the bottom of the box fell into his palm. He flipped over the box and Charlotte saw a yellowed square of what looked like paper inside the hidden panel.

Conrad removed the paper and turned it over to reveal a glossy black and white photograph of a teenage girl standing on a boardwalk. Above her head large scripted letters spelled *ger's* and beneath that in smaller letters *Taffy*. The hand on her shoulder implied someone stood to her right, but that person had been torn from the photo.

"My love," he said, his eyes welling with tears. "I thought I lost you."

"That's why you wanted the box? For a photo?" asked Seamus.

Conrad held it up.

"It's Lily. Lily Talliferro. She was the love of my life. We had this photo taken on the Atlantic City Boardwalk not long before I lost her."

A dark-haired girl stood smiling in the photo. She wore a light-colored dress, her long sleek hair lying neatly across each shoulder.

Charlotte moved closer to Rock, following the photo with her gaze as he waved it in the air while he spoke.

"We were going to get married—"

Charlotte grabbed the corner of the photo. Rock scowled and tugged on it, but she didn't let go.

"Um…anyway…her family disappeared. I was going to give her this box I made for her, but she was gone. Witness protection. Her father worked for the mob and he flipped. I've been looking for her for fifty years."

"So you *are* in the mob," said Jackie pointing at him.

"Me?" Rock laughed. "I said *her* father. And mine for that matter, but not me."

"Your son told us if we didn't get the box you'd bump us off."

"He *what?*" Rock's face turned red as he roared the words. In his surprise, he released the photograph to Charlotte who'd continued to tug at it. "I'm going to kill him. I should have *never* told him about his grandfather. He's been obsessed for years."

"Who's his grandfather?"

"I can't say. We were put in witness protection as well, shortly after Lily's family. Even Rocky doesn't know our real last name."

"Should you be telling us you're in witness protection?" asked Declan.

He chuckled. "Probably not. Simone would kill me. But everyone is dead now—"

"Simone!" yipped Seamus, cutting Rock short. "Wait. Who's Simone?"

Jackie looked at him. "What are you all wound up about?"

"She's my contact with the U.S. Marshals," said Rock. "Funny story, actually…apparently, when she was a newbie, she goofed and ended up sending a ton of WitSec people to this same area of Florida."

"WitSec?" asked Jackie.

"Witness Security. She sent people from rival gangs and whatnot. Set them up just a few towns away from each other in some cases. Big mess. They stationed her here for life, just to keep an eye on us all."

Seamus' jaw slowly fell. "Holy mother of—"

"Funny thing," continued Rock, oblivious to Seamus' reaction. "She showed up on my door yesterday asking about this box, which was strange. Hadn't seen her in years. She really knows *everything*..."

Jackie stared at Seamus. "Do you *know* this woman?"

"Huh?" Seamus looked at her as if he'd just awoken. "Who? Simone? No. Just an interesting story, don't you think?"

"I guess..." Jackie squinted at him and then turned to Rock. "So...you're *not* going to kill us?"

Rock's expression clouded. "No. I spotted the box in the newspaper and Rocky offered to get it for me. He didn't say anything about *threatening* anyone. I don't know if you noticed, but he's a bit—"

"We know," said the other four in unison.

Rock cleared his throat and offered a stiff nod.

"What about the lady in the greenhouse? The one you had moved," asked Seamus.

Rock turned to him. "The Lady—hey...I can't shake the feeling I know you. Have we met?"

Seamus shook his head and tilted his face towards the floor. "No..."

"Wait..." Rock gasped and pointed at him. "You're the Russian who was destroying my rose bushes."

Seamus sighed. "Yeah. I might have done a little reconnaissance on you..."

Rock chuckled. "That accent was terrible."

"Agreed."

"My son must have really had you in a tizzy to drive you to spying on me. I'm going to *kill* him." He grimaced. "Anyway, *The Lady* you said? In the greenhouse? That's my prize-winning lily. She's at the garden show right now. I started breeding a hybrid in honor of Lily, of course, and it became quite an obsession for me."

"What about Artie? Did you kill him?"

"Artie, my tennis partner? I'm meeting him at the club tomorrow. I plan on killing him, yes..."

"You killed him in *tennis*..." mumbled Seamus.

Rock's eyes grew large. "You thought—"

"I've seen this photo before," said Charlotte, interrupting, her eyes riveted on the image. She looked up at the others and gasped. "And I just remembered where I saw it—"

"My house."

Everyone turned as Tilly entered, a torn photo in her nutmeg-colored hand.

"Tony," she said, staring at Rock.

"*Lily?*"

Rock's mouth fell open and the two of them stood, staring at each other.

"Tilly's missing from his photo," Charlotte said, holding the picture in the air and pointing at it.

"Tilly?" echoed Rock.

"I took the name Tilly because it rhymed with Lily and had a *T* for Tony."

"Remember your nickname for me?" he asked.

She smiled. "Rocky."

Rock's face broke into the largest grin Charlotte had ever seen.

"My love," he reached Tilly in two long strides and they embraced, his voice breaking with emotion. "I thought I'd never find you."

"I tried to find *you*—" she began.

"My father flipped too. They sent us to Lakeland."

"They sent me here."

They clung to each other, rocking back and forth in apparent bliss.

"I never married," she exclaimed.

"I—" Rock fell silent. As the silence continued, Tilly began to struggle to free herself.

"Wait, wait, wait…" she said, waving her hands in the air.

"Come on, Lily, it's been *fifty* years."

"You *married* some broad?"

"Yes, but I never loved her the way I loved you. We divorced not long after Rocky was born."

"You had a kid?"

"Awkward," mumbled Seamus.

"Tell me, how long did you wait before you married some hussy?"

"Lily, my love, I was young. You were gone. Everyone else was doing it…"

Tilly spun on her heel and stormed out of the house.

"Tilly!" called Rock, racing after her.

The others looked at each other as Tilly and Rock's voices faded in the distance.

"So…that was interesting…" said Charlotte.

Jackie turned to the box, sitting half broken on her table, pieces sticking out from every side. "And I have this *stupid* box back again."

"Well, look at the bright side," said Charlotte pointing to the hanging plant. "That touching reunion is all captured on video."

"Can I still kill Rocky?" asked Seamus.

Epilogue

Charlotte called for Gloria, but found only Abby, half asleep on her bed with her back legs stretched out behind her like a frog.

The house felt quiet without Gloria in it.

She needed to get ready. Declan would arrive soon to take her to a celebratory dinner. But first…she needed to update the chalkboard wall. She'd solved the switched lawn ornaments, found Witchy-Poo, discovered the person threatening Gloria and returned the mystery box to its rightful owner.

What a week.

Heading back down the hall, she noticed a pile of something on her counter top. A mound of money sat on top of a note scrawled on white paper. She slipped the note out from the pile.

Dear Charlotte,

Thank you so much for all your help and for giving me a place to stay during my ordeal. I've left you payment for your services. My house is a disaster. I'm moving to the beach. I've always wanted to live on the beach. Hope to see you soon!
Love,
Gloria

Charlotte picked up the pile of money and realized each bill was a crisp hundred. Thirty of them.

Three thousand dollars. What a payday. No, no. She

couldn't possibly accept so much money. Granted she had been attacked, but still...

The smile melted from Charlotte's face.

Such crisp bills...

She found her purse and pulled from it the first hundred Gloria had given her. Another new bill. The date on each was over fifteen years ago. Every single one. She hadn't thought the newness of the first bill was odd at the time, but in combination with thirty others...all with old dates...Gloria's new house at the beach...

No wonder Jason couldn't find the bank money his father hid in his grandmother's house.

Gloria found it first.

THE END

Thank you for taking time to read *Pineapple Mystery Box!* If you enjoyed it, please consider telling your friends or posting a review on Amazon or GoodReads or wherever you like to roam. Word of mouth helps poor starving authors so much!

Read Pineapple Port Book Three: *Pineapple Puzzles*

Bonus: Pineapple Puzzles

Chapter One

Two months earlier.

Alex walked into The Striped Goldfish and felt cool, heavy air settling on sun-warmed skin. A skinny man in his mid-fifties sat alone at the bar in a pair of khaki shorts and over-sized Jimmy Buffett t-shirt. In front of him sat a full beer and an empty shot glass. It was three o'clock in the afternoon.

Alex moved to the bar and sat one stool away.

"What can I getcha?" asked the young bartender, his eyes never leaving his phone.

"I'll take a beer. Whatever's on tap."

The bartender finished thumbing his text message, slipped the phone into his pocket and reached to pour a frosted glass.

The man in the Buffet t-shirt spoke.

"Still hot out there?"

"Not too bad. It's been worse," said Alex.

"You aren't kidding. Sometimes I question why I came to Florida in the first place."

"Are you originally from farther north?"

"Isn't everyone? Connecticut."

"Philadelphia, myself."

"See?"

Alex held out a hand. "I'm Alex."

"Pat."

"How long you been here, Pat?"

"In the *bar,* or in Florida?" he asked, chuckling.

"Florida."

"Twenty years. You?"

"Just a few. Retired?"

"I guess you could say I'm semi-retired. I worked for the railroad up in Connecticut. Down here I started making jigsaw puzzles."

"Jigsaw puzzles?"

"Outta wood. I sell them at the craft fairs. Got a

website I don't understand. Got some in stores."

"Wait." Alex took a sip of beer. "You're not Pat *Conley* are you?"

Pat grinned. "In the flesh."

"Wow. I've seen your stuff. You're kinda famous. Weren't you and your puzzles on TV or something a few years back?"

"Yeah, well—"

Alex snapped in the air. "Bartender, get this man another round. Me too, for that matter. I'll have what he's having."

The bartender tucked his tongue into his lower lip, staring as if considering the value of the request, and then nodded.

Alex peppered Pat with questions about the jigsaw puzzle making business and the man answered each inquiry with delight. He never asked about Alex, but then, Alex found most people never thought to steer the conversation away from themselves if given the chance to remain the center of attention.

The shots of bourbon appeared and disappeared like runway models. Alex threw back the first, but for subsequent rounds, dribbled the contents of the shot glass down the leg of the bar stool to the wood plank floor.

It would be important to stay sober.

"I'd sure love to see how you do it," Alex said, as Pat finished expounding on his time creating a puzzle for Mick Jagger's grandchild. Or it might have been James Brown's grandkid. Alex wasn't really listening.

"You should come back to the shop," said Pat, his tongue thick with bourbon.

"Could I? Hey, you need a ride? I have my car."

Pat looked at the door. "I walked here. DUI last year.

Lost my license. It was a trap. Cop was *waiting* for me—"

"No problem, no problem. I'll drop you off and you can show me your stuff."

Pat grinned—leered, really—his eyes at half-staff. "Sure sure." He turned to call for the bartender.

"Don't worry about it. I've got the bill."

"This is my kinda day." Pat slid from his bar stool.

Alex paid and palmed Pat's shot glass as the young man ran the card. After signing the receipt Alex held the door open for Pat as they headed for the car. The jigsaw king weaved, giggling at the effort it took to continue forward.

"I might've had one too many today."

"Happens to the best of us."

Alex opened the passenger door and helped Pat inside. Three minutes later they pulled into the driveway of Pat's moss green, cement block rancher.

After a wobbly trip from the car to the front porch, Pat hummed the theme to *The Brady Bunch* as he fumbled for his keys. The door popped open and they entered.

Inside, the walls were covered with intricate wooden puzzles, assembled, mounted and framed.

"Look at that," said Alex, whistling with admiration.

"That's one of my favorites." Pat thrust his finger in the direction of a large wooden map of the world with each country's puzzle piece stained a slightly different shade. "Took me three years to finish that."

Alex had already wandered to the slider doors leading to the back yard. "No kidding. Is that a pool out there?"

Pat nodded. "You bring your bathing suit?"

"No, but I wouldn't mind sitting out back and getting a little air. Evening breeze is picking up."

He nodded again. "Whatever you like. Grab us some beers from the fridge and I'll lead the way."

Alex gathered one Miller Lite from the fridge and handed the can to Pat before wandering to the edge of the pool.

"Hey Pat."

Pat, about to flop into a lounge chair, paused. "Yeah?"

"You've got a gator in your pool."

"What?" Pat shuffled toward the pool. His eyes grew wide. "Hoo!"

In the shallow end of the pool, a large alligator floated, eyes and nose breaking the surface.

"What the—"

Alex opened a pocketknife. Before Pat could say another word, Alex grabbed him by the shoulder of his t-shirt sleeve, stabbed him twice in the neck and pushed him into the pool. The attack took less than three seconds. Not a single drop of blood had fallen on the cement surround.

Pat surfaced sputtering, an ever growing halo of blood encircling his body.

"Did I fall in?" he asked, swimming toward Alex. "Help me out of here."

He doesn't even realize he's been stabbed. Doesn't know he's bleeding to death faster than he's swimming.

To Alex's surprise, Pat *did* manage to paddle to the edge of the pool. He reached out his hand for help and his mouth opened but he was too weak to speak. Alex watched as the man's eyelids grew heavy. His arm, hooked on the side of the pool, kept Pat afloat, even as his face submerged. It slid in tiny staccato jerks across the pavement as the weight of his body pulled.

A moment later, the alligator was on him. It grabbed Pat by the leg and jerked him under.

Alex stepped forward to watch, curious how the hungry beast would proceed, but the water was too bloody to see.

"I told you if you were patient you'd get fed."

A few details to arrange . . .

Alex returned to the car, retrieved a boxed cardboard puzzle featuring a field of jellybeans, and tossed a handful of pieces in and around the pool.

Alex sat on the end of the lounge chair and watched the pieces bob in the bloody water.

Get *Pineapple Puzzles on Amazon*

To keep up with what I'm writing next, visit my humor blog/author site and sign up for my newsletter at:
http://www.AmyVansant.com

Amazon:
http://www.amazon.com/Amy-Vansant/e/B001K8WXV0/

Twitter:
https://twitter.com/AmyVansant

Goodreads:
https://www.goodreads.com/amyvansant

Facebook:
https://www.facebook.com/TheAmyVansant

For questions or delightful chit-chat:
Amy@AmyVansant.com

ABOUT THE AUTHOR

Amy Vansant is a *Wall Street Journal* and *USA Today* best-selling author who writes with an unique blend of thrills, romance and humor (occasionally with a touch of time travel or fantasy).

She *has* rocked water aerobics at a fifty-five plus community, but has yet to play bingo. She's heard it's vicious.

Other Books by Amy Vansant

Pineapple Port Mysteries
Funny, clean mysteries full of unforgettable characters.
Plenty of thrills without anything TOO rough.
View the Series (Nine+ Books)

Kilty Romantic Comedy/Thrillers
Funny, suspenseful romances with a touch of time-travel.
See the whole series (Eight+ Books)

Slightly Romantic Comedies
New Adult/Adult zany romantic romps
Slightly Stalky (I) *Slightly Sweaty* (II)

The Magicatory
YA Fantasy

OTHER BOOKS
Moms are Nuts (editor: humor anthology)
The Surfer's Guide to Florida (non-fiction: out of print)